W9-BPM-526

"TERRIFIC.
—Dave Barry

"ENTERTAINING."
—Orlando Sentinel

"STYLISH."
—Randy Wayne White

"SUSPENSEFUL."
—The Flint Journal

"ZANY."
—Publishers Weekly

ST. MARTIN'S
MINOTAUR
MYSTERIES

GET A CLUE!

Be the first to hear the latest mystery book news...

With the St. Martin's Minotaur monthly newsletter, you'll learn about the hottest new Minotaur books, receive advance excerpts from newly published works, read exclusive original material from featured mystery writers, and be able to enter to win free books!

Sign up on the Minotaur Web site at:
www.minotaurbooks.com

"Great characterizations, a thorough knowledge of his locales, plus an easy-breezy style that's hard to resist make Bob Morris's *Jamaica Me Dead* another must-read. A new mystery series that's smart, funny, and slightly off-kilter."
—*Bookloons*

BahamaraMa

"I was wondering when Bob Morris would finally get around to writing a novel, and it was worth the wait. *Bahamarama* is sly, smart, cheerfully twisted, and very funny. Morris is a natural."
—Carl Hiaasen, *New York Times* bestselling author of *Skin Tight*

"Bob Morris, a terrific writer and Florida boy, has created a marvelous tale that perfectly captures the nation's strangest state. Like Florida itself, *Bahamarama* is wild, weird, unpredictable, populated by exotic denizens—and funny as hell."
—Dave Barry, *New York Times* bestselling author and Pulitzer Prize winner

"Chasteen makes a fine hero, one who lives by his own rules...a highly enjoyable way to pass an afternoon."
—*Miami Herald*

"Morris captures the islands and local people well...a great bullets-and-beaches book to pack on your next trip."
—*Caribbean Travel & Life*

"This book stands out. It's a fun and engrossing read from an author who expertly knows the lay of the land and the sea."
—Michael Connelly, *New York Times* bestselling author of *The Narrows*

ALSO BY BOB MORRIS

BahamaraMa

AVAILABLE FROM
ST. MARTIN'S/MINOTAUR
PAPERBACKS

Jamaica Me Dead

BOB MORRIS

St. Martin's Paperbacks

JAMAICA ME DEAD

Copyright © 2005 by Bob Morris.
Excerpt from *Bermuda Schwartz* © 2006 by Bob Morris.

Library of Congress Catalog Card Number: 2005051257

ISBN: 0-312-99748-5
EAN: 9780312-99748-9

Printed in the United States of America

St. Martin's Press hardcover edition / October 2005
St. Martin's Paperbacks edition / October 2006

St. Martin's Paperbacks are published by St. Martin's Press, 175 Fifth Avenue, New York, NY 10010.

10 9 8 7 6 5 4 3 2 1

FOR DEBBIE...
AGAIN AND ALWAYS

JAMAICA ME DEAD

1

It was the first game of the season at Florida Field, and in typical fashion the Gators had scheduled something less than a fearsome opponent. This year it was the University of Tulsa. Midway through the second quarter the score was already twenty-seven us, zip for the Golden Hurricanes.

Reality would come home to roost in two weeks when we faced off against Tennessee, but for now the future appeared glorious, and the only thing in life that even mildly concerned me was why a football team from Oklahoma would call itself the Golden Hurricanes.

I turned to Barbara Pickering and said: "Don't you think they ought to call themselves something more geographically appropriate? Like the Golden Cow Patties?"

It got laughs from the people sitting around us.

"Or the Golden Tumbleweeds," said a woman to my left.

Barbara looked up from her book.

"I'm sorry," she said. "Did you say something?"

It was Barbara's first time at Florida Field. In fact, it was her first time at a football game. I was trying hard not to be offended by the fact she had not only brought along a book—*A House for Mr. Biswas,* by V. S. Naipaul—she was actually reading it. I had never seen anyone reading a book at a football game.

A man sitting in front of us turned to Barbara.

"Honey," he said. "Please tell me that's a book about football."

"Well, actually, it's about the Hindu community in Trinidad and how this poor downtrodden man, Mr. Biswas, so badly wants a house of his very own, yet—"

I gave Barbara a nudge. She stopped.

"You'll have to forgive her," I told the man in front of us. "Barbara's British."

Barbara gave the guy a smile so stunning that his ears turned red. I could relate. I do the same thing whenever she smiles at me.

I reached under my seat and found the pint flask of Mount Gay that I had smuggled into the stadium. I poured a healthy dollop into my cup. Then I pulled a wedge of lime from the plastic baggie in my pants pocket and squeezed it into the rum.

The man in front of us turned around again. Mainly because I had succeeded in squirting the back of his neck with lime juice.

"You'll have to forgive him," Barbara told the man. "Zack has scurvy."

Moments later, the Gators scored. I stood to cheer with the rest of the crowd. Barbara took the opportunity to stretch and yawn and work out the kinks. She glanced at the scoreboard.

"Oh my, only two minutes left," she said. "Perhaps we should go now and beat the crowd."

"That's just until halftime."

"Meaning . . ."

"Meaning, with TV time-outs and the Gators' passing game, I'd say we can look forward to at least another two hours of this. Good thing the relative humidity is 187 percent. That way it will seem like a whole lot longer."

She faked a smile. Even her fake smiles are pretty damn stunning.

Just then I heard someone yell: "Yo, Zack!"

Monk DeVane was standing in the aisle, waving for us to join him.

"Come on, there's someone I want you to meet," I told Barbara.

"An old college friend?"

"Yeah, we go way back."

Barbara put her book on her seat and we began edging our way toward the aisle.

Monk DeVane had been my roommate when we played for the Gators. Like me, he had knocked around in the pros a few years before getting hurt and calling it quits. He opened a car dealership, but it went belly-up. So he tried selling real estate and tried selling boats and tried selling himself on the idea that he could stay married. Last I heard there had been three wives, but I had lost track on exactly what he was doing to make a living.

Monk's real name was Donald, but one Saturday night on a bye weekend during my freshman year, when I had gone home for a visit, Coach Rowlin decided to conduct a curfew check at Yon Hall. He caught Monk in bed with not one but two comely representatives of Alpha Delta Pi.

While Coach Rowlin booted players off the team for missing practice or talking back to a coach, and did it in a heartbeat, bonking sorority girls at 2 A.M. was not high on his list of misdeeds. At the following Monday's team meeting, when Coach Rowlin handed out punishments for a variety of weekend infractions, he gave Donald twenty extra wind sprints.

"You boys need to be saving your strength during the season," Coach Rowlin told us. "Not engaging in wild-monkey sex."

Donald had been Monk ever since.

Despite all Monk's ups and downs over the years, he seemed none the worse for wear. Still fit and handsome, his sunstreaked brown hair was considerably longer than I remembered, and he had grown a beard. It was spackled with just enough gray to lend a note of dignity.

Monk stuck out a hand. I took it without thinking, and a moment later I was grimacing under his grip. Monk had a Super Bowl ring. I didn't. He liked to remind me of that by catching my hand in just the right way for his big gold ring to bear down on my knuckles.

I wrenched away and introduced him to Barbara. Monk pulled her close and wrapped an arm around her.

"How about you dump this joker you're with and come up to

the skybox and have a drink with me? We're throwing a little party."

"This skybox of yours, is it air-conditioned?" asked Barbara.

"Cool as Canada, with an open bar and food that'll make your eyes bug out."

"Since when do you have a skybox?" I said.

Monk grinned.

"Since never. It's the president's skybox."

"As in president of the university?"

"As in," Monk said.

"Traveling in some pretty swank circles these days, aren't you?"

"Well, it helps that I work for Darcy Whitehall."

Monk saw the look on my face. On Barbara's, too.

"Yeah, *that* Darcy Whitehall," he said. "I'd like for you to meet him, Zack. Plus, there's something I need to talk to you about."

I had seen Darcy Whitehall that very morning at Publix when I went to pick up a few things for our pregame tailgate lunch. He was staring at me from the cover of *People,* along with a host of other celebrities the magazine had proclaimed "Still Sexy in Their Sixties."

Barbara spoke before I had a chance to.

"We'd love to join you," she told Monk.

After that, things went straight to hell.

2

We cut under the stands and headed for the elevators that would take us to the skybox level. The concrete breezeways echoed with the boisterous buzz of game day, and we wove through a happy crowd all decked out in variations on a theme of orange and blue.

I had been coming to Gator games since I was in diapers, and the seats I now held season tickets to originally belonged to my grandfather. I felt right at home at Florida Field, but it seemed an odd place for the likes of Darcy Whitehall.

Darcy Whitehall was Jamaican, a white Jamaican, part of a family that could trace its roots on the island back to colonial days. He had made his name as a young man in the music industry. Catching reggae's early wave of popularity, Whitehall had started a music label and signed a number of musicians who hit it big.

Since then, he had branched out and was now best known as founder and figurehead of Libido Resorts, a collection of anything-goes, all-inclusive retreats scattered throughout the Caribbean. The first one, in Jamaica, just up the coast from Montego Bay, immediately gained notice as the ultimate swingers' haven. Naked volleyball. Group sex in hot tubs. "Formal" dinners for three hundred where the women were clad only in pearl necklaces and high heels, and the men wore black bowties, but not around their necks.

In recent years, Libido had tried to present a more refined image, no doubt to justify the many thousands of dollars it cost to stay there for a week. Gourmet dining. Serene spa treatments. Yoga pavilions under the palms.

Turn on the television and there was Darcy Whitehall, an icon of rakishness, strolling along a dazzling stretch of beach, an umbrella drink in one hand, a gorgeous young woman on his arm, telling would-be guests: "Yield to Libido."

The pitch was upscale, but the subtext was the same as it always had been: book a week at Libido and you'll definitely get laid.

As we approached the elevators, Monk gave us laminated badges that said "Skybox Access." We clipped them on, and I stood up straight and tried to look presentable. We would soon be mingling with all sorts of movers and shakers. The conversation would be dignified, the company refined. And I wouldn't have to pour my rum out of a plastic flask hidden underneath my seat.

I was wearing my sit-in-the-sun-and-swelter outfit—flip-flops, khaki shorts, and a T-shirt from Heller Brothers Produce that I had chosen because it had a plump, juicy navel orange on the chest that was my nod to sporting Gator colors. The T-shirt also bore a variety of stains—Zatarain's Creole Mustard, Louisiana Bull hot sauce, Big Tom Bloody Mary Mix—which spoke to the success of our tailgate lunch and the zealousness with which I enjoyed it.

The skybox elite might sniff that I was underdressed, but I wasn't concerned. Barbara was at my side and, like always, she looked dazzling. Her outfit was simple—something beige and linen—but she wore it with a grace that few women can claim. She had recently cut her long dark hair and was wearing it in a swept-back style that fell just above her shoulders. I was still getting used to the look, but it was tugging at me in all sorts of pleasing ways.

Barbara caught me staring at her and smiled and gave my

hand a squeeze. I knew she was thrilled by the chance to meet Darcy Whitehall. It had nothing to do with his sexiness or his celebrity. Well, maybe it had a little to do with that. But for Barbara it was mostly a matter of business. I saw the look in her eyes. Her mind had undoubtedly slipped into overdrive as she tried to figure out a way to leverage this lucky encounter into an opportunity for *Tropics*.

Tropics is Barbara's baby, her pride and joy, a classy travel magazine that covers Florida and the Caribbean. She launched it on a shoestring and, against long odds, carved out a niche in the market, thanks both to the quality of the magazine and her very considerable will. The success of *Tropics* has allowed her company, Orb Communications, to start tourist magazines on several islands—*Barbados Live!* and *St. Martin Live!* among others—along with occasional custom publications for cruise ships and resorts.

She's done well, very well. Still, in the publishing world she's small-fry, and she's on the road often, roping in new advertisers, stroking old ones, and promoting her magazines with dauntless zeal.

I knew she had long tried to land the Libido account, but had made little headway. Now to have this opportunity fall in her lap, well, I was pretty sure she'd forgive me for making her sit through a football game.

We got on the elevator and as the doors closed behind us I thought about Monk DeVane working for Libido Resorts. It was like the fox getting hired to run the henhouse.

"So what do you do for Darcy Whitehall?" I asked Monk. "You the Vice President for Rubbing Suntan Lotion on Female Guests?"

Monk laughed.

"No, I'm in the security business these days, Zack."

"Ah, you make sure the female guests don't get hit by falling coconuts."

"It's slightly more complicated than that," he said. "We'll talk about it."

The elevator *dinged* as we reached the skybox level. The

doors slid open and a crush of people began pushing their way on before we could get off. Not the sort of behavior you'd expect from this exclusive crowd.

It helped that Monk used to be an offensive guard. He bulldozed a path out of the elevator. We followed him into the narrow hallway that led to the skyboxes. It was packed with people, all heading for the elevators.

But something was off, way off. This was not a jolly football gathering. No, these people looked scared, on the edge of panic.

I saw the lieutenant governor using his wife as a battering ram to get to the elevators. I saw a fairly famous golfer elbowing his way through the fray. I saw the junior U.S. senator from Florida desperately yanking open a fire door. As people split off to follow him down the stairs, the alarm shrieked a soundtrack to the mayhem.

A short round woman collided with Monk. He caught her as she tumbled and helped her to her feet.

"You alright?" Monk said.

The woman gasped, words hanging in her throat. She shot an anxious look back toward the skyboxes.

"There's a bomb," she said.

3

The bomb was in skybox 14, row 1, by a floor-to-ceiling window that looked down on Florida Field. It was fastened under the seat of a leather-console chair. Sitting in the chair, gripping the armrests, was Darcy Whitehall.

I wasn't the best judge of whether Whitehall really was as sexy as *People* insisted, but there was no denying that he had a presence about him. Pale blue eyes and a mane of silver hair, he reminded me of an aging rock star who hadn't lost his chops. His face bore the deep lines of indulgent living that on some lucky bastards only seem to enhance their good looks. Darcy Whitehall was one of them, a guy who would go to his grave looking good.

Unless, of course, the bomb beneath his butt did him in. In which case we'd all be waltzing off into the hereafter a bit less photogenic than we might have wished.

Whitehall was taking slow, deep breaths, like they teach you in yoga, trying to stay calm. He seemed to be doing a pretty good job of it, considering that just a few minutes earlier he'd received a call on his cell phone from a man who said: "There is a bomb under your chair. One move and you're a dead man."

Except for a handful of people, everyone had evacuated the skybox. I recognized William B. Barnett, the tanned and dapper president of the University of Florida. Flanking him were a pair of UF campus cops. They stood by a counter filled with God's own hors d'oeuvres—fat shrimp in remoulade sauce, beef tenderloin crusted with cumin and peppercorns, and sushi of every description.

Not that I would consider snacking at a time like this. Well, I'd already considered it, actually, but dismissed it as bad form. Rare are the occasions when my self-restraint shines through, but this was one of them.

A young man and woman stood a few feet from Darcy Whitehall. The woman was in her twenties and nothing short of beautiful. Exotic, smoky features and long black hair. She was crying, wiping away tears with a sleeve of her sheer linen blouse. She wore it loose outside of a long embroidered skirt. Stylish, classy.

The young man wore a charcoal gray suit and wire-rim glasses that gave him an air of seriousness well beyond his years. He had an arm around the woman, trying to comfort her.

Monk kneeled on the floor by Darcy Whitehall, who was still clutching his cell phone.

"When did you get the call?" Monk said.

"Couldn't have been more than a couple of minutes or so after I sat down, while you had stepped away," Whitehall said.

"You recognize the voice?"

Whitehall shook his head no.

Bill Barnett shifted anxiously between the two campus cops. The cops looked pretty nervous, too, out of their element. But then, we all were.

Barnett checked his watch.

"Bomb squad should be here by now," he said. "Been seven minutes since I called 911."

Down on the field the Gator band was marching in formation to start the halftime show. Speakers around the skybox blared the Florida fight song.

Monk said, "You done anything to get the rest of the stadium emptied?"

Barnett shook his head.

"Not yet."

"Well, you've got people pouring out of the skyboxes screaming about a bomb. Got to do something or else there's going to be pandemonium down there."

As Barnett pulled out a cell phone, Monk told him, "Blame it on the weather."

The president paused, puzzled. The weather outside was gorgeous—puffy white clouds against a perfect blue sky.

Monk said, "Say the weather service has issued an advisory that there's a squall line moving in from the Gulf. NCAA has a rule says that if there's lightning spotted within six miles of a stadium, then the teams have to leave the field. You have to tell them something or else eighty-five thousand people are gonna go ape shit."

Barnett nodded and made the call. Given Florida's freakish out-of-nowhere thunderstorms, it was surely plausible.

I had to admire the way Monk was handling things. He was cool and focused, in control of the situation, a far cry from the break-all-the-rules hellraiser I'd known in college and in the years we played in the pros.

I watched as Monk moved aside a few shopping bags and a briefcase that sat by Whitehall's chair. Then he flattened himself on the floor and looked under the chair. He crooked his head to get a good view of whatever was underneath it. No one in the skybox said a word.

Barbara pulled me close. I put an arm around her. Part of me wanted to turn us both around and march out the skybox door, but the other part felt obliged to stay there with Monk, at least until the police arrived.

Monk stood up. He looked at the young man and woman.

"Alan, Ali . . . I want you to step slowly away and exit the skybox."

The young woman said, "What about you?"

"I'm staying here with your father," Monk said.

The young woman, sobbing now, flung herself at Monk, burying her head in his chest.

"Please, please, no," she said. "Don't let this happen."

As Monk comforted her, he spoke to the rest of us: "I want all of you to get out of here. Except you, Zack. You mind sticking around?"

"No problem," I said.

Barbara looked up at me, her eyes wide. I kissed the top of her head and hugged her and turned her away so we could have a moment.

"You be alright?"

"Yes," she said. "But I really need to get back to our seats."

I looked at her.

"I left my book there, Zack," she said.

"Your book? You want to go back for your book?"

"Why, yes, I do. It's a first edition. It's signed by Naipaul. It's very dear to me, a gift from my mother, and I fully intend to . . ."

I turned her toward the door.

"Just go," I said. "We'll worry about the book later."

I watched as she left the skybox and disappeared down the hallway, followed by Bill Barnett, the two campus cops and the skybox attendant.

The young man and woman said their good-byes to Whitehall, but as they moved to the door, the young woman turned on the young man and shouted: "It's all your fault! If you hadn't decided to . . ."

"Ali!" Darcy Whitehall silenced her. "That's enough. This has nothing to do with your brother."

The woman held his look for a moment, then stepped into the hall. The young man stood in the doorway, anguish in his eyes.

"Dad," he said. "If this is about me, I'm sorry. I'll quit. I'll drop out. I'll . . ."

Whitehall put up a hand to quiet him.

"You'll do no such thing," Whitehall said. "It's not your fault. I'll be alright. Now go."

The young man stepped away. That left just me, Monk, and Darcy Whitehall in the skybox. With a bomb.

Some fun party this was turning out to be.

4

Outside, the band stopped playing and I heard the stadium announcer telling the crowd the game had been postponed "upon advisement of the National Weather Service." There were boos and catcalls, but they quieted down as several dozen state troopers moved through the stadium, and everyone began heading toward the exits.

As Monk stepped over to the window and gazed out on the stadium, Darcy Whitehall looked me up and down.

"So, you're the one Monk's been telling me about, are you?"

"Zack Chasteen," I said, sticking out my hand. Whitehall gave it a shake.

"Forgive me for not getting up," he said.

"Gee, what's the world coming to? Put a lousy little bomb under a guy's chair and good manners go out the window."

Whitehall smiled.

"Reminds me of that movie," he said. "*Lethal Weapon* something-or-other. The second one, I think."

"The one where Danny Glover sits down on the toilet and there's a bomb rigged to the seat?"

Whitehall nodded.

"Mel Gibson walks in, checks it out, and Danny Glover looks

at him and says, 'Tell me I'm not fucked.' And Mel Gibson says, 'Don't worry, guys like you don't die sitting on toilets.' "

"Compared to Danny Glover you got it good," I said. "Your pants aren't down around your knees. And you don't have to listen to Mel Gibson make wisecracks."

Whitehall laughed.

"Nor do I intend to die at a bloody football game."

"Makes two of us," I said.

Monk turned from the window and stepped next to the chair.

"You want to take a look at that thing down there, Zack?"

As if I knew a bomb from a Bundt cake. But I kneeled and looked under the chair and tried not to think about what could happen if Whitehall was overcome by a sudden butt twitch. Might ruin my schoolboy complexion.

There wasn't much to see. Just a rectangular box, a shoebox it looked like, fastened to the bottom of the chair with duct tape. No wires. No ticking clock. Nothing that shouted: Bomb! Which made it all the scarier.

I stood up.

"Beats heck out of me," I said, "but I'm guessing it's not a new pair of Nikes in there."

Monk looked at Darcy Whitehall.

"We're going to get this worked out," he said. "Just sit tight."

"I intend to," Whitehall said. He looked at me. "So, Mr. Chasteen, assuming we put this bomb business behind us, Monk tells me you'll be coming down to Jamaica."

I looked at Monk. He winced, then shrugged an apology.

"Sorry," Monk said. "But that's what I wanted to talk to you about, Zack. I need some help."

"Doing what?"

"Backing me up, lending a hand, doing whatever needs doing security-wise."

The whole thing was coming at me from so far out in left field that I couldn't think of anything to say. I just stood there.

"I think it's rather obvious that I require some looking after," said Whitehall. "And you strike me as a man who would be a good hand in a tight spot. We could use you."

Monk said, "It will only be for a couple of weeks, Zack, just until I can find someone who . . ."

"Who what? Knows what they're doing? Hell, Monk, I don't have any experience in the security business. And I damn sure don't know anything about bombs."

"Doesn't matter," he said. "I just need someone I can trust. That's why I'm asking you, Zack. How about it?"

Before I could answer, there was a commotion in the hall and I turned to see the Alachua County Sheriff's Department bomb squad coming through the door.

5

ctually, the bright yellow letters on the back of the black
T-shirts said "Anti-Terrorism Unit." But unlike a S.W.A.T.
team with its macho bravado, they moved in slowly, quietly,
their group demeanor geared toward instilling a sense of calm.

I counted six of them, seven if I included the dog, a German
shepherd. Once inside the skybox it rested on its haunches,
looking up at its handler. The dog's long pink tongue lolled
from its mouth, drool dripping on the skybox floor.

The other members of the unit rolled in handcarts and dol-
lies filled with all sorts of high-tech gear. Some of it wasn't so
high-tech. I saw bolt cutters and sledgehammers, too.

A trim man in a crew cut approached Monk and I. He eased
us away from Whitehall's chair and introduced himself as Captain Kilgore.

"We're going to take care of a couple of quick things, then
I'll need to ask you some questions," he said. "After that, I want
you out of here."

Kilgore signaled the shepherd's handler, who unleashed the
dog. It went straight for Whitehall's chair, sniffing and pawing
the floor, and otherwise signaling that there was something
down there that might blow up and go boom.

"Heel, Sweeney," said the handler, and the dog returned to his side.

Sweeney? The dog didn't look like a Sweeney. It looked like a Duke. All German shepherds do. Duke, or Rex, or King maybe. Sweeney was what you called a bloodhound. I'd have to take it up with the bomb squad's nomenclature department.

Kilgore turned to the only woman in the unit, a blonde with her hair tied back in a ponytail.

"OK, Syzmeski, you're primary. Suit up," said Kilgore.

She looked like a Syzmeski. Thick-faced and squarely built, the sleeves of her T-shirt rolled up just like the guys. Her biceps bulged just like theirs, too.

Two men held the jacket and pants of a military-green Kevlar suit. They helped Syzmeski into the heavy outfit. Then she lumbered toward one of the carts and removed a stubby black wand, sort of like the kind they use at airport-security stations. She flipped a switch on the side of the thing.

One of the men opened a laptop computer. He studied the screen.

"It's showtime," he told Syzmeski, and she moved toward Whitehall's chair.

Another of the men knelt on the floor in front of Whitehall, cradling in his arms a Kevlar blanket.

"Sir, if you don't mind, I'm going to drape this around you," the man said. He unfolded the blanket until it covered Whitehall from his shins to his shoulders.

"Is it to protect me or you?" said Whitehall.

"Both," said the man. He smiled and looked Whitehall in the eyes, holding his gaze. "You doing OK?"

Whitehall nodded. He glanced down at the woman as she stuck the black wand under the chair.

"What in the devil is that thing?"

"An RTR4," said the man kneeling on the floor. "Real-time X-ray. Whatever it sees is gonna pop up on the computer over there."

Whitehall thought about it. Then he said: "Excuse me, miss."

Syzmeski looked up at him.

"Yes?"

"As long as you're down there, would you mind giving my prostate a quick look-see?"

Syzmeski bit back a smile. She got back to work.

Kilgore zeroed in on Monk and me.

"OK, one of you fill me in on what I need to know," he said.

I let Monk do the talking. He stood there, casual as could be, hands in his pockets, giving Kilgore the lowdown. He might have been talking about the game. Just seeing him like that made me relax a little. Things might actually turn out OK.

The guy studying the computer screen called out: "No signs of fragmentary."

"That's a good thing," the guy kneeling by the chair told Whitehall. "That's a real good thing."

"So what next?" said Whitehall.

"Well, after Syzmeski finishes playing tourist down there, we'll figure a way to get you out of that chair. It's mostly a matter of keeping steady pressure on the seat while you step away."

"You make it sound like a walk in the park."

"Well, sir, it's a scenario we've worked on in the past."

"A scenario. Meaning you've never actually encountered the real thing."

"No, sir. Not actually."

I backed up to the counter. No one was paying any attention to me, so I sampled one of the shrimp. It was sweet and briny, and the remoulade sauce had a nice tang to it. Maybe a little light on the horseradish, but far be it from me to complain. I didn't want the shrimp to feel lonesome, so I tried a piece of tenderloin and followed it with a couple of spicy tuna rolls and generous dabs of wasabi.

I checked out the bar. Mostly top-drawer labels. Johnny Walker Blue. Some small-batch bourbons. Grey Goose and Beefeater. But they'd cheaped out on the rum. Bacardi Gold. Monkey piss, meant for umbrella drinks.

I was going in for another shrimp when I heard Syzmeski holler: "Goddamn . . . !"

I looked up to see the box with the bomb in it dangling

from a piece of duct tape under the console chair. It hung there, vibrating.

"It's engaged!" Syzmeski shouted.

She flung herself backward. So did the guy kneeling by the chair. The rest of the squad scattered, too, bailing out through the skybox door. Captain Kilgore rolled behind a row of chairs and pulled Monk down with him.

Darcy Whitehall sat rigid, eyes wide open, looking right at me as I dived behind the counter, toppling trays of food and bottles of liquor.

I crash-landed on the tile floor.

And waited.

6

It would be wrong to call the bomb a dud, because it succeeded in scaring hell out of us. Still, it wasn't much of an explosion. Just a muffled pop, like a firecracker going off beneath a pillow. Then came a flash and a hiss and a lot of smoke. It stunk up the place and stung my eyes, but that was as bad as it got.

I stood up behind the counter, wiping bits of shrimp and sushi off my clothes. The greenish splatter of remoulade sauce complemented all the other stains on my T-shirt. I smelled like bad rum. Wasn't the first time.

Darcy Whitehall sat in the chair. He looked shaken but hadn't stirred.

"You OK?" I said.

He nodded.

The bottom was blown out of the chair. Pieces of cardboard lay scattered around the skybox, along with fragments of plastic and bits of wire.

I stepped around the counter and started to pull the Kevlar blanket off Whitehall.

"Hold it!" shouted Kilgore. He sprung up from the floor, Monk at his side. "There might be a secondary. Just hang tight. Don't let him move."

Whitehall blew out air, exasperated.

"Well, if I must continue sitting in this bloody thing . . ." He looked at me. "Did you destroy all the liquor in your mad leap for cover?"

"Think there might be a few bottles left back there."

"Then would you mind fetching me a tumbler of scotch?"

Kilgore turned on him.

"I don't think drinking is a good idea. Not at a time like this."

"On the contrary," said Whitehall, "it's a splendid time. It appears that I am still breathing air. Less than a minute ago, I had my doubts."

Kilgore let it slide, but he didn't like it.

I went behind the counter and poured Whitehall three fingers of Johnny Walker. I delivered it to him and watched as he finished two fingers of it on the first pull. Monk stood beside us, edgy, ready to get out of there.

Kilgore was with Syzmeski, who sat hunched up in her Kevlar suit behind a row of chairs. The guy who had been kneeling beside Whitehall was with her. The others in the unit were moving back inside the skybox.

Syzmeski looked mad enough to spit nails.

"Just a box of fucking squibs," she said. "Some asshole . . ."

"You OK to eyeball it?" Kilgore said.

"Yeah, I'm good," Syzmeski said.

She got down on her back and slid under Whitehall's chair.

"Nothing here," she said. "Looks clean."

"OK then people, let's shit and git," said Kilgore. He slung the blanket off Whitehall and helped him to his feet.

The other bomb-squad guys fell aside as Kilgore led Whitehall out the skybox door. Monk and I followed them into the hallway.

A cop was standing by the elevator, holding the door open and waving us to get on.

"We got another couple hours of work up here, picking up the pieces, trying to figure out what the hell this is all about," said Kilgore. "We're going to have lots of questions for you."

"I daresay I won't have many answers, but I will cooperate

in whatever way I can," said Whitehall. "Meantime, I can't thank you enough for your service."

He raised the tumbler of scotch and gave Kilgore a crooked smile.

"Cheers, Captain," he said.

Kilgore tilted his head.

"Back at ya," he said.

The three of us stepped onto the elevator. The door closed behind us. We all exhaled at once. Then came one of those long, awkward elevator moments when no one says anything. The elevator started heading down.

Darcy Whitehall drained his scotch. He smacked his lips.

He said, "I knew the bastards were bluffing."

7

And what bastards would those be?" said Barbara.

"I don't know. The elevator doors opened and it was a madhouse with the cops and everything. I had about two minutes with Monk before we found you, and then they were gone."

It was long after dark. Barbara and I were on the road and heading back to my place. It's a two-hour drive from Gainesville to LaDonna, a big chunk of it on a dismal stretch through the Ocala National Forest, where the most common forms of wildlife are rednecks in pickups foraging for beer.

As if in retribution for Monk's smoke screen of an excuse for evacuating the stadium, a hellacious thunderstorm had indeed swept in from the Gulf. The roads were slick and I was going slow, the windshield wipers on my old Wagoneer not wiping nearly fast enough to keep up with the downpour.

Barbara was still in a funk. The cops hadn't let her go back to our seats to get her copy of *A House for Mr. Biswas*. The book had been one of the last things Barbara's mother had given her before she died. And the fact that it was a signed first edition made it . . . well, the money didn't really matter since it was something Barbara never intended to part with.

"So when do you head down to Jamaica?" Barbara said.

"First thing Monday morning. Meeting Monk in Mo Bay."

"So soon?"

"Monk wanted me to fly out with them tonight on Whitehall's jet. I told him I needed a day to get ready," I said. "You OK with all this?"

Barbara shrugged.

"As OK as I'm going to get."

"I don't have to go."

"Zack, please. You know you have to go. It's your nature."

"Meaning?"

"Meaning you just don't have it in you to turn your back on a friend. Even if it means getting killed."

"So you're not OK with it."

"I'm OK with the helping a friend part. But the getting killed part? No, I'm not OK with that, Zack. I'm not OK at all."

"I don't plan on getting killed."

"Funny, I don't remember you planning on that bomb being in the skybox either."

She turned away and looked out the window. There wasn't anything to see. Just rain and darkness.

I flipped on the radio, found a news station and caught the tail end of a story about what had happened at the stadium. The thing that exploded under Darcy Whitehall's chair was no longer being called a bomb but a "bombing device." A little bit of spin from the university and the cops, trying to diminish the fact that someone had sneaked it into the stadium past several layers of security and placed it in the skybox.

A spokeswoman for the Alachua County Sheriff's Department was saying, "Whoever assembled it knew what they were doing. It was expertly rigged. With more explosives it could have caused a great deal of damage." She said FBI investigators had been called in to examine the remains of the device.

Commercials came on and I flipped off the radio.

Barbara loosened her seat belt so she could lean against the passenger door and stretch out her legs on the seat.

She said, "There are a few things I don't understand."

"The BCS ranking system? Quark physics? Why human beings invent things like Splenda?"

Barbara flashed me her cut-the-shit look. I cut it.

"Why would someone plant a bomb that wasn't very much of a bomb? Seems like a great deal of risk."

"Just to show that they could," I said. "To get attention."

"Darcy Whitehall's?"

"Who else? The phone call came to him. The bomb was under his chair."

"Do they have any idea at all what might have prompted something like this?"

"Like I said, Monk and Whitehall were pretty tight-lipped about the whole thing, but Monk said he'd fill me in on everything when I got down there."

We crossed over the St. Johns River in Astor and the rain let up a bit. I put the Wagoneer on cruise control as we hit the long straightaway on the Barberville Road.

"Something else I don't understand," Barbara said. "It seems like whoever planted the bomb was leaving a whole lot to chance. I mean, anyone could have sat down in that chair, couldn't they have?"

"I thought the same thing. But afterward I heard Bill Barnett telling the cops that all the seats were reserved with name tags on them. Apparently, it was a very well-behaved crowd, the type of folks who pay attention to stuff like name tags and where they are supposed to sit."

"The Distinguished Alumni Association."

"Excuse me?"

"The event in the president's skybox. It was to honor the newest members of the Distinguished Alumni Association. Alan Whitehall was one of them."

"Darcy Whitehall's son? The kid in the suit?"

Barbara nodded.

"He's not a kid. He's thirty-two. The youngest-ever inductee into the association. That's why they all came up here from Jamaica. The university held the ceremony at a luncheon at the president's house. It ran a little long and they didn't make it to the skybox until well after the game had started. And that's why it was almost halftime before Darcy Whitehall finally sat down in his chair."

"How do you know all that?"

"I spoke with Alan and his sister while we were waiting for the rest of you to get blown to smithereens," Barbara said. "Plus, I picked this up."

Barbara reached for her purse and pulled out a brochure. She switched on the dome light and read from it.

" 'As founder of Homes for the People, Alan Whitehall has brought hope to thousands of the Caribbean's most unfortunate residents. In just ten years, his nonprofit foundation has aided in the construction of more than seven hundred and fifty single-family residences and fought to improve basic living conditions in blighted neighborhoods throughout the region. Born and raised in Jamaica, Whitehall graduated summa cum laude from the University of Florida's Warrington College of Business Administration and . . .' "

Barbara stopped reading and switched off the dome light.

"The rest is pretty much straight bio, but you get the idea," she said. "He's made quite a name for himself."

"Nice guy?"

"From what I could tell. I mean, the setting wasn't really conducive for casual conversation. But he's a rich guy, or at least the son of a rich guy, and he builds houses for poor people. So I guess that translates into nice guy."

"What about the sister?"

"She had her back up about something, that whole scene with her brother in the skybox."

"Why was she blaming him?"

Barbara shook her head.

"No idea," she said. "I only know one thing."

"What's that?"

"I loved that outfit she was wearing."

I looked at her.

"You loved the outfit."

"Yes, it was darling. The two of us, we talked about it."

"While everyone else was running around worried about a bomb, the two of you were talking about her outfit?"

Barbara smiled.

"That skirt, she made it herself. Lovely, wasn't it?"

"Lovely," I said.

And I thought: They are an entirely different species. They will walk this earth long after we with the Y-chromosome are gone. And they probably deserve to.

"I know something else, too," said Barbara. "I am suddenly exhausted."

She undid her seat belt, flipped around in the seat, and rested her head on my thigh. She looked up at me.

"Are you a member of the Distinguished Alumni Association, darling?"

"So far that honor has eluded me," I said. "Maybe if I started wearing nicer T-shirts. Something without food stains on them."

Barbara squirmed around and got comfortable.

"Well, I love you anyway," she said. "And, for the record, I think you have a very distinguished lap."

I woke up early that Sunday, just before dawn. Barbara was still asleep, so I slipped out of bed and into some clothes and headed for the kitchen to make coffee, trying to tread lightly down the hall so the oak floors would creak as little as possible.

The lusty aroma off the lagoon mingled with the sweet scent of gardenias on the bush by the bay window. Mourning doves coo-cooed from under the front porch eaves. Two more arguments against installing central AC in the house my forebears had built.

I'd been going back and forth about the AC. In the cool of the morning, it seemed an atrocity to cut vents in the ceilings and run ducts behind the walls and let the relentless mechanical drone of a compressor drown the outdoor sounds. But come the swelter of afternoon, which extended long into evening, it seemed foolish not to embrace the temperature-altering benefits of what my grandfather referred to as "Dr. Gorrie's goddam ice machine." According to him, Florida had been on a slow slide to ruin ever since the invention of air-conditioning had made living indoors somewhat tolerable down here.

It was September. Only two more months of Florida summer before the interlude that qualified as neither fall nor winter, but simply not-summer. I figured I could endure the heat for a little while yet and protect the house from the indignity of so-called improvement.

There was a light on in the kitchen. I stopped in the doorway. A woman I'd never seen before was tending a pot on the stove.

She was lean and rangy, her brown hair falling halfway down her back. She wore a khaki shirt and khaki pants, like she was going on safari or something. She was pretty enough, in an outdoorsy way, humming a tune as she watched whatever was in the pot boil.

Boggy had mentioned something about a friend coming to visit. Beyond that, my illustrious housemate had been typically vague regarding the details. Boggy plays a close hand when it comes to women. Hell, he plays a close hand when it comes to everything.

The woman in the kitchen spotted me and smiled.

"Oh, you must be Zack," she said. "I'm Karly Altman."

She stuck out a hand, and I stepped across the kitchen to shake it.

I peeked into the pot on the stove. It held a simmering jumble of roots and stems and leaves. The aroma was somewhere between suitcase-full-of-dirty-socks and floor-that-has-just-been-mopped-with-Pine-Sol.

I said, "That some of Boggy's bush tea?"

Karly Altman nodded.

"He got up early and gathered it, then went out to the nursery to check on the irrigation. I'm supposed to take him a cup when it's ready," she said. "Only, how do you know when it's ready?"

"When the paint starts peeling off the walls," I said.

Karly Altman smiled. She had a great smile—big and honest, and when she smiled her eyes did, too.

"Boggy said it was medicinal."

"So's this," I said, measuring a big scoop of Café Bustelo and packing it into the espresso machine.

Karly gave the pot on the stove a stir, unleashing another wave of odors so pungent that both of us had to stifle back coughs. She leaned against the counter, leaving the bush tea to simmer on its own.

"So," I said, "how do you know Boggy?"

Karly cocked her head. She looked amused.

"Is this the part where you grill me?" she said.

"Excuse me?"

"Boggy warned me that you might ask a lot of questions. He says you get in everyone's business."

"Oh, he did, did he?"

"Yeah, he did. He called you something. I can't remember it exactly. Gommy-something."

"*Guamikeni*. It's a Taino word. Means 'lord of land and water.'"

"Whoa, impressive."

"Not really. It's what the Taino called Christopher Columbus when he showed up out of nowhere and started getting in their business. Everything pretty much went down the toilet for them after that. I think Boggy calls me that sometimes just to be a smart-ass."

"Like if someone calls their boss Hitler."

"A tad extreme. But like that, yeah."

"Taino humor."

"Such as it is."

She shrugged.

"Whatever. It's your place. You're entitled to ask questions and know who your houseguests are."

"I am indeed," I said. "So how do you know Boggy?"

She smiled.

"I met him a few weeks ago when he was in Miami. He dropped by Fairchild."

"Fairchild? The botanical gardens?"

She nodded.

"I work there," she said. "Curator of palms."

"How about that," I said. "My grandfather and David Fairchild were good friends. Went on collecting expeditions together—Malaysia, New Guinea, Madagascar. My grandfather used to drag out the photo albums and show me all those far-off places."

Karly Altman looked impressed.

"Well, that explains a lot. I was wondering how you came to

have so many different specimen palms out there on your property," she said. "This place is amazing, just amazing. Boggy said there used to be a town here or something?"

"Yeah, LaDonna, it was called. Founded back at the tail end of the nineteenth century. That's when my great-grandfather built the house."

"So what happened to everyone?"

"Government kicked them out. Started buying up land to buffer Cape Canaveral and the space center, turned everything surrounding LaDonna into national park. They made people sell, but my grandfather fought them on it. He contended that his palm nursery represented a unique business that was tied to this piece of land and couldn't be restarted anywhere else. Said the government was robbing him not only of his homestead but his livelihood. A federal court agreed with him. When my grandfather died, I inherited the place."

"So now you're the one and only resident of LaDonna?"

"Well, I guess there's two of us counting Boggy."

Karly found some mugs in a cupboard and set them on the counter. I heated milk to go with the Café Bustelo.

She said, "You don't mind me asking, what exactly is the relationship between you and Boggy?"

"Well, it's damn sure platonic, I can tell you that."

She laughed.

"Believe me, I didn't think otherwise," she said.

There was something in the way she said it that led me to believe she and Boggy shared more than a common interest in palm trees. Barbara and I had gotten home so late the night before that I hadn't checked out the bedroom situation. Were the two of them sleeping together? Not that I would get into their business or anything.

Karly said, "What I meant was, does he work for you?"

"Hunh," I said. "If you know Boggy at all then you know him well enough to understand that he doesn't really work *for* anyone. When I was running boats, taking people out fishing and diving, I called him my first mate. But it's not like there's a hierarchy. Fact is, most times I feel as if I'm working for him."

She nodded.

"I know what you mean. He just has this way about him. Not like he's superior or anything. More like, he's beyond everything. He just knows so much."

Yep, they were sleeping together.

I said, "All I know is that he's the only reason the nursery is what it is today. Back when I was playing ball, I couldn't really take care of the place. After I left the Dolphins and started my charter business, Boggy and I were both too busy to give the nursery the attention it deserved. Then I lucked out and got thrown in prison."

"Boggy told me about that. He said you were eventually cleared of everything, even got a special commendation from the governor."

"Yeah, but it cost me two years, and I almost lost this place," I said. "The only good thing about it, Boggy spent that time getting the nursery back in shape. Worked his butt off—pruned, planted, put in new irrigation, went out and found people who would pay top dollar for exotic palm trees. Made Chasteen Palm Nursery profitable again."

I poured the hot milk in a mug, mixed the coffee with it, and poured in way more sugar than is good for me.

I looked at Karly Altman and said, "You're pretty good, you know that?"

"What do you mean?"

"I was the one started out asking the questions, but you turned it around on me. Now back to you and Boggy," I said. "I remember that he went down to Miami a few weeks ago. I didn't know he had gone by Fairchild Gardens."

Karly found a strainer in one of the drawers. She poured the bush tea through it, filling two mugs. The stuff left behind in the strainer looked like soggy lawn trimmings.

"Yeah, Boggy just showed up unannounced one day. He was asking the tour guides so many questions that they finally directed him to me. He told me about you and the nursery, and it sounded so intriguing that I had to come have a look for myself. Plus," she said, "I found him quite intriguing as well. I've never met anyone quite like him."

"That's because there is no one quite like him," I said. "Last of his kind and all that."

She picked up the mugs and stepped for the screen door that opened onto the backyard and, beyond it, the nursery. She stopped and looked at me.

"Do you really believe that?" she said.

"Sure," I said. "What's not to believe?"

"I don't know, it's just that after I met Boggy and he told me, you know, about his background, I started checking into it. Even called a professor friend at the University of Miami, head of the Caribbean Studies department. She said there is no way that he's a full-blooded Taino. She said there are no more Taino. They died out years ago, way back in the sixteenth century."

I held the screen door open for her. She stepped outside.

"Better not let Boggy hear you say that," I said. "He tends to get bent out of shape when people tell him he's extinct."

She smiled.

"OK, *Guamikeni*," she said.

She turned and walked away, the smell of Boggy's infernal bush tea lingering in her wake.

9

I went down to the boathouse with my coffee and got out the cast net and took it to the end of the dock. The sun was up now, and I could see fish working in the shallow waters of the lagoon.

After a couple of really lame throws, in which the net collapsed and caught nothing but oyster shells, I finally hauled in a half dozen mullet. I took them to the boathouse and filleted them in the sink of the kitchen I had built just the week before.

While the kitchen in the mainhouse was a perfectly fine kitchen, it had one major drawback—it was stuck on the back of the house and I couldn't look out on the water while I cooked. And since looking out on the water is just about as pleasurable a thing as I can imagine, along with cooking and eating and drinking and, well, that other thing, I had moved around some storage lockers and thrown out some clutter and created a kitchen in the boathouse.

Nothing fancy, but I was proud of it. A rehabilitated Viking stove that ran off propane tanks. A secondhand refrigerator with a quirky icemaker. For a counter, I had lain two-by-eights across a couple of sawhorses. The cabinets came from Target— a dozen plastic crates nailed to the wall. I was feeling somewhat slighted that *Architectural Digest* hadn't called to schedule the photo shoot.

By the time Barbara got out of bed, I was putting the final touches on LaDonna Benedict—poached eggs on fried green tomatoes topped off with homemade Hollandaise. I rolled strips of mullet in cornmeal, fried them in peanut oil, and artfully arranged them around the tomatoes and eggs. I don't like space to go to waste on a plate so I gave us each a healthy mound of grits. Not just any grits, but Rockland Plantation stone-ground white grits that I have to order all the way from Mt. Pleasant, South Carolina, because the best grits that grocery stores in Florida can come up with are lesser grits, from Dixie Lily or Quaker Oats. Rockland Plantation grits are grits with gumption. You cook them in milk for almost an hour, and they make other grits taste like pablum.

We sat in the big Adirondack chairs at the end of the dock, eating off wicker trays. I pulled a bottle of champagne from the ice bucket and fiddled with the wire basket around the cork.

"Are we celebrating something?" asked Barbara.

"Uh-huh," I said. "The fact that we are sitting here. Just the two of us. Enjoying each other's splendid company."

"Works for me. Especially since it might be my last free-and-easy gasp for the foreseeable future."

I stopped fiddling with the cork.

"Look, if this is about me going down to Jamaica . . ."

"It's not."

"It's not?"

"No. Believe it or not, Zack darling, there are things aside from you that do occasionally torment me, and one of them is called Aaron Hockelmann. He is flying in tomorrow."

Aaron Hockelmann was owner and cofounder of Hockelmann-Glass, or H + G as it is known in the magazine business. His publishing empire, which started in Germany with a stable of racy newsweeklies and gobbled its way through Europe, had recently been amping up its U.S. presence, buying titles left and right, and launching several more. Hockelmann—the trades called him "Aaron the Baron"—had been courting Barbara for the past year with offers to buy Orb Communications and install her as vice president of a new travel division at H + G. He had privately suggested to her that he was thinking about launching a new travel magazine, one that would go head to head with the likes of *Condé Nast Traveler* and *Travel & Leisure.*

It was a tantalizing scenario and one that had caused Barbara no small amount of conflict. While *Tropics* had won all sorts of awards for design and editorial content, it remained smallish in terms of circulation, hovering around 150,000. It lacked the necessary oomph to pull in the most desirable big-money advertisers, the "non-endemics," as Barbara called them, clients like brand-name vodkas or big clothing-store chains, who would sign on to buy a year's worth of back covers or multiple full pages at the front of the book.

Instead, Barbara and her sales staff were forever on the road, flogging the product, trying to cobble together co-op ads from small hoteliers or kissing up to Caribbean tourism ministers in hopes they might loosen their islands' advertising purse strings. For all Barbara's resiliency, it occasionally wore her down.

And now here came Aaron the Baron, dangling a bucket of money and the allure of an international stage. While Hockelmann promised Barbara that he would leave *Tropics* and the rest of Orb Communications intact, that hadn't been his style in previous acquisitions. Grabbing the gold ring meant Barbara would lose control of something she had created and built and truly loved.

I popped the cork and reached for Barbara's glass.

"Just a wee dribble for me," Barbara said.

"I don't believe in wee dribbles," I said, filling her glass and mine.

I took a healthy sip. I didn't roll it around on my tongue or let it rest at the back of my mouth so I could savor a hint of pear or lemongrass. I just sucked it down. It went well with the fish and the eggs.

It was fake champagne, actually, something from Spain that had cost me twelve dollars. It was the perfect fake champagne for swilling on a dock on a hot day in September while you are admiring the love of your life.

Barbara was twisting a strand of hair around her right index finger the way she always does when she is thinking hard about something. Maybe twisting the hair massages a point in her scalp that connects with a nerve ending that leads to her prefrontal cortex and helps her think. Whatever, it is one of about a zillion things she does that endears her to me, and sitting there watching her and drinking good, cheap, fake champagne, I was a happy man.

"Do you know what I am thinking?" Barbara said.

I put my fingers on my temples, closed my eyes, and pretended to concentrate.

"Yes," I said. "You are thinking that as a reward for this most excellent breakfast you would like to take me by the hand, gratefully lead me to the house, and jump my bones."

"You're a lousy mind reader."

"I wasn't trying to read your mind, I was trying to plant a suggestion."

"Lousy gardener, too," she said. "Actually, I was sitting here thinking that I really must be an awful, heartless, self-centered mercenary who cares only about her own well-being and bottom line."

"Little harsh on yourself, aren't you?"

She shrugged.

"In the wake of all that happened yesterday the only thing that really concerns me today, aside from your leaving, of course, is that I did not get a chance to actually meet Darcy Whitehall."

"Which undoubtedly would have led to you charming him and him signing a long-term contract to advertise in *Tropics* and the world would be a happier place."

"Undoubtedly, because if Darcy Whitehall came on board then other big players would surely follow and I wouldn't be so tempted by the likes of Aaron Hockelmann," she said. "And here I am, with so many larger things swirling all about, and all I can think about is my own puny circumstances. Am I awful or what?"

"No, not at all."

"Oh good," she said. "I didn't really think so."

She took a tiny sip of champagne. I finished off my glass and poured some more.

"Don't worry, Toots, I can grease the skids for you with Darcy Whitehall. After all, I am now one of his bodyguards."

"Toots?"

"Bodyguard talk. I'm getting into character."

Barbara chewed her lip, studying me.

"That's something I don't understand, Zack. Bodyguards are big and thick and dumb and like to play with guns. Since when are you bodyguard material?"

"It's nothing I've ever aspired to, believe me, but Monk needed help in a hurry."

"So what will you do actually? Shadow Whitehall wherever he goes and keep the bad guys at bay?"

"Something like that, I guess. It's not like I've ever done this before. And Monk didn't give me a lot of details. He was anxious to get out of there."

"There was no one else he could get?"

"Guess not. He says it might take a couple of weeks to find the right person who can do it full time. I told him I'd fill in until then."

"But why you? Why not some rent-a-cop or something? There must be tons of them out there looking for work."

"Monk trusts me. We go way back."

Barbara looked out at the lagoon. Then she looked at me.

"You keep saying that. 'We go way back.' But you haven't seen the guy in what, seven or eight years . . ."

"About that long, yeah."

"And he suddenly shows up out of nowhere and asks you for a favor, a really huge favor, and you drop everything to run off and . . ."

"You're still not right with this, are you?"

"I'm trying, Zack, I'm trying. But you have to see it from my standpoint."

"Which is?"

"Some stranger waltzes in and you waltz off."

I sipped some champagne. It had gotten a tad too warm and lost some of its fizz. I put it down.

"Let me tell you about Monk," I said. "He was like a big brother to me. He grew up poor, in the Panhandle. His parents pretty much abandoned him and he got into all kinds of trouble. Went straight into the army out of high school and when he got out he played junior-college ball somewhere out in the Midwest. He was good, good enough to land a full ride at Florida.

"He was six or seven years older than the rest of us. At first, I wasn't so hot about him being my roommate. I mean, he was this old guy. It was like living with a semi-adult. But I learned a lot from him, a whole lot."

"Look, Zack, you don't have to explain. Really, I . . ."

"I want to explain. I want you to understand. Because Monk and I *do* go way back. There *is* a bond between teammates. Doesn't matter that we haven't seen each other for years."

I picked up my glass of champagne and dumped what was left in the water.

"I went to his first wedding. It was the year before he stopped playing ball. Married a New Orleans Saints cheerleader named Rina. I was one of the groomsmen. Hell of a wedding, that was. Then they split up after a few years, and I kind of lost track of him after that.

"Word was he'd fallen on some pretty hard times. When that kind of thing happens, a guy sometimes just burrows down, doesn't want his old friends to come knocking. Now he seems to be pulling everything back together. If he needs help I'll give it to him."

We were quiet for a moment. Then Barbara said, "I'm sorry. I never meant to question your friendship. I know you are loyal to the core."

She leaned across the table and kissed me. The sun was beating down hard now. The lagoon was flat. Not even the hint of a breeze.

"There's another reason Monk asked me to go down there," I said. "It's probably because he knows I don't have any . . ."

I stopped.

Barbara said, "You don't have any what?"

"What I started to say was, I don't have any attachments."

"Well, it's true," Barbara said. "You don't."

"It's not true," I said. "There's you."

Barbara smiled. She reached out and took my hand.

"Yes, there *is* me," she said. "But I don't ever want you to feel as if I am tying you down."

"Gosh, you mean I bought you those fur-lined handcuffs for nothing?"

Barbara swatted at me.

"Stop it," she said. "You know what I mean. And if you really did buy fur-lined handcuffs, then you should bloody well take them with you to Libido. Lord knows you'll find plenty of willing wenches down there."

"You worried about that?"

"Not in the slightest," she said.

"Right answer," I said.

Then she took me by the hand and led me to the house. She was much better at reading minds than I was.

10

After Barbara left I did some things that needed doing before I could leave for Jamaica, which is to say I mostly just piddled around, burning time and trying to convince myself that I was indispensable around the place. Truth was, all I needed to do was pack my bags. Boggy could take care of everything while I was gone.

The previous year had been a prosperous one, at least by my standards, thanks largely to the proceeds of what Barbara generously called my "Bahamas investment venture." It had been slightly short of legal, but since no one had lost money except those who deserved to lose it, and they were now either dead or in jail, I didn't feel much in the way of guilt.

Besides, it was the sort of enterprise that, had I been forthcoming about it, would have created a great deal of extra work for an already overburdened IRS. That's why I had thoughtfully decided not to bother them with the details of it. Just call me Good Citizen Chasteen.

I sank much of the cash from that venture into my favorite investment—fiberglass. There were two new boats in my boathouse, a 27-foot center console that I use for offshore fishing and the occasional dive trip, and a 17-foot flats boat that's ideal for working Redfish Lagoon, the mangrove-lined sanctuary that spreads out for miles behind my house.

I showed the boats some attention and talked to them and told them not to miss me while I was gone. Then I hosed down my trawler, *Miz Blitz,* let her engines idle for a few minutes, shut them down, and went off looking for Boggy.

I finally found him at the south end of the nursery, atop a small bluff that overlooks a narrow finger of the lagoon. It is one of only a few small chunks of open space on the property. Everywhere else is crammed full of palm trees.

Boggy and Karly Altman were on their knees, digging dirt from near the base of a tall, scraggly solitary palm tree and placing it in several glass jars marked with labels. They stood as they saw me approaching.

In all the years I've known Boggy, I've never been able to figure out what attraction he holds for women. But they attach themselves to him like holy on the pope, which is especially curious when you consider that he stands five-foot-four with a face that looks like it was molded out of Silly Putty and a physique somewhere between that of a suitcase and a bowling ball.

"He's like a little brown god," is how Barbara once described Boggy. "You just want to hug him."

Beats hell out of me.

Karly Altman stood at least a head taller than Mr. Huggable, and she was beaming at me.

"Congratulations," she said.

"Thank you," I said. "What did I do?"

"Why, it's your carossier," she said. "It has fruited."

"Hmmm," I said.

"Aren't you excited?" she said.

"Mere words can't express," I said.

I looked at Boggy. He nodded at the tall scraggly palm.

"That's the carossier," he said. Then he turned to Karly. "Zachary, he just own the place. About palm trees, he does not know shit."

Karly looked at me with unmasked pity.

"You mean to tell me you don't have a clue what it is you

have here?" she said. "No wonder you can't grasp the immensity of the occasion."

"Clueless, graspless, don't know shit. That's me," I said.

"I'm sorry," she said. "I tend to lose sight of the fact that not everyone's a palm nut like I am."

She wiped dirt from her hands and rapped her knuckles against the trunk of the palm tree.

"*Attalea crassipatha.* One of several species of the American oil palm. Native habitat, southwestern coast of Haiti. Number of specimens known to exist in the wild, no more than thirty. Number of specimens successfully propagated in private nurseries, zero," she said. "But we're about to change that."

"We are?"

"Oh, yes. Just look at those," she said, pointing to the top of the palm. A yellow stalk protruded from the tree's crown. It was studded with dozens of tiny white flowers. Bees were buzzing around them.

"The blossoms should fall off in the next week or so, and I'll bag the stalk in plastic mesh after that," she said. "Otherwise, we run the risk of losing the fruit to birds."

"Can't have that," I said.

"Then it will take four to five weeks for the seed pod to mature and be ready to plant," said Karly Altman.

She grabbed one of the jars of dirt.

"It's critical that I analyze the soil. I'll need to set up a small lab to do that. I was hoping to use a portion of your kitchen," she said. "Is that OK?"

"Sure," I said. "I won't be needing it. I'm getting ready to leave for . . ."

"Great," said Karly Altman. "And would it be OK if we built a potting house? We can probably make do with the scrap lumber and screen that's in the storage shed. Boggy said he could slap something together."

"That's fine. I'd offer to help you, but I'll be . . ."

"Oh, this is so exciting. Thank you, thank you, thank you," said Karly, giving me a hug. "Now I have to go send out some e-mails. This is big news. A carossier fruiting in Florida. Who could have ever imagined?"

"It's really that big a deal, huh?"

"Omigod, it's giant," she said. "Wait until the International Palm Society finds out. There will be all kinds of people swarming in here to get a look."

She gathered up the jars of dirt, put them in a cardboard box, and hurried off toward the house. Boggy and I watched her go.

"Woman's got a lot of enthusiasm," I said. "Didn't know it was possible for someone to get that excited over a palm tree."

"She has a big spirit," Boggy said.

I looked at Boggy.

"So, you and her . . . ?"

Boggy didn't say anything. And his face gave up nothing. It never does.

"Aw, c'mon," I said. "What's the deal with the two of you? Is it serious?"

It sounded stupid the minute I said it. With Boggy everything is serious.

So we stood there atop the bluff, enjoying the view. To the west the lagoon sprawled out like a giant jigsaw puzzle, a dazzlement of curlicue islands and snakelike sloughs. From the east came the Atlantic's low grumble. The surf was choppy and the water was the gray-green it gets after a summer's worth of hard rain and outflow from the lagoon.

Minutes went by. Neither one of us spoke. Boggy is one of exactly two people in the world with whom I can feel comfortable in the quiet. Barbara is the other one.

Finally, Boggy said, "Barbara, she wants me to go with you."

"So you know what's going on, about me heading down to Jamaica?"

Boggy nodded.

"Barbara found me as she was leaving and told me about it," he said. "She is much troubled, Zachary."

"Funny, she didn't act much troubled when I last saw her."

"Sometimes she puts on a face for you because she knows that is the face you want to see."

"And what? She puts on another face for you?"

He shrugged. He didn't say anything.

"Well, she's got nothing to worry about," I said. "I'll be back before she knows I'm gone."

"So you do not wish me to go with you?"

"I can handle it," I said.

Boggy turned and faced me. He looked long and hard into my eyes. His gaze seemed to bore into some deep core of me that not even I can penetrate. He does this every now and then. It is more than mildly creepy.

Then he turned away and said, "It will not be quite so easy as you expect, Zachary."

"That a fact? Or is this one of your hunches?"

"It is what it is," he said.

"You know, it really ticks me off when you say crap like that. You might as well be writing newspaper horoscopes. Nothing is ever as easy as anyone expects. And everything is what it is. Tell me something I don't know, how about it, instead of all the mumbo jumbo."

Boggy didn't say anything. He folded his arms above his little potbelly and looked west across the lagoon.

"No way," I said. "It doesn't work like that. You don't just throw stuff like that out there and then clam up and let it hang. Give up what you've got."

But I didn't get anything else out of him. When I walked away he was still standing there, gazing into the distance at something I couldn't see.

11

Monday morning I got up long before sunrise and drove to Orlando and caught a flight to Miami. I was glad to be flying early, well ahead of the afternoon thunderstorms that close in from the coasts and collide with a fury and make flying in Florida such a come-to-Jesus experience.

The pilot banked the plane east, took us out over Port Canaveral, and we cruised south along the condo corridor. An hour later, the Miami skyline poked itself out like jailbait in a bikini and drew us thither.

Miami International has two redeeming features. One is a killer Cuban cafeteria, La Carretta, on Concourse D. I grabbed a stool at the take-out counter and ordered café con leche and a crab relleno. Then I sat there admiring the airport's other redeeming feature—a steady stream of Latina lovelies from the Caribbean basin and beyond.

Had Barbara been with me, we would have rated the contenders as they walked past and speculated about where they came from.

"Pink tube top with the black capris. An eight-point-five. Puerto Rico."

"What is it with you men and tube tops? She's slutty. Barely a six. But those shoes of hers, they're darling. Brazil. She's definitely from Brazil."

I ordered a pastelito, filled with sweet guava paste and cream cheese, and another café con leche. Someone had left behind a copy of the *Miami Herald*. I flipped through it.

The *Herald*'s news staff had been caught short in its coverage of the bomb in the skybox for Sunday's edition, but had more than made up for it in Monday's paper. There was a flashy piece stripped across the top of the front page under the headline: "Resort Mogul No Stranger to Danger." It portrayed Darcy Whitehall as a consummate risk-taker both in business and in his personal life. It told how he had beaten the odds as a music producer, then cut his own path as a renegade hotelier. And it showcased his penchant for adventure—trans-Atlantic sailboat races, diving with whale sharks in Belize, hot-air ballooning across the Andes.

The story jumped to a full page inside with lots of photographs of Whitehall from over the years—palling around with Peter Tosh and Mick Jagger backstage at a 1980s-era concert, soaking in a hot tub at Libido with a bevy of fetching babes, dancing with a pair of leggy supermodels at a South Beach nightclub. There were quotes from various people who knew him, but nothing in the way of explanation, or even reasonable speculation, as to why someone might have planted the bomb.

A paragraph near the end of the story, however, caught my attention.

"While Whitehall has never taken an active role in Jamaica's often-bloody political arena, his son, Alan, is no stranger to public life. Having founded a high-profile relief program that provides low-income housing throughout the Caribbean, the younger Whitehall has set his sights on a seat in the Jamaican parliament and was recently nominated by the ruling People's National Party to stand as a candidate in the Trelawney Northern district."

My "Ah-ha!" moments are few and far between, but this was one of them. I thought back to the scene in the skybox, the little incident between Alan Whitehall and his sister. She'd blamed

Alan for the jam their father was in. Then she'd stormed away and left him with Darcy.

"If this is my fault, I'm sorry," Alan had said. "I'll quit. I'll drop out."

Had he been referring to his budding political career? Did someone want him out of the race? And was that dud-of-a-bomb their way of underscoring the seriousness of their intentions?

All questions I could ask Monk DeVane soon enough.

12

A half hour later I was at the gate for Air Libido. It was part of Darcy Whitehall's empire, a charter operation that flew guests to the islands on which his various resorts were located.

And what an operation it was. Instead of the typical airport hellhole of molded plastic seats and crummy carpet, the Air Libido waiting area resembled a beachside tiki bar. There were comfy divans, rattan chairs, and even a couple of hammocks strung between fake palm trees.

Perched on a stool by the boarding gate, a guy in dreadlocks was strumming the guitar and singing Bob Marley standards. The check-in counter resembled a little grass shack by the sea.

All in all, it was a masterful piece of marketing. Air Libido stood out like an orchid in a sandspur patch. Vacationers on their way to other airlines walked past Air Libido and thought: Man, next time I want some of that.

The flight to Montego Bay was already boarding. A young man and a young woman were working the check-in counter. Both looked like catalogue models ready for a frisky day at the beach.

The young man wore his flowered shirt open, all the better for displaying his pecs and abs. The young woman wore a gauzy blouse over a halter top and shorts, all the better for displaying her everything.

I handed the young woman my ticket and she gave me a boarding pass. Then she held up a tray and offered me my choice of rum punch or a bottle of Red Stripe beer. Not even ten o'clock in the morning and on Air Libido it was already time to cut loose.

I reminded myself that I was heading to Jamaica on a serious mission, a possible matter of life and death, a situation in which it might be a good idea to keep my wits about me.

I took a Red Stripe.

Boarding the plane was like walking into a party that had started long before I got there. The buzz was lively, the cabin speakers were blasting reggae, and several people—including a couple of the flight attendants—were boogeying by the bulkheads. The island vibe was so pervasive that I halfway expected the copilot to step out of the cockpit and pass around a giant spliff.

The crowd was about what I expected. The women wore a little too much makeup, the men a few too many gold chains. All of them were laughing just a little too hard and talking just a little too loud and straining just a little too much to have a good time.

It was like spring break for grownups, which made it slightly pathetic. Everyone seemed to be checking out everyone else, maybe deciding who they would pick when it came time to choose sides for naked volleyball.

My boarding pass said A-14, the window seat. A woman was sitting in it. Another woman sat next to her. Both were in their early thirties, I'd guess. Both had bottle-blond hair, lots of it, done up in a way that ought to be illegal outside of Texas or Tennessee. And both had devoted much time and consideration to their travel outfits, which were tight and revealing. They were pretty enough, if you like that over-the-hill-Hooter's-girl kind of look.

"I hope you don't mind I took your seat," said the woman by the window. "We wanted to look out on all the pretty water."

"Not a problem," I said. "I can use the extra room to spread out."

They gave me the once-over.

"Well, I guess you *can*," said the one in the middle seat. "You're a long tall one, aren't ya?"

I've been hearing that all my life, and I've never been able to come up with a suitable reply. So I just smiled and strapped myself in and sat back with my Red Stripe.

"Yoo-hoo, over here, hon," said the woman by the window as she waved down a flight attendant carrying a tray full of rum punches. They each took one and passed over half a dozen empty cups in return.

The woman in the window seat leaned forward and looked at me and said: "So where you from?"

"Florida," I said.

"Well, we're from Knoxville . . ."

Knew it.

"You ever been there?"

I nodded my head yes. I didn't bother telling them how I had been there twice when the Gators played Tennessee. We'd won one and lost one and I'd blown out my knee for the first time in the one we'd lost.

They talked. A lot. They both worked in "the financial industry," which I took to mean they were probably bank tellers. Lynette and Darlene, that was them.

Darlene leaned closer to me.

"You traveling by your lonesome?" she asked.

I nodded.

"Well, I hear there isn't no one who gets lonesome at Libido," she said.

I shrugged.

"I hear things can get really wild and crazy," she said.

I nodded.

"But that's why we're going there, isn't it? To get wild and crazy."

I wasn't sure if I should shrug or nod, so I did a little of each. Darlene looked at me.

"What's a matter? Cat got your tongue?"

I shrugged.

"That's OK," she said. "I like the strong silent type."

She snuggled up against me. Lynette elbowed Darlene.

"Girl, just cool your jets," she said.

Then she leaned across Darlene and patted me on the knee.

"Just never you mind her," Lynette said. "Darlene, she just got divorced a while back. And she's hornier than a trumpet. Isn't that right, Darlene?"

"Toot-toot," said Darlene.

The two of them laughed.

I closed my eyes. I pretended to sleep. The plane took off. Pretty soon I didn't have to pretend anymore.

13

Monk DeVane stood waiting for me on the curb outside customs at Sangster International. He was easy to spot. He wore a bright pink Libido polo shirt and white pants. He saw me and gave a big wave.

The sidewalk was hot and loud and thick with people. Dozens of cab drivers and hustlers worked the crowd with typical Jamaican zeal and rat-a-tat spiels. Several of them were in my face before I was halfway to Monk.

"Welcome to Jamaica, mon. You need a drivah? I got da wheels, mon, I got da wheels," one said, falling in step with me. "Where ya be needing to go?"

"Sorry," I said. "I've already got a ride."

Another one tapped my elbow and spoke low.

"Welcome to Jamaica, mon. You need ganja? You need crank? I be ya pharmacy, mon."

I pulled away and reached the curb where Monk was grinning at me. I was still getting used to his gone-tropo appearance—the shaggy hair, the untrimmed beard. He looked like a particularly hirsute Jeff Bridges, a big guy with a big jaw and broad shoulders.

"Welcome to Jamaica, mon," Monk said.

"What are *you* selling?"

Monk laughed.

"Misery and heartbreak," he said. "Not sure exactly what I might have gotten you into here, Zack."

"That bad?"

He wiggled a hand—so-so.

"Still hard to tell," he said. "Afraid it might be one of those calm-before-the-storm things."

"You figured out who's creating the storm?"

Monk glanced to either side, cautious. It seemed a tad melodramatic, but what did I know? Maybe the bad guys were watching us. I had to get into the bodyguard mind-set, be suspicious of everyone.

"Not now," Monk said. "We've got plenty of time to talk about that on the way to the resort. I'll fill you in on everything."

Just then a familiar trill shattered the sidewalk chatter.

"Hey, you! Over here . . ."

I turned to see Darlene and Lynette, watching us from alongside a big pink bus. The Libido Resorts logo was emblazoned down its side and the other passengers from our flight were filing onto it.

Darlene put her fists on her hips and gave me a cute little pout.

"Aren't you coming with us?" she said.

"I'll be along," I said.

Lynette wagged a finger at me and winked.

"Alright, but don't you forget about us," she said. "We're gonna party."

They giggled and waved and got on the bus. Monk turned to me and cocked an eyebrow.

"Looks like you're about to get lucky, my friend."

"Believe I'll pass, thank you."

"Don't tell me you've turned into a one-woman man, Zack."

"Sad but true," I said. "Think it suits me, actually."

"That's great. I'm happy for you."

"Like hell you are," I said. "Where's your car?"

Monk smiled.

"Man, you know I always follow the Chasteen rules."

When Monk and I were roommates, I had shared with him my grandfather's three simple rules for surviving life in Florida and the rest of the tropics: "Walk slow. Marry rich. And always park in the shade."

"Unfortunately," Monk said, "I can't slow down or I'll go broke. And I don't plan to get married again, or I'll go broker. But I can damn sure find a decent parking space. It's way on the other side of the lot, under the trees."

He pointed to the far end of the terminal, maybe a hundred yards away, where a stately row of royal poinciana trees was in full audacious orange bloom.

I grabbed my two duffels. I had overpacked, not knowing exactly how long I'd be staying or what the dress code might be for a bodyguard.

"Let's go," I said.

Monk stopped me.

"Naw, I'll go get the van and pick you up."

"I don't mind walking," I said. "Be good to stretch my legs."

But Monk wouldn't have it.

"Save your energy. You're going to need it. Besides, it's an hour's drive to the resort. You might want to take a leak first."

"Ah, the power of suggestion."

Monk put a hand on my shoulder.

"Look, Zack," he said. "I want you to know how much I appreciate you coming down here. Means a lot."

"Now, don't get sappy on me. I just wanted to beef up my resume."

"We haven't talked about money," Monk said.

"I'm not worried about that."

"I know you aren't," he said. "But I'll make it right for you. Promise."

He gave me a slap on the shoulder and headed off across the parking lot. I stepped back inside the terminal and found a men's room and took care of everything that needed taking care of.

Then I made my way back to the curb, passing through the hawker gauntlet again. I turned down two offers of ganja and two offers from drivers wanting to show me all the sights in addition to selling me ganja.

The Libido bus was long gone. I stood on the curb, looking across the parking lot, trying to spot Monk. He'd said he was driving a van. I was betting it was a pink van, just like the pink bus and Monk's pink polo shirt.

Branding is everything these days. I was hoping my little stint as a bodyguard didn't mean I'd have to wear one of the pink polo shirts. Pink doesn't favor me. I'm a khaki-and-white kind of guy. Occasionally I will put on the plumage and wear something navy blue, but I always feel shifty about it for weeks afterward.

I glanced toward the royal poinciana trees at the far end of the terminal. They don't call them royal poinciana trees down in the islands. They call them flamboyants. It's a much better name. It says exactly what they are when they are in bloom—an in-your-face orange.

Only . . . these flamboyants were suddenly more orange than any I'd ever seen. They were consumed by orange, an inferno that billowed up from the pavement and above the trees, followed by a massive gray plume that lapped at the sky and swept out in all directions.

In the next instant came the roar and the shockwave of the explosion. I crouched behind a taxi, shards of glass and shreds of metal scattershot all around.

Then deathly silence. And then people screaming.

I leapt out from behind the taxi and ran to the parking lot. I hadn't made it more than twenty yards when the second explosion came, followed almost instantly by a third.

I hit the pavement, landing behind a concrete balustrade where a young woman lay unconscious, her clothes singed, her face bleeding. The asphalt must have been a hundred degrees, but the air around us was suddenly even hotter. Green needles on a nearby stand of casuarinas crinkled and turned black.

I scooped up the young woman and retreated toward the terminal, casting a glance back toward the flamboyant trees. They were gone. So was the far end of the parking lot. All that remained was a gaping hellhole ravaged by flames.

This time the bastards weren't bluffing.

14

I am sorry about what happened to your friend," said the man sitting across the desk from me.

We were in a small stuffy office at the Mo Bay headquarters of the Jamaica Constabulary Force, and he was a smallish black man wearing a short-sleeved white shirt and a black tie—Inspector Eustace Dunwood. His close-cropped hair had a tinge of gray and so did his tidy mustache.

"Has anyone figured out how it happened?"

"Not really," Dunwood said. He spoke in the measured tones Jamaicans use with foreigners who can't begin to understand their lyrical patois. "There are witnesses who say they saw a van, one belonging to the Libido resort, explode."

"That would have been Monk's."

Dunwood opened a manila envelope, fished around inside, and pulled out a charred leather wallet. He handed it to me. I opened the wallet. The plastic window that held the driver's license had been singed, but I could make out what was left of the license's green logo. "The Sunshine State," it said. Below it was Monk's name—Donald Wilson DeVane Jr.

"Is this the only thing of his that you have?"

Dunwood took a deep breath and exhaled.

"For now. Our investigators are still trying to determine what is what."

My gut ached. I could have been in the van with Monk. It could have been shreds of my former existence that Eustace Dunwood was carrying around in a manila envelope.

"How many others?" I said.

"At least three. Maybe more. A half dozen vehicles destroyed. It's fortunate the blast occurred where it did, at the far end of the parking lot. Otherwise it would have been much worse."

I handed Monk's wallet back to Dunwood. He stuck it in the envelope. He set the envelope atop a small stack of papers. He tapped the papers, straightening them, then squared the stack with the corners of his desk. It was the neat and orderly desk of a neat and orderly man.

"There are a few questions I must ask," he said.

"Please, go ahead."

"You stated that Mr. DeVane was at the airport so that he might give you a ride to the Libido resort, correct?"

I nodded.

"And he met you outside of customs and the two of you chatted there on the curb for a few minutes."

"Yes, that's right."

"So why is it that you did not accompany him to the van?" Dunwood said.

"He told me to wait for him on the curb. He said it was a pretty good drive to the resort and suggested I might want to use the men's room before we got started."

"And did you?"

"Did I what? Use the men's room?"

Dunwood nodded.

"Why yes, I did."

"Did anyone see you use it?"

I looked at him.

"Exactly what are you getting at here?"

Before Dunwood could answer, the door to the office opened without anyone knocking on it and in walked two men, white guys.

The younger of the two, he might have been thirty, showed a

lot of white teeth in a face that was tan and smooth. He wore a blue blazer with some kind of fancy crestlike insignia, white polo shirt, khakis with sharp creases, and leather loafers with socks that matched the pants. He looked as if he had just stepped off a golf course, a very private golf course.

"Inspector," he said, nodding at Dunwood. He stuck out his hand for me to shake. "Jay Skingle, U.S. Embassy, assistant consul for Homeland Security. Got here as soon as we could. On behalf of the ambassador, I'd like to express our sympathy over your loss and any hardship you might have suffered. We stand by to do whatever we can to assist you in this matter."

His words flowed out like oil from a can. A born diplomat.

The other guy didn't introduce himself. And Skingle didn't bother to do it for him.

The other guy moved to a corner and leaned in it. He was a small man, quite slender. He wore plain brown pants and a plain beige shirt. His face was all angles, like something a cubist painter might draw, with a sharp nose, boney cheeks, a sharp brow—the very definition of a hatchet face.

Skingle sat down in a chair next to mine and gave me the once-over, his expression pinched. Guess the bloodstains on my shirt didn't do it for him. Dunwood had told me the girl I'd pulled from the parking lot would be alright.

"I understand you were a friend of Mr. DeVane's," Skingle said.

"That's right. We used to play ball together."

"And you came here on vacation?"

I shook my head.

"No, I came to help Monk out."

"Doing what?"

"I was still waiting to find that out," I said.

"But did it involve his work with Darcy Whitehall?"

"Yes," I said. "It did."

Skingle shot a quick look at the guy leaning in the corner.

"Some sort of security work, right?" Skingle said.

"That's right," I said. "Did you know Monk?"

"No, no, not at all," said Skingle. "But I was aware that Mr. Whitehall had recently hired him, on a consultant basis."

Eustace Dunwood cleared his throat.

He said, "If you don't mind, I was in the midst of interrogating Mr. Chasteen when you arrived."

I looked at him. Interrogating?

"Carry on, then," Skingle said.

He made a steeple of his hands and placed them under his chin. He reminded me of every frat boy I'd ever known in college. I didn't feel like talking to him. Or Dunwood. Matter of fact, I didn't feel like talking to anyone. Or being interrogated.

I stood.

"Sorry," I said. "But I'm not up for this right now. I need to make some phone calls, let a few people know what's going on."

"Now listen here," said Dunwood. "There are still a number of matters we need to discuss."

"Like what? Who I took a leak with at the airport? Go interrogate someone else about that."

Dunwood started to say something, but Skingle stopped him.

"Please, Inspector, you must understand that Mr. Chasteen is under a great deal of strain at this time. I'm sure he will be more than happy to make himself available to you when he has had a chance to collect himself, won't you, Mr. Chasteen?"

"Whatever," I said.

Skingle stood from his chair, brushed off the seat of his khakis, and shot the sleeves of his jacket.

"Mr. Chasteen," he said, "in situations of this nature, the embassy is charged with seeing to it that next of kin is notified. May I assume you will take care of that?"

I nodded.

"Also, regarding the proper disposition of Mr. DeVane's remains, there will be some necessary paperwork, which the embassy will assist you with. We will be in touch with you at the appropriate time."

"Fine," I said.

Skingle turned to Dunwood.

"As for you, Inspector, I would be remiss not to mention that the U.S. Embassy will be closely monitoring the handling of this affair."

Dunwood said nothing.

"And I would be further remiss not to mention that you can expect the embassy to lodge a formal complaint with the prime minister's office regarding the Jamaica Constabulary Force's lack of initiative in controlling certain groups that present a clear and present danger to the well-being of U.S. citizens in your country," said Skingle. "I refer specifically to the NPU."

"No reason to believe the NPU had anything to do with this," said Dunwood.

"No reason to believe they didn't either," said Skingle.

Skingle gave the guy in the corner a look, and the two of them walked out the door. Dunwood turned to me.

"Where will I be able to find you, Mr. Chasteen?"

"Suppose I'll head to Libido and check in with Darcy Whitehall."

"Taxis are out front," he said.

I started for the door.

"One more thing, Mr. Chasteen," Dunwood said. "Don't be telling that embassy man anything you don't tell me. We clear on that?"

"Yeah," I said. "Real clear."

15

Outside, the air was still heavy from the heat of the day and smelled of diesel and dust. It was almost dark and the streets of Mo Bay were busy, people rousing for the evening. Trucks honked, music played loud. Taxi drivers leaned against cars, smoking cigarettes and talking.

I looked down Union Street, past the old Cable & Wireless building and Raj Mercantile and the Scotia Bank. Church bells were ringing from the other side of Sam Sharp Square. I saw a tiny sliver of the sea. The sun was a half hour gone. The sky was the color of a day-old bruise, and the water showed not a bit of blue.

I felt dirty and grimy. It would be good to take a hot shower and slip into some clean clothes. Only . . .

Zack, you damn fool.

In the madness at the airport I'd left my duffels behind. No way they were still sitting on the sidewalk, but maybe it was worth a shot to swing by there on the way to Libido.

I signaled the closest taxi driver. He hopped in his car and pulled my way. Just before he reached the curb, a horn blared and a black Mercedes vectored in from Union Street and cut off the taxi. Gold letters were monogrammed on the front door—D. W.

The passenger's window went down on the Mercedes. Looking out at me was Darcy Whitehall's daughter, Ali.

"Get in," she said.

I gave the taxi driver a shrug, sorry, and he responded with a string of enchanting colloquialisms regarding my parentage, mating habits, and personal hygiene. There were several references to goats.

I settled into the backseat of the Mercedes. It slid into traffic.

The driver was a sinewy black man with salt-and-pepper dreadlocks that fell like thick pieces of rope below his shoulders. His helmet of hair rubbed up against the Mercedes' headliner.

Ali turned around in the front seat, her big dark eyes rimmed with red.

"What about Monk?"

I shook my head.

"Oh my God, no," she said.

She let out a wail and buried her face in the headrest, slamming a fist against the seat.

"No, no, no."

She slumped in the seat and sobbed.

We drove like that for a while. We went past the airport. I didn't mention anything about my bags. Wouldn't have done Ali any good for us to stop there. And even if we had stopped, we couldn't have gotten anywhere near the terminal. It was blockaded with armed troops stationed at the barricades.

The driver snaked the Mercedes into a roundabout and exited on the Al, the coastal road to Runaway Bay and Ocho Rios. We passed clumps of sunburned tourists walking along the sidewalk. Small hotels, big hotels, every kind of restaurant and a joint on the shoulder called Bushman's Jerk Shack. A crowd of people stood outside it. I could smell the reason why. If I'd had any appetite at all I would have been right there with them.

A few miles down the road, Ali pulled herself together. She turned around in the seat again. She smiled. She was a lovely young woman.

"We didn't have a chance to meet properly the other day. I'm Ali." She pointed to the driver. "And this is Otee."

I caught his glance in the rearview mirror. We exchanged nods.

"Tell me about it," said Ali.

And so I did. When I was done, Ali was quiet for a while. Finally, she turned to me again and said: "Monk told me you were a famous football player."

"I played. The famous part is debatable. My career didn't last that long. Bad hinges," I said.

Ali looked confused.

"My knees gave out," I said.

"Oh," she said.

We rode for a bit. Then she said: "Did he play the game well? Monk, I mean."

"Yeah, he played it very well. Had a Super Bowl ring to show for it."

"And you do not?"

"No," I said. "I do not."

"Why is that?"

"Because I played for the Dolphins."

"The Dolphins of Miami."

"That's them," I said.

"They are a bad team, the Dolphins?"

"No, we weren't bad. We always seemed to start the season strong and fizzle at the end. My last year we went nine and seven. But we lost the last four in a row and didn't make the playoffs. We had to play the Patriots and the Bills in the snow. We sucked in the snow."

A day like today and we were riding along in a car talking football. The real salvation of sports is not the victories or the devotion to a team. It's the blessed distraction. It gives us something to talk about when we can't bear to talk about the bad stuff bearing down on us.

Otee looked at me in the rearview mirror.

He said, "Da real football, mon, you ever play dat?"

"Soccer, you mean?"

"Yah, mon, what da whole resta da world call football."

"No, I didn't play it."

"Didn't tink so," he said. "Big stout man like you be suckin' air."

"Stout?"

"Yeah, mon, you stout."

I didn't say anything. I didn't feel stout. I was carrying two hundred thirty pounds on my six-foot-four frame, just ten pounds more than my old playing weight. I ran. I worked out. I watched my carbs. Well, sometimes. Like maybe every fifth meal.

"Wot position you play, mon?" Otee asked.

"Strong safety."

He nodded. Probably had no better idea what a strong safety did than I did about a midfielder or a left wing or a sweeper.

We rode along for a bit, and then Ali said: "We could use some of that now."

Otee looked at her.

"Wot dat we could use?"

"Some strong safety," she said. "That's what we really need."

Maybe that was my cue. Maybe I should have spoken up and told her not to worry. Maybe I should have tipped my hat and slipped my thumbs under my belt and said something like: "Well, ma'am, don't you worry that pretty little head of yours, because that's exactly what I'm here to give you."

But I didn't say anything. I sucked in my stomach. I sat up tall in the seat.

Stout, my ass.

16

The A1 hugged the coast, shooting straight through flat country-side. To our left, the sea lay hidden behind the walled compounds of private estates and big resorts. To our right, the terrain began its ascent toward the mountains.

I'd visited Jamaica several times over the years, but had lingered mostly along the coast. I had very little firsthand knowledge of the island's wild interior. Not many people do, including the majority of Jamaicans. But I knew there were vast stretches of the hinterland, from the Cockpit Country to the John Crow Mountains, which remain virtually uncharted, as hostile and impenetrable as they were hundreds of years ago when Jamaica was a colonial outpost in the conquest of the Caribbean.

I couldn't see the mountains from the car. Yet, I had a real sense of their presence, a feeling that something dark and threatening loomed out there.

Then again, maybe it was just my own dark mood. An old friend was dead. And I was alone, heading into uncharted territory of my own. I kept shifting around in the backseat of the Mercedes, but no matter how I fidgeted I couldn't make myself comfortable.

After an hour or so we neared the bluffs around Repulse Bay. The road steepened. A canopy of Jamaican cedars hid the night sky. The afternoon showers were long gone, but water still dripped from the trees.

We rounded a bend and the high beams of the Mercedes lit up a concrete wall on our left. It was tall, eight feet at least. It was painted pink and ran as far ahead as I could see. The grounds along the wall were landscaped with stately Royal palms and clusters of bougainvillea. The grass was thick and manicured.

Spotlights drew attention to big letters that were inset on the wall. They spelled out "Libido."

The spotlights also drew attention to something else. When she saw it, Ali shot up in her seat.

"Damn them!" she said. "They're at it again."

Alongside the Libido logo, black spray-painted letters announced: "NPU say go!"

Otee slowed the Mercedes. As the car edged along the wall, we saw a succession of graffiti, all written by the same hand. Sometimes it was just the three letters "NPU." Elsewhere there were slogans: "NPU say no to Babylon!" and "NPU say stop da exploitation!"

Then the high beams picked up three figures along a section of the wall that lay ahead. Two of them turned toward us, frozen in the headlights. The other one crouched beside the wall, working furiously with a can of spray paint.

"Stop them!" shouted Ali.

Otee whipped the Mercedes off the road, driving along the shoulder. We hit bumps and hollows in the grass, and Otee kept tapping the brakes. We couldn't go very fast. I bounced around in the backseat.

As we closed in, the crouching figure slung the spray-paint can aside and stood by his accomplices. Three boys, barely in their teens—one of them, the spray painter, barechested and wearing red running shorts; the others in baggy pants and T-shirts. All three of them wore yellow-and-red bandannas pulled tight against their heads.

We were about fifty yards away when the shirtless one reached down, picked up a rock, and flung it at the Mercedes. It struck dead center in the windshield and sent out a spiderweb of shattered glass. Otee hit the brakes, and I heard Ali scream as I tumbled onto the floorboard, the car spinning in the wet grass, crashing into something, and slamming to a stop.

I pulled myself up and saw Otee leap out his door, saw him pull a pistol from his waistband, saw him lean across the hood of the Mercedes, using it to steady his aim. But the three boys had already bolted across the road and disappeared into the underbrush.

I got out of the car. The Mercedes had crashed into one of the palm trees. The front door on the passenger's side was crumpled. I helped Ali slide out on the driver's side.

We joined Otee by the wall. And we looked at the words that had been written there, the paint still fresh and gleaming.

"NPU say go!"

17

They call themselves Nanny's People United—NPU. Officially, a political party. But just hoodlums, as far as I'm concerned, committing crimes and calling it politics."

We sat in the living room of Darcy Whitehall's cliffside house at Libido, just Darcy Whitehall and me. Otee had deposited me there, then left to escort Ali to her cottage elsewhere on Libido's sprawling grounds.

It was one swell house—soaring ceilings, bamboo floors, exotic hardwood furniture, everything opening onto a broad deck that wrapped around the place. Airy and expansive, the house seemed to draw in the outdoors and create the impression it was floating above the sea. It was like something the Swiss Family Robinson might have built if they had good taste and a decent design budget.

The wall opposite me was filled with badges of honor from Whitehall's storied career in the recording industry—framed albums that had gone platinum, photos with all sorts of famous musicians, a row of trophies that included several Grammies.

"Nanny's People?" I said. "Sounds like it ought to be the name for a day-care center, not a political party."

"Oh, this Jamaican Nanny, she was about as tough as they come. You never heard her story?"

I shook my head no.

"Granny Nanny, they sometimes call her," Whitehall said. "Jamaica has seven national heroes. She's one of them."

"Like George Washington or Thomas Jefferson."

"No, actually, not like them at all," said Whitehall. "There's really no one in America like our Nanny."

Whitehall wore a faded blue polo shirt and cream-colored pants that could have been pajamas, baggy and made out of cotton with a drawstring waist. He was barefoot. Mr. Casual Elegance.

He reached into a pocket and came out with a roll of cash. He peeled off a bill and handed it to me. It was for five hundred Jamaican dollars, about eight bucks U.S. given the current exchange rate. The face on the bill was of a gaunt, fierce-looking woman, wearing a turban and a necklace of bones and leaves.

"That's Nanny. Someone says, 'Hey, mon, lemme hold a Nanny,' means they want you to give them five hundred J's."

I handed Whitehall the bill. He tucked it away.

"Nanny was a leader of the Maroons," Whitehall said. "You know about them, I assume."

"That's what they called the runaway slaves who lived up in the mountains and fought the British. Back in the 1700s."

Whitehall nodded.

"Didn't just fight the British, they beat the British, with Nanny leading them all the way. Descendants of those original Maroons still live up there. Got Maroon villages scattered all over Cockpit Country. They have their own autonomous government, their own leaders, their own way of life. Might as well be a separate country up there."

"And these Nanny's People, the NPU, they're based in the mountains, too?"

"Oh, they're everywhere. In the city, in the mountains. They've spread like a brushfire. Got some woman they call Nanny Two, stirring them up and making them do what they do."

"So what's their beef with you?"

Whitehall arched an eyebrow, gave me an ironic smile.

"Why, I am the Great Oppressor, of course."

"Because you own big resorts?"

"Exactly. According to the NPU, tourism equals slavery. Rich white people come here, and poor black people wait on them. No different than the plantations. What they neglect to see, of course, is that without the money tourism brings here, there would be no roads, there would be no airports . . ."

A voice interrupted him.

"No AIDS, no pollution, no homogenization of the culture."

I turned to see Alan Whitehall standing at the entrance to the living room. Otee stood just behind him.

"What, the NPU has brainwashed you, too?" said Whitehall. "Or are you spouting their nonsense just to win a few more votes in the countryside?"

He said it with a smile, and Alan Whitehall returned it as he joined us in the living room. He embraced his father warmly.

"I might stand miles apart from the NPU on most matters," said Alan, "but there are some things on which we share a common ground. And the negative impact of wholesale nonsustainable tourism is one of them."

"I don't know what this talk is about nonsustainable tourism. All I know is that the people who come and stay in our hotels make it possible to pay the bills," said Whitehall. "What would you do, man, bite the hand that feeds you?"

"Oh no, Father, I would never bite it. But take a friendly little nip from time to time? Just to keep you honest? Sure, I'll do that."

Whitehall jostled his son's shoulder in mock anger. There was clearly a lot of affection between the two of them whatever their political differences might be. Alan shook my hand.

"My condolences for the loss of your friend," he said. "I did not know Mr. DeVane well, but no one deserves to die in such a fashion. Such a horrible thing."

Alan Whitehall bore only the slightest resemblance to his father. Like Ali, his features were dark, the Creole blend so common in the islands. Where Darcy Whitehall was dashing and devil-may-care, Alan was bookish and buttoned-down.

Darcy Whitehall gestured us to the bar. He made drinks. The two of them had gin and tonics. I saw a bottle of Appleton Estate Reserve twenty-one-year-old rum. Costs sixty bucks a bottle in the States. When you can find it. I had some that.

We stepped out onto the broad deck that wrapped around the house. Otee stationed himself between the living room and the deck, his pistol snug in the waistband of his pants.

Far below us, waves crashed against cliffs that fell away to a perfect crescent of white-sand beach. Lit up at night, Libido's layout resembled a wagon wheel cut in half. Pathways radiated out to clusters of villas. The hub was a long low complex near the beachfront with a couple of restaurants, a nightclub, a spa, and a fitness center.

"I know you must have many questions, Mr. Chasteen," Darcy Whitehall said.

"Just one," I said. "Who killed Monk DeVane?"

Whitehall shook his head. It was a long moment before he finally said: "I've no idea."

I'm no good at masking what I'm thinking. Whitehall said: "You look surprised by that."

"That's because I am," I said. "I just assumed you might have some suspicions about who's responsible for all this. Someone you've crossed, someone you've done business with, someone who has it out for you. Back at the skybox, in the elevator, when you said you knew the bastards were bluffing . . ."

Whitehall cut me off with a dismissive wave of his hand.

"Just a figure of speech," said Whitehall. "I wasn't referring to anyone in particular."

"What about Monk? Didn't the two of you talk about who might have planted that fake bomb in the skybox? Didn't he have his suspicions?"

Whitehall sipped his drink. He held my gaze.

"No," he said. "We never discussed that at all."

I didn't believe him. I looked at Alan Whitehall. He seemed to be studying his father with the same skepticism I felt, but he didn't say anything.

"OK," I said. "What about these Nanny's People characters? They obviously don't have warm, fuzzy feelings about you."

"No, they don't. If I had to suspect anyone, then it would be them. Not only do they have their grievances with me, they are fielding a candidate to oppose Alan in the parliamentary election," said Whitehall. "However, my son, the politician, disagrees."

"I don't think they had anything to do with it," Alan said. "The NPU has been vocal, but it hasn't been violent."

"Not yet, anyway," said Whitehall. "But this is Jamaica. Politics leads to bloodshed like honey to the bee. Which is where you come in, Mr. Chasteen."

I took a sip of my drink. The twenty-one-year-old rum is the oldest that Appleton puts on the market. They make a forty-year-old batch, but don't let us riff-raff have any, saving it as gifts for presidents and prime ministers and heads of state.

"I know you came here as a favor to Monk DeVane, not out of any allegiance to me," said Whitehall. "But I would be greatly obliged if you stayed. Just to help out for the short term, until all this gets settled."

I took another sip of my drink. Wonder how often any of those presidents and prime ministers and heads of state ever pour a big glass of the good stuff, kick back and enjoy it. The world would be a better place . . .

"I am fully aware that you don't have any particular expertise in such matters," Whitehall said.

No denying that. I was completely out of my league. But I saw no need to second my shortcomings. I sipped some more rum. I let it puddle in my mouth before I swallowed it. It burnt good going down.

"Monk held you in high regard and that's quite good enough for me," Whitehall said. "Still, please know that I forgive you should you choose to walk away from all this."

I drained the last of the rum.

"Appreciate that," I said. "But if I were to walk away, then I couldn't forgive myself."

Darcy Whitehall smiled. He took my glass.

"Let me get you a refill," he said.

18

We all had another drink. Darcy Whitehall offered a toast to Monk's memory. We talked and talked, but I didn't learn much more about who might be running around setting off bombs and killing people.

I did learn a lot about Libido. Darcy Whitehall steered the conversation away from Monk's death and toward the resort business. He gave me an overview of his operation—about two hundred and fifty acres at the Jamaica property, the largest in his chain of resorts, with a maximum occupancy of three hundred guests and a staff of four hundred. Then he and Alan started talking about amortization of capital outlays and tax-deferment strategies, and unable to hold up my end of the conversation, or even wanting to fake it, I called it a night.

"Meet me for breakfast," said Darcy Whitehall, "and we'll decide where we go from here."

He told Otee to take me to where I would be staying.

"Give him a quick tour of the place," said Whitehall. "Then stop at the main guardhouse and make sure Mr. Chasteen has everything he needs."

Several golf carts were parked outside. Otee pointed at one and we got in it and drove off, zipping down the hill that created a buffer zone between Whitehall's house and the resort proper.

We passed thickets of bamboo and ginger, heliconia and antherium. The sweet smell of frangipani was thick on the air. Giant philodendrons arched overhead with fronds the size of market umbrellas. Tree frogs croaked a racket.

The guest villas were so well hidden behind all the plants that I could barely make them out. Idyllic, open-air affairs, they gave their occupants the impression of bunking down in a private Eden.

Otee pulled the golf cart into a mulched parking lot and got out.

"Dis where all de action is come night," said Otee.

He set out down a footpath and I followed him. I heard music and the throbbing beat of a bass line coming from the direction of the beach. As we drew nearer, I spotted a long pavilion, a low glow silhouetting the people dancing inside. At least, I think they were dancing. A few of the couples appeared to have progressed to more intimate rhythmic diversions. It was hard to tell in the dim light.

Ahead of me, Otee stopped on a wooden footbridge. Squeals of laughter cut through the night.

I joined Otee and looked down on an artificial stream that rushed out of a shrub-luscious glade. It was a flume ride, like you'd find at a water park, made of poured concrete, its smooth sides painted turquoise. Big round lights lined the bottom, and the shallow water sparkled as it whooshed under the bridge.

The squeals of laughter drew closer.

"Here come da show," said Otee.

They came in groups of twos and threes and fours and more, shooting down the flume, all of them naked and all of them having a wild old time. Most of them were just in it for the ride, whooping and hollering as they went. For others it was a grope-fest, and they had latched on to each other in wonderfully creative ways as they negotiated the flume's banks and turns.

Some went down on their bellies with partners riding their backs. Some went down sitting upright in long human chains, their legs wrapped around each other. I spotted one guy gleefully coursing along in tandem with a slim brunette woman, his hands clutching her perky boobs, manipulating them as if they were steering knobs.

There was a brief lull in the parade. And then another couple came into view.

"Oh, yah," said Otee. "Dose two got it figured out."

The man was riding on his back, hands behind his head, comfy as could be. The woman was straddling his lap, facing forward. She worked her hips with intensity of purpose, leaving little doubt what the two of them were up to.

All in all, it was an impressive display. The woman's blond hair was plastered down her back. She smiled and waved as they shot under the bridge.

"Hey, there!" she called out.

It was Darlene, the friendly woman from Tennessee who had sat next to me on the plane. I waved back as she and her partner disappeared around a bend in the stream.

Otee gave my arm a tug and took off down the path ahead.

"Got to see how dose two finish it," he called out as I hurried after him.

We passed a sign that said "Libido Lagoon" as the footpath opened onto a free-form pool the size of three tennis courts. It had been designed to look like some tropical version of aquatic paradise—water trickling down limestone walls, lots of ferns, and lots of naked people lounging on terraced ledges and paddling around in the pool.

A faux volcano belched smoke and kept the pool enshrouded in a haze of watery mist. Small caves honeycombed the limestone walls. They were dark but I could catch an occasional glimpse of movement from within and could well imagine what was going on in there.

A few dozen people were gathered at one end of the pool, by a broad waterfall with a ten-foot drop. It was fed by the flume we'd crossed just moments before. Bodies were spilling over the lip of the waterfall to the delight of the people in the pool.

Otee stopped by the edge of the pool. I pulled alongside him and watched as Darlene and her partner shot out from the flume. For an instant the acrobatic duo hung there, conjoined like alley cats. Darlene threw up her arms in a perfect V, and the guy matched it from beneath her—a brilliant piece of choreography that was greeted with tumultuous cheers and applause from the crowd as the couple splash-landed, wrenched apart upon impact.

Otee nodded his admiration.

"Now dat's a flying fuck," he said.

19

Back in the golf cart, we putted away from Libido's glitzy reception hall and followed a narrow road marked "Staff Only." It led us past several squat stucco buildings and storage sheds before coming to an enormous pile of rubble—charred timber and crumbled blocks.

"What happened there?"

"Used to be the maintenance building," Otee said. "Had a fire took it down a few weeks back."

Otee pulled the golf cart alongside a long concrete block building. A couple of off-duty security guards sat out front playing cards. We got out.

Otee spoke to the guards, and we stepped inside, passing a control room where a bank of monitors flashed sequences of shots from security cameras placed around the resort. One of them offered interesting angles on activity in the lagoon area. Others showed similar goings-on elsewhere on the property.

A guard sat in a swivel chair watching the monitors. He yawned.

"How da show?" Otee asked him as we walked past.

"Same ol'," said the guard. "Sell tickets, I'd be a rich man."

We walked through a small locker room and stopped at a

steel door with a digital lockbox on it. Otee punched in a code, opened the door, and we stepped inside.

Otee flipped on a light. The room wasn't much bigger than a good-size closet, and it was filled with guns—rifles in racks along one wall, pistols on shelves along another.

Otee closed the door behind us.

"Just got a new door and lock," Otee said. "Someone got in here a couple weeks back. Took five of the AR-15s, half dozen of the Glocks."

"Any idea who it was?"

"Could have been anyone. One of the guards, someone else," Otee said. "Mr. Whitehall, him no like the regular guards carrying guns. It scare the guests. But they here if they need them. You mek a choice what you want. Got Glock, the G36. Got Beretta, the 92 full or compact. Me, I like the Browning."

He patted the pistol in his waistband.

"I'm alright, thanks," I said.

"What you say?"

"I don't want a gun."

Otee considered me as if I had just told him I ate mud for breakfast and crapped brownies for lunch.

"You don't want a gun?"

"No," I said. "I don't."

"You watch out for Mr. Whitehall, you need a gun, mon."

"Not me."

"Dis Jamaica. Mon get in a jam he need a gun."

"I get in a jam, I'll figure something out."

Otee studied me for a long moment, then he nodded me out of the room, pulled the door shut behind.

"Dead man want to do what a walking dog can," he muttered.

"What's that mean?"

"Means if you die you can't even lick yer own ass. Dat's what it mean."

"I'll take my chances."

Otee said, "Yeah, you'll damn sure be doing that."

20

We got back in the golf cart, continuing our way up a steep hill, the golf cart straining against the incline, finally stopping at a cluster of wood-frame duplex cottages.

"Dat where you mek a bed. Numbah five," said Otee, pointing at a door on one of the cottages.

"This where Monk stayed?"

"Numbah six," said Otee. He nodded at the adjoining door. "All his tings still inside."

He jerked his head in the direction of the cottage.

"Go look at da place, see if it suits ya."

The door on number five was unlocked. I went inside and flipped on a light and looked around. Nothing fancy. A tiny sitting room out front, a tinier bedroom in the back, and in between, a narrow galley kitchen. The furniture was worn and the mattress was thin, but the paint was new and the place smelled clean. It would do.

When I stepped outside, Otee was on the porch, holding two leather pouches. He reached into one of the pouches and sprinkled whatever was inside it along the edge of the porch. Then he sprinkled some more in front of my door.

"What's that?"

"Tobacco seed," he said. "Keep Monk duppy away."

I knew about duppies, what folks of the Caribbean call the wandering souls of the dead. And I knew better than to disrespect such beliefs. Duppy lore is firmly entrenched on all the islands. To mock it is to engender all sorts of bad ju-ju. Not worth it. Besides, when it comes to wandering souls and the spiritual world and things that go bump in the night, I figure it makes sense to pay tribute on all fronts, just to cover your butt.

"Tobacco seed, huh. Why's that keep duppies away?"

"A duppy, him ain't good with figures," Otee said as he continued sprinkling. "Can't count past nine. Duppy get to the porch, see all dis tobacco seed, and him want it, him want it bad. Him pick it up and start counting it, and when him gets to nine him have to stop and start counting all over again. It vex him. Sooner-later him just go way."

He opened the second pouch and began sprinkling something from it, something white.

"Salt?"

Otee nodded.

"Duppy no like salt. Mek him heavy so he cannot fly." He finished sprinkling the salt. "Used to be all us Africans could fly. You know dat?"

"No, I didn't."

"Yah, mon, true-true. We could fly like hell we could. Could fly everywhere, free like bird. But da white man, da slavers, dey gave us salt and when we get off de boats in Jamaica we could not fly home to Africa."

Otee finished spreading the salt, then tucked away the two pouches.

He said, "Duppy got nine days."

"Nine days?"

"Someone die, they duppy got nine days to roam around, do what they want, take what they want with them to the grave. Dat ninth night, the duppy he finally rest."

Otee got in the golf cart. He punched the pedal and it rocked forward.

"Thanks for that," I said.

"Yah, mon," he said. "But you gonna wish you had one dem guns."

21

I spent nearly an hour on the phone in the living room. I tried calling Barbara. On her cell, at her house, at her office just in case she was working late. No luck. I left messages on all of them, telling her I was OK and not to worry.

After half a dozen calls to various far-flung friends and God knows how much in long-distance tolls, I finally found Rina Murray, Darcy's first wife. She was still living in New Orleans and now had her own real estate business.

"Christ, I wouldn't wish something like that on anyone," she said after I'd told her what had happened. "Not even Monk."

I didn't say anything.

"That sounds awful, I know, but he stuck me with a lot when he left, Zack. I spent the first five years paying off debts that were in both of our names, the next five getting out from under things he hadn't even told me about. Man had more secrets than the CIA. Can't imagine what kind of shape those other two wives of his are in, not if he did them like he did me."

"You know how I'd get in touch with them?"

"Yeah, I've got their numbers laying around here some-where. Might take me a while to put my fingers on them. They both used to call me every now and again, asking if I'd seen him after he'd run out on them. We should have formed a club or something."

"Monk have any kids that you know of?"

"Think he had a couple by the last one. Annie, her name is. Lives somewhere around Tampa. The two of them were still married, I think. She called here a few months ago, wondered if I might have heard from Monk. Poor thing was broke. I wound up sending her a little something just so she could make her bills."

"Anyone else I need to get in touch with?"

"Not that I can think of," Rina said. "I mean, besides his old teammates, but you know most of them. Then there were some of his old Army buddies. Monk was still pretty tight with one of them back when we were married. Connigan. Scotty Connigan. That was his name. But I wouldn't know how to find him."

"Well, you come across any numbers, keep 'em handy. I'll get back in touch with you so I can notify folks about it," I said.

"Look, Zack, don't you worry about that. I'll make the calls," she said. "Sounds like you've got enough on your hands."

"You sure about that?"

"Yeah, I'm sure. And I'll see about a memorial service or something. Guess it should be in Florida, with his wife and kids," Rina said, her voice breaking. "Hold on, let me get some goddam Kleenex."

When she came back on, she said: "Never thought I could shed tears again over that son of a bitch. But no one deserves to go like that, Zack. No one. Not even Monk DeVane."

We said our good-byes and I told her I would call in the next day or two, as soon as I knew anything more.

It was late and I knew I should sleep, but I was wound tighter than the knob on a cheap alarm clock. I thought a shower might do some good, relax me a little bit.

I got undressed and stepped in the tub and turned on the spigot full blast. When things got steamy I yanked on the shower valve and let the needles of water beat against my neck and shoulders. Not as good as a deep-tissue massage, but not bad.

I stretched and got out the kinks and did some yoga neck rolls that Barbara had shown me. Said they were good for relieving stress. They worked. Sorta. But if Barbara had been in the shower with me then we could have engaged ourselves in a stress-reliever that would have worked a whole lot better.

I dried off, stepped into the living room, and tried all of Barbara's numbers again. Nothing doing.

I went back to the bedroom. There was an AC unit in one of the windows, but I didn't turn it on. It was warm out but not unbearable, with a breeze off the ocean coming through the front screen door, moving through the cottage, feeling almost cool against my just-out-of-the-shower skin.

The lightbulb in the middle of the ceiling was confounding a couple of moths. I turned it off and the moths flitted away.

I lay on the bed in the dark, face up, arms at my side. I closed my eyes. I thought tranquil thoughts. I visualized Redfish Lagoon, behind my house in LaDonna, its surface smooth and unruffled.

So calm. So peaceful.

Such a load of horseshit.

I got out of bed, wrapped a towel around me, and stepped next door, to check out Monk's place.

22

The layout on the other side was just like on mine—same generic furniture, same color curtains and paint on the walls—but it bore Monk's presence. A pair of worn running shoes just inside the door, a T-shirt and gym shorts draped on the doorknob, as if Monk had gone for a run and was letting things air out for the next time. A quart bottle of drinking water sat on the coffee table, uncapped, a few swallows left in it.

Monk had just stepped away. And then he was gone for good. Poor bastard.

There wasn't much to see. No books or magazines scattered about. Monk had never been much of a reader. In the kitchen, dishes were washed and stacked neatly in the drying rack. A towel was folded over the faucet.

I looked inside the refrigerator. Empty, except for more bottles of water, a carton of eggs, a withered mango, and a plateful of something covered with aluminum foil. I decided it didn't bear investigating.

I stepped into Monk's bedroom and turned on the light. The bed was made, its corners tucked tight. The room was tidy as could be.

I opened the closet door. There were shirts and pants on hangers, including two pink Libido polos, like the one Monk was wearing the last time I saw him. I found a couple of white polos that looked as if they'd fit me, along with one of his old scrimmage jerseys from the Saints, and took them off the hangers. I tried on a pair of khaki pants. A bit loose around the waist but they'd do. I took one of Monk's leather belts, too. A blue Kelty backpack hung on the clothes rack. It was empty. I stuck everything in it.

I rummaged around in a wooden dresser that sat at one end of the closet and found a pair of khaki shorts and some bathing trunks. I added them to my borrowed wardrobe. I let Monk's underwear stay where it was. It didn't really creep me out to wear the shirts and pants of a dead man, but I drew the line at underwear whether the guy was dead or alive. I'd free-ball it until I could get to a store and buy some of my own.

The bottom drawer of the dresser doubled as Monk's filing cabinet. It was filled with manila folders and crammed with papers. I saw old bank notices and car-payment booklets. I'd go through it later. Maybe I'd come across something that would be helpful in settling Monk's affairs, a life-insurance policy or a secret savings account that might help out that ex-wife of his in Tampa. I really wasn't counting on finding anything like that. Still, it couldn't hurt to sort through things.

I peeked in the bathroom. Monk's Dopp kit sat open on the formica bureau. I recalled reading somewhere that the Dopp in Dopp kit came from the name of a German immigrant to Chicago in the early 1900s, Charles Doppelt, whose nephew was in the leather-goods business and named that particular style of small zippered bag after his beloved uncle. Then again, maybe the nephew didn't really think too much of the old guy. Why else would he attach his moniker to something made to carry everything from jock-itch salve to hemorrhoid cream.

I wondered what Charles Doppelt might think of someone who went snooping in someone else's Dopp kit. He'd probably turn up his German immigrant nose at it. Screw him. I fingered my way through Monk's private stuff: dental floss, tweezers, toenail clipper, travel-size containers of talcum powder and aftershave, aspirin, Maalox. The usual.

I stepped into the bedroom and stopped at a small desk by

the door. I hadn't noticed it on my way in, but sitting square in the middle of the desk was a black, faux-leather organizer, one of those day-by-day calendar/journal things. Gold letters, embossed on the front cover, read "Ideal Executive Daybook."

I picked it up and flipped through it. A newspaper clipping fell out. It was a month old, from the *Jamaica Gleaner,* a page of legal ads. Someone, Monk I presumed, had circled one of the announcements in black ink. Under the heading "Notice of Ownership," it read: "Regarding Township 14, Range 7 West, Section 24, Trelawney Parish, 254 hectares, as bounded by Old Dutch Road and Fishkill Morass; notice is hereby given that said parcel is fully and lawfully owned by Libido Resorts, LLC, in accordance with all covenants of the Commonwealth. All other claims hereupon are rendered null and void, and all unlawful occupants therein are hereby instructed to vacate said parcel."

Sounded like fancy language for an eviction notice. I stuck the clipping in the back of the daybook and finished flipping through it. The pages were stiff, as if the organizer had been seldom used. There were only a dozen or so entries, dating back to early May, which would have been shortly after Monk first arrived at Libido. They were written in a neat, deliberate hand, in the same black ink that had circled the legal ad in the *Gleaner.* Phone numbers, to-do lists, that sort of thing.

Two entries caught my eye, if for no other reason than Monk had marked them in big letters and set them off with asterisks. One was for just a couple of days earlier:

****K.O.****
MARTHA BRAE
1019 CHRIST CHURCH LANE

K.O. The only thing I knew that that stood for was knockout. And who was Martha Brae?

The last entry was for today, September 6. It listed my flight number and arrival time. Beneath that was written:

****EQUINOX INVESTMENTS****
314 DOVER RD MB

I'd never heard of Equinox Investments, but I was guessing MB stood for Montego Bay. Brilliant deduction, Zacklock. I stuck the daybook in the blue Kelty backpack along with the clothes I had taken from Monk's closet.

Maybe the entries meant something, maybe they didn't. They were strings, the only strings I had. Might as well tug on them and see if they unraveled something.

23

I slept better than I had any right to and woke up feeling like a new man. A new man who was famished.

Darcy Whitehall had mentioned something about breakfast. Wonder when he liked to eat it. I glanced at the clock. A little after six. A tad early for civilized dining. How to kill time until mealtime? Life's most pertinent question.

I put on Monk's bathing trunks and the old Saints scrimmage jersey, slipped into his running shoes, and set out on a slow jog across the Libido grounds. Ten minutes later, after following a dirt path that wound down a hill, I reached a secluded stretch of sand along a pocket-sized cove. It was separated from the rest of the resort by VW Bug–sized boulders that jutted out from the shore. The sun was still low, the water dark and opaque, not yet flaunting its tropical striations.

A stately arc of coconut palms rimmed the beach just beyond the high-tide line. Contrary to Boggy's assessment of my taxonomical knowledge, I was slowly learning which kinds of palm trees were which. I couldn't spout off genus and species, but I could look at the trees along the beach and know that they were not just any coconut palms. They were Jamaica Tall Palms.

Used to be Jamaica Talls flourished throughout Florida, but

lethal yellowing disease has pretty much done them in. Nowadays when you see a coconut palm in Florida it is most likely the shorter, stubbier Malayan Greens or Malayan Golds, perfectly decent palm trees, but lacking the oh-wow factor enjoyed by the statuesque eighty-foot-tall beauties along this beach.

As I stood there admiring the scene, a voice from behind startled me: "Welcome to my beach."

I turned to see Ali Whitehall smiling at me from the porch of a stilt house nestled in a thicket of pepper trees just a few yards away. I had walked right past it, but hadn't even seen the place, so much was it a part of the landscape.

"Your beach?" I said.

"Yes, Ali's Beach. That's what Father named it when he bought the property." She pointed to a bluff at the far side of the beach. "Way over there, past the promontory, where you can't see it, that's Alan's Beach. He's on one side, I'm on the other. The prodigal son, the black-sheep daughter. Fitting, I suppose."

I didn't know how to respond to that, so I didn't.

"Out for your morning constitutional?"

"Something like that," I said. "I'm supposed to meet your father for breakfast. What time does he usually get started?"

"Oh, he's not much of a morning person. Sleeps in 'til at least nine, then works out for an hour. Never breakfasts before eleven," she said. "But I've got a pot of tea going. If you'd like some."

"I'll take my caffeine any way I can get it," I said.

I stepped onto the porch and followed Ali inside the house. It was a small place, a great room/kitchen downstairs with a loft bedroom above it. She walked back to the stove and I looked around. Bolts of fabric were stacked everywhere, bright colors and wild prints, with swatches of this and that flung over chairbacks. An easel displayed sketches of women's gowns and dresses. More sketches were scattered on the hardwood floor. A trio of mannequins stood by a window, two of them draped in exotic, floor-length ensembles, the other in something brief and frilly.

Ali returned with two big mugs of tea. We sat at opposite ends of a rattan couch.

"Interesting stuff," I said, nodding to the mannequins. "You have your own line of clothing?"

"I wish," said Ali. "So far it's a private collection. Just for me. I've been after Father to let me open a boutique here on-property, but he hasn't shown much enthusiasm for the idea." She made a face, sighed. "Figures."

"Well, I know of at least one customer you could count on. Barbara couldn't stop talking about that outfit you were wearing the other day in Gainesville. Had the circumstances been a little different, I think she would have bought it off your back."

Ali's face lit up.

"Oh, really? How sweet of her," she said. "Barbara's your wife, right?"

"No, just friends," I said. "Well, more than friends, but . . ."

"No need to explain," said Ali. She smiled. She looked at my shoes, my shorts, my shirt. "You're wearing Monk's clothes."

"Yeah. Lost my luggage. Had to borrow something of his."

"I saw you coming down the hill, and at first I thought you were him." She closed her eyes. Then she opened them and squared around on the couch to face me. "Monk and I, we were together you know."

"Together?"

She gave me a look. It finally sunk in.

"Oh," I said.

"I thought maybe he'd mentioned it."

"No," I said. "He didn't."

A flicker across her face. Disappointment? Whatever, she recovered quickly.

"We'd been seeing each other for several weeks. No one knew about it. Monk was adamant that no one find out. Especially not Father."

"So why tell me?"

"I don't know. I just felt like telling someone. Monk's gone, you were his friend."

I sipped my tea.

"You don't approve, do you?" said Ali.

"It doesn't really matter whether I approve or disapprove.

You're an adult. So was Monk. Adults make their own choices. And live with them."

"That means you don't approve."

"He was old enough to be your father, Ali. Sorry, but something about that is just a little off for me."

Tears welled up in her eyes. She wiped them back and looked at the floor.

"I loved him," she said softly. "We talked about leaving here, going off somewhere together, just the two of us."

"Sorry it didn't work out for you."

She looked up at me.

"No, you aren't," she said. "You're just saying that."

I finished my tea in a hurry. When I was done, Ali didn't ask if I wanted any more.

24

I showed up at Darcy Whitehall's house just before eleven. He was waiting for me at a table on the deck, freshly showered, rosy-cheeked and vigorous. He wore a black silk bathrobe with some kind of Oriental design. I'd never sat down and eaten breakfast with someone whom I would describe as dashing. Darcy Whitehall was.

I wasn't. I had changed out of the running clothes and was now wearing a pair of Monk's pants and one of Monk's shirts. They hung on me as if they had been handed down and I was still growing into them.

A waiter served us ackee and saltfish. It's the national dish of Jamaica, and for good reason. The yellow clumps of ackee resembled scrambled eggs, but had a sweet nuttiness that tangoed seductively with the saltfish. I was trying to take tiny bites and pace myself. Wasn't working.

Below us, things were just beginning to stir. Beach attendants hauled out Jet Skis and Hobie Cats. A small legion of men, the fluff crew, raked corduroy strips in the sand. Here and there, guests were making their way toward the beachside dining pavilion. Some were already in the pool. Another long day of debauchery had just begun.

A waiter refilled my cup with coffee. I drank some.

"Good stuff," I said. "Blue Mountain?"

Darcy Whitehall shook his head.

"No, Peet's. Major Dickensen's Blend. I have it shipped from California. I find our Blue Mountain a bit thin for my taste."

"Glad to hear you say that. I thought it was just me."

"Of course, being the proud Jamaican that I am, I insist that we serve Blue Mountain in our restaurants and sell it at our gift shop. Guests buy it by the caseful. Thirty dollars U.S. a bag."

"Whatever the market will bear."

"Exactly." He sat back in his chair and let out air. "Only these days, I'm afraid it is I who can no longer bear the market."

I didn't know where he was going with that, so I let it hang. There was one more corn muffin left in the breadbasket. I took it.

Whitehall said, "Had I known twenty years ago what I know today, I would have done some things a little differently."

"You and me both," I said. "I would have been a punter."

It didn't register with Whitehall. He was lost in his own reverie, a bittersweet one by the look on his face.

"When it all started out, it was so daring, so provocative. It was almost as if we were on a grand and noble mission. Imagine—a resort where you could lose all inhibition, play out any sexual fantasy you wished. We were creating something new, breaking the mold, flaunting the conventional. Now, it seems, the conventional has caught up with us."

"I'm not so sure about that," I said. "Where I come from, they don't have naked flume rides on every block. And last I checked, Disney kinda frowned on it if you bonked your seatmate coming down the homestretch of Splash Mountain."

Whitehall smiled.

"I suppose what I mean is that Libido's success, its expansion to other islands, has diluted the experience. As a business model, it has succeeded beyond my wildest expectation. But as a source of enduring pride? Believe me, Mr. Chasteen, I never set out to be the figurehead of a nonstop fuckfest."

"But there is the money."

"Yes," he said. "There's that."

The waiter appeared with more coffee. We both took refills.

When he was gone, Whitehall said: "So, what's your opinion of Alan?"

Before I could answer, Whitehall said: "Forgive me. That's a horrible question to ask. Puts you in an awkward position, me being his father and all."

"Not at all," I said. "You have every right to be proud of him. He's quite an impressive young man."

"You're familiar with his work for the homeless?"

"A little bit," I said. "He's made quite an impact, improved a lot of lives."

"Which will continue on a greater scale when he's elected to parliament. I fully believe he could be prime minister one day. Alan's marked for great things, and I will do everything within my power to see that he achieves his dreams."

"What about Ali?"

Whitehall made a face. Not quite a scowl, more like a grimace. Whatever, it wasn't pleasant.

"Still trying to find herself," he said. "Flits from one thing to the next. A bit too much like her mother, perhaps."

"Tell me about her mother."

It took Whitehall a moment to get the words out.

"She's dead," he said.

"Sorry," I said. "I didn't know."

"It's alright. No reason why you should."

He didn't offer any details, and I didn't feel like it was my place to pry. Whitehall sat back in his chair.

"If it's all the same to you, I'd appreciate it if you could help Otee keep watch over Alan for the next few days. Tomorrow, he's supposed to head up to Benton Town to make a speech, and I am most concerned about his well-being."

"Fine by me. But who'll be keeping watch over you?"

"Oh, I have no intention of going anywhere for the foreseeable future. I have plenty of work that needs to get done here in my office," Whitehall said. "Resort security will be just fine. I hardly think whoever is behind all this intends to storm the place and drag me away."

I finished off my coffee. The waiter immediately appeared and took the cup.

"So," I said. "Who *is* behind all this?"

Whitehall crossed his legs and smoothed out his silk robe.

"I told you last night, I really have no idea."

"Yeah, I know you told me that. No offense, but I really don't believe you."

"Why would I lie about it?"

"I'm not saying you're lying. I just don't think you're being totally forthcoming," I said. "If I'm going to stick around and help you out, then you'll need to lay everything on the table."

A gold cigarette case sat on the deck rail. Whitehall opened it, took out a cigarette, and tapped it on the case.

"Who is Martha Brae?" I said.

"Martha Brae?"

I nodded. Whitehall smiled.

"It's not a who, actually, it's a town," Whitehall said. "Little place in the hills above Falmouth. It's the name of a river, too. They do raft trips down it for the tourists, that sort of thing. We run excursions there from the resort. Why do you ask?"

"Saw the name mentioned in some of Monk's things," I said. "Thought it might mean something."

"Means nothing to me. I don't know anyone who lives in Martha Brae."

He pulled a box of matches from his robe and lit the cigarette. He sat there smoking it.

"I'm down to five a day," he said. "Been trying to break the habit."

"What is Equinox Investments?" I said.

It got a reaction out of Whitehall, but he recovered quickly. He took a drag on the cigarette and exhaled slowly.

"Another habit I've tried to break," he said.

"Excuse me?"

"Oh, nothing," he said. "What do you know about Equinox?"

"Only what I've read," I said.

Wasn't a complete lie.

"It was mentioned in Monk's things as well?"

I nodded.

Whitehall sat there smoking his cigarette, brooding. A

minute passed. A banananquit flew onto the deck rail, then flitted to the table and began pecking at the sugar. Whitehall waved it away.

He stood up from the table.

"I really need to get to work," he said. "What are your plans for the day?"

"Thought I'd head into Mo Bay, drop by the airport, see if they've found out anything more than they knew yesterday."

"You want Otee to drive you?"

"No, I'll be alright on my own."

"Fine then, I'll arrange a car," said Whitehall, stepping away. "Check back with me when you return."

25

I went back to the cottage, hoping to get through to Barbara before I drove into Mo Bay. I tried her cell phone. No answer. I called Orb Communications and was eventually connected with her assistant, Steffie Plank.

"Barbara's in Berlin," Steffie said.

"Berlin?"

"Yes, you know, as in Germany. As in decadent hub of European avant-gardism. As in Aaron the Baron's headquarters for impending world domination."

Steffie is bright and talented, destined for great things, and Barbara lives in fear that she will jump ship for the heady nexus of the New York publishing world. That's why Orb Communications was paying her tuition in the M.B.A. program at Rollins College. It wasn't as if Steffie really needed an advanced degree. Barbara was just hoping it would make her stick around a little longer.

"I didn't know Barbara was going to Berlin."

"Neither did Barbara. But Hockelmann showed up here in his jet, took a quick look at our place, then told Barbara he wanted to show her his," Steffie said. "His place, that is. In Berlin."

"Glad you clarified that," I said. "I was getting a little worried."

"Maybe you ought to be."

"What's that supposed to mean, Steffie?"

"Oh, nothing."

"Steffie . . ."

"Let's just say that Aaron Hockelmann is not nearly the ogre that the press makes him out to be. He's kinda cute, actually."

"Cute?"

"Well, in a bland, Aryan, all-business kind of way. He's not awful. That's all I'm saying."

"So you think you could work for him?"

Steffie didn't answer right away.

"I don't know. Part of me doesn't want Barbara to sell the company. The other part of me thinks it could be pretty exciting," Steffie said. "What has she said to you about it?"

"That's she's on the fence, not quite sure what to do."

"Well, an impromptu trip to Berlin, a little glitter and razzle-dazzle, just might be the thing to help her make up her mind."

"Just might," I said. "So how come Barbara didn't take you along with her?"

"You know, I was wondering the exact same thing," Steffie said. "I think maybe it had something to do with the fact that she wanted a little one-on-one time with Mr. Hotty Hockelmann in the lushly appointed cabin of his private jet. Maybe she was thinking they could form their own European Union or something."

"Funny, Stef."

"I thought so." She paused. "When are you going to make an honest woman out of her, Zack?"

I was wondering how long it would take before Steffie hijacked our conversation toward this particular topic. Barbara and I had been seeing each other and no one else for several years without entertaining any talk of marriage. I was OK with that, and I was pretty sure Barbara was, too. But it seemed to upset Steffie's notion of the way things ought to be. Kids today. Jeez.

"Barbara's already an honest woman," I told her. "And I'm surprised that an otherwise enlightened and progressive individual such as yourself would trifle in such backwards, sexist terminology."

"Cut the crap, Zack. You know what I'm talking about."

"Yes, I do."

"The exact words she longs to hear."

"I'm not so sure about that."

"Why? Have you asked her?"

"No, I haven't."

"So when are you going to?"

"When am I going to what?"

"Ask her to marry you, dammit."

"Is this something that Barbara and you have sat around and discussed?"

"No, not in so many words. Not at all, actually. But I don't have to talk to her about it. I know how she feels about you, Zack. We all do. It's written all over her," said Steffie. "Besides, it's not as if the two of you are getting any younger."

"Appreciate you reminding me of that," I said. "Feel like I've aged twenty years since yesterday."

We talked about what had happened at the airport. And when I was done, I asked Steffie: "Did Barbara know about it before she left for Berlin?"

"No," she said. "I don't think so. It didn't come on CNN until after 5 P.M. and she left a couple of hours before that. She and Hockelmann were probably out over the Atlantic by then. Sipping cocktails. In the lushly appointed cabin of his private jet. Just the two of them . . ."

"I gotta go, Stef."

"Ask her, Zack," she said.

26

The car Darcy Whitchall arranged for me turned out to be a big black Mercedes, just like his, only minus the mono-grammed initials on the doors.

I opened the sunroof, opened all the windows, turned the air conditioner on high, and put the Mercedes on the A1 for Mo Bay. I found a radio station that was playing roots reggae, not the dancehall crap, and turned it up loud. The sky was blue, the Caribbean was, too, and a couple of times I almost forgot exactly why I was in Jamaica and why I shouldn't be slapping the seat in time with the music and having a good time.

Seeing the airport brought it all back to me. Flights had resumed, but the parking lot remained off-limits, with armed troops still manning the perimeter. Cars and trucks were parked helter-skelter along the main access road, which was bumper-to-bumper. Would-be passengers were making the long haul to the terminal with their luggage. Horns were honking, tempers were short.

A couple of strip malls near the airport had capitalized on the moment by renting parking spots for about twenty bucks. I paid for a space, left the Mercedes, and made the fifteen-minute trek to a checkpoint by the main entrance where only ticketed passengers, employees, and those with official airport business were permitted to pass through.

"I'm part of the investigation," I told one of the soldiers.

A slight exaggeration maybe, but I might as well try to see where it could get me. The soldier eyed me suspiciously.

"Who you with?" he said.

I was trying to figure out what bogus official-sounding acronym I could throw at him when I spotted Eustace Dunwood speaking with some uniformed patrolmen in the airport parking lot.

"Just tell Inspector Dunwood that Zack Chasteen is here to see him," I said.

The soldier motioned me to step aside and then went off to have a word with Dunwood. Dunwood looked my way, studied me for a moment. He waved the patrolmen away and gave the soldier a nod. The soldier had me put my name on a sign-in sheet and a few moments later I was standing with Dunwood in the parking lot.

"You find someone to verify that I was indeed taking a leak at the airport yesterday when Monk DeVane was walking to his car?"

"No, guess I'll have to take your word for it," Dunwood said. "What you doing here?"

"Just thought I'd check in, see if there was anything I needed to know."

"Well, if there were then I wouldn't be the one to tell you," Dunwood said. "All they got us doing is combing the airport grounds, seeing what we can find. Your people are in charge."

"My people?"

"FBI, Homeland Security, whoever else they flew in last night. They the ones calling the shots now."

"That piss you off?"

Dunwood looked at me.

"Pissed off, pissed on, doesn't matter," he said. "You seen the hole?"

"The hole?"

"The one the bomb dug out."

I shook my head.

"Well, you come all this way you might as well get a look at that," he said.

We walked across the parking lot, toward where the flamboyant trees once stood, making our way around chunks of pavement and twisted shards of metal.

We stopped just short of a dozen or so U.S. Marines spaced along a row of plastic orange barricades. Beyond them I could see the hole—maybe a hundred feet across, a dozen feet deep, like the beginnings of a hellacious swimming pool.

Wasn't much to say. I had this image of Monk getting in the van, starting the engine . . . I tried to put it out of my head.

Twenty or thirty people were in the hole, combing through dirt and debris.

"Biggest piece of that van they found was part of the bumper, no bigger than this." Dunwood held his hands about a yard apart. "Just picking out tiny pieces now. It's like the whole van just vaporized."

"What's your thought on who did this?" I said.

Dunwood sucked his lip, shook his head.

"Got to figure it was directed at Darcy Whitehall, after what happened up at that football game the other day," he said. "Got to be tied to that. Your friend just got in the way."

"So who has it in for Darcy Whitehall?"

"That's just it, I can't think of anyone right off," Dunwood said. "He's pretty much a hero in these parts. Local boy made good, all that. Gives a lot of people jobs, puts money back into the community."

"What about the NPU? We came across some of them last night, painting slogans on the wall at the resort."

"Flies on the cow's ass," said Dunwood. "They a damn nuisance more than anything. Just like that embassy man came to see you in my office."

"Jay Skingle?"

"Same one. He filed his report just like he said he would. Had it into the prime minister's office first thing this morning and we're already catching the heat. Blamed us for a lapse in airport security and said we'd been lax in our monitoring of domestic terrorist organizations."

"The NPU a domestic terrorist organization?"

Dunwood looked at me.

"They are now," he said. "Thanks to that embassy man."

"Inspector!"

We turned to see two of the patrolmen Dunwood had been talking to earlier approaching us from the other side of the parking lot.

"Just found this," one of them said, handing something to Dunwood. He looked at it then showed it to me: A big gold ring. On the face of it, tiny diamonds in the shape of a football. A Super Bowl ring.

"That's Monk's," I said. "Where did you find it?"

Both the patrolmen pointed to the other side of the parking lot.

"By the fence," one of them said.

I looked at the fence. I looked at the hole. A hundred yards, easy. My god, what a blast it had been. I closed my eyes.

"You alright?" Dunwood said.

"Yeah, I'll be fine."

He took a plastic bag from his pocket, put the ring inside it.

"I'll give you a call if we find anything else," he said. "I need to turn this in."

27

On the way back to Libido, entering Falmouth, I saw the sign that said: "Falmouth, Capital of Trelawney Parish."

I pulled off the Al, followed a road to Water Square, and parked near a historical marker. Back in the nineteenth century the site had held a huge stone reservoir where all the townspeople came to get their water, but it had been leveled and was now a public garden. Not much of one—it seemed in serious need of the water that once resided there—but a nice thought anyway.

Across from Water Square sat Albert George Market, named for Queen Victoria's two sons, a tumbledown collection of craft stalls, shops, and produce stands. After a few minutes of asking around, someone finally figured out what I was asking for and pointed me in the direction of the Government House annex, a two-story white clapboard building next door to the Anglican Church.

I wandered around inside it for a few minutes before finding the office of deeds and surveys. Behind the tall counter, a young woman sat at a computer, the only person in the office. She looked up and smiled.

"May I help you?" she said.

I'd brought Monk's daybook with me. I opened it and

showed her the legal notice that had been cut out of the *Gleaner*.

"Can you show me on a map where I might find this piece of property?" I said.

The young woman studied the notice, then took it with her to the computer. She punched something in, then started scrolling down, studying the screen. A few minutes later she returned from the counter.

"Do you have your own map?" she said.

"No."

"Then I must charge you two hundred J's for a parish geographic survey map," she said. "Or an aerial map is two thousand."

"Parish map will be fine," I said.

I gave her the money and she produced the map from a drawer. She unfolded it on the counter and took a moment getting her bearings. It was a pretty big map. She finally spotted the area she was looking for and circled it with a pencil.

"It's right here," she said, showing it to me.

"Can I drive there?"

"Hmmm," she said. "Partly, yes. You go to Oyster Bay, take the B11 south about six miles, past Lucy Bend. Old Dutch Road, it will come in on your left. It's not marked. You might have to ask for it. Old Dutch Road, it's just an old cattle-cart road. You have to walk it a few hundred yards in and that's where the property begins. You can look down the hill, see the morass."

"That's Fishkill Morass?"

The woman nodded.

"That's it," she said.

I thanked the woman for her help and headed for the door.

"Wait, wait, wait," she said. "I just thought of something."

I turned and went back to the counter as the woman sorted through a stack of papers on her desk. She found a folder, opened it, and pulled out another newspaper clipping.

"Part of my job is to file all the legal notices about Trelawney Parish that run in the *Gleaner*," she said. "This just came in today, that same piece of land."

She handed it to me. The heading said "Notice to Sell." The legal description was for the same piece of property. The notice said: "Owner, Libido Resorts LLC, hereby registers intent to sell said parcel to Equinox Investments. JD$350,000,000."

I did the math.

"Three hundred fifty million J's, that's five million U.S.?"

The woman made a face, looked at the notice.

"Must be a typo," she said. "More like three hundred fifty thousand J's, if that. Nobody pays that for land on a morass."

Apparently Equinox Investments did. But Darcy Whitehall hadn't wanted to talk about that.

"What can you tell me about Equinox Investments?"

"Nothing. I don't know the name."

"Can you make a copy of this?" I said, handing her the Notice to Sell.

"Surely," the woman said.

She walked to a back room and returned a minute or so later with the copy. She handed it to me and smiled.

"That'll be fifty J's," she said.

28

I followed the woman's directions and, sure enough, after driving back and forth several times on the same steep and winding stretch of highway, I had to ask for help finding Old Dutch Road.

"Just up da hill, here," said an old man who was walking along the B11, a machete in one hand, a small dog at his side. "You carry me, I show you. My daughta and her child they live off the Old Dutch Road. I'm coming from Gallville to see her."

He picked up the dog and was sitting with it in the front seat of the Mercedes before I could object.

"Dis Sir William," he said, meaning the dog. "Got no teeth."

Sir William grinned at me, showed its gums. Seemed healthy enough for a toothless dog. And pretty cute for one that seemed to have a serious case of mange.

We drove for about a mile and then the old man said: "Stop da car."

He and Sir William got out. I got out with them.

"Dis Old Dutch Road," he said, pointing his machete at a rutted path of clay that snaked into the underbrush.

We were at the top of a hill. Beyond other hills to the north I could just barely see a patch of the Caribbean down in Oyster Bay. It was cool up here, the temperature a good ten degrees lower than it had been in Falmouth. It was quiet, too. Not another car had gone by on the B11 since we had pulled over.

The old man and the dog set off down Old Dutch Road and I followed them.

"Jes sightseeing?" the old man said.

"Yeah," I said. "Out stretching my legs."

"Dis a good place to stretch them," he said.

He was right about that. Old Dutch Road was surely the crookedest road I'd ever followed. It went up and down, around and around, then seemed to switch back just to admire itself. There wasn't a flat part to it, and I was grabbing hold of every tree limb that presented itself just to keep my footing.

Sir William scampered ahead and the old man kept up with him. They stopped at a clearing, waiting for me to catch up. By my guesstimate we were well into the two hundred and fifty-four hectare parcel of land that had been described in the legal notice.

The clearing was a narrow strip that stretched a hundred yards in either direction. Goats and skinny cows grazed on part of it. Another part, less than an acre, had been tilled, and whoever had done the tilling had invested some serious sweat equity. Rocks and a few small boulders were piled along the edges of furrowed loam. Rows of corn, beans, and squash struggled to make a meager stand.

I smelled a wood fire burning and saw smoke coming from a far end of the clearing. I spotted a dozen or so makeshift dwellings—blue tarpaulins stretched over saplings, some lean-tos thatched with palm, the beginnings of a small frame house. I heard children laughing and shouting.

Past the clearing ahead of me, I could see down the hill to where, several hundred feet below, Fishkill Morass filled a wide depression in the terrain until the next hill began. As swampy a swamp as you could ever hope to see.

"This where your daughter lives?" I asked the old man.

"Yah, dey making a home here. 'Least until someone come to run them off. My daughta, she want me to come live here, too. I see I like it, maybe I will," the old man said. "You going to walk down there with me? Smells like they got a pot of goat stew on the fire. Dey nice people, don't mind a visitor."

"No," I said. "I appreciate it, but I think I've stretched my legs enough."

The old man raised his hand good-bye and headed off across the clearing, Sir William racing ahead of him and yapping as a group of children ran to meet them. A woman followed them, a hoe in one hand, waving to the old man with the other. I turned and headed back to the car.

As I recalled from some cobwebby corner of my brain, the same corner that had swallowed everything I ever knew about algebra, a hectare equaled about two-and-a-half acres. Which meant a two hundred and fifty-four hectare parcel was equal to, oh, let's call it a little more than six hundred acres. Which translated to just about eight thousand dollars an acre. For a rocky, hardscrabble chunk of land well removed from the main road and bordered by swamp. With some serious squatters on it.

Someone was getting robbed by this deal-in-the-making, and it didn't appear to be Darcy Whitehall.

29

It was dark by the time I got back to Libido. I went up to Darcy Whitehall's house to check in with him. Otee met me at the door.

"Him back in his office working. Say he want no interruption," Otee said.

"We still on for tomorrow? I understand you and I are supposed to go with Alan when he makes a speech somewhere."

"Yah, mon, to Benton Town. Way up in da mountains."

"What time we heading out?"

"Don't know dat," Otee said. "Best check with Alan."

He told me how to get to Alan's house. It sat on the west end of the resort property, about a ten-minute walk on a well-lit footpath that wound down along the beach then cut up to a rocky promontory. The house was perched at the end of the point, on stilts just like Ali's, but minus all the vegetation it looked stark and alone.

Alan opened the door and waved me in, a phone to his ear. I followed him to the living room as he spoke to the person on the other end.

"I'd say we're about eighty percent there on our funding for the Mandeville project," he said. "I'm still trying to get the suppliers to knock off another ten percent in costs, and I'm asking

Scotia Bank to cover the rest with a no-interest loan. If that all comes together . . ."

He put a hand over the receiver and said to me: "Sorry. It's a reporter from the *Gleaner.*"

"No problem," I said.

Alan went back to his conversation. I looked around the place. One word came to mind: austere. A wooden desk in a corner with a laptop in the middle of it, no clutter of papers or files. A round dining table with four cane-back chairs. Wood floors, no rugs. No television, no stereo, no art on the walls. The only adornment—a floor-to-ceiling bookcase along one wall, filled with hardbacks, nonfiction mostly, and a few framed photos.

It wasn't exactly cold—the killer view provided décor plenty—but it was the kind of place where a guy like Gandhi would have felt right at home.

I heard Alan saying, "Yes, that's right, we have at least fourteen homes already under way there, and with luck there will be another dozen added to it. Can you excuse me for just one moment?"

He put a hand over the phone again and said: "Zack, I'm sorry, but this could take a while."

"That's OK. I just wanted to know what time we need to head out in the morning."

"Oh, let's say by eleven. That'll put us there by one o'clock with time to spare."

He went back to the phone. I showed myself out the door.

On the walk back to my cottage I swung by the resort's beachside restaurant and hit the buffet line—jerked pork, corn pudding, and sliced mangoes. The tables were all filled with couples, or couples with other couples, or people getting ready to be couples. I could have sat by myself but I didn't want to risk someone sitting down with me and trying to make friends. So I wrapped the food in a plate and took it with me. I ate it sitting on the cottage porch. It was gone in about five minutes. That included picking my teeth.

I went inside, took off my clothes, and stepped in the

shower. The water was hot. It felt good. I kept inching up the temperature, letting it get good and steamy, fogging over the glass shower stall, turning the tiny bathroom into a sauna.

I do some of my best thinking in the shower. And I was sorting through the pieces of the day—Darcy Whitehall's circumspection, the scene at the airport, the property off Old Dutch Road—when I heard laughter. More like giggles, actually. Women's giggles.

I turned off the faucet, slid open the shower door. And there, looking in from the bedroom, stood Darlene and Lynette. They were all dressed up for a big night out, and they looked fairly fetching. Skimpy dresses, little left for the imagination.

I fumbled for the rack, came up with a face towel and used it to cover up as best I could. More giggles from the two of them.

"You don't have to be shy," Lynette said. "We already saw you."

"Boy, did we ever," said Darlene.

They looked at each other and whooped it up.

Lynette said, "We were standing here trying to decide if we should step in there and join you."

"It's a very tiny shower," I said.

"Uh-huh, and you're a very big boy," Darlene said.

They laughed some more, really cracking each other up. I stepped out of the shower, found a larger towel, and wrapped it around me.

The two of them looked around the cottage. They weren't impressed.

"Excuse me for saying so," said Lynette, "but this place is a dump compared to ours. How come they stuck you up here?"

"I'm on a tight budget," I said. "It was all I could afford."

They both looked at me with real sympathy. Then Darlene perked up and said: "Well, honey, it is time to put on your party clothes. We're gonna go out and play."

"Or," Lynette purred, "we could stay in and play."

Darlene eyed my bed and made a face.

"Our bed is bigger," she said.

"Plus," Lynette said, "there are mirrors on our ceiling."

"And in our bathroom they gave us all these body oils," Darlene said. "We got hot oils and cold oils and soothing oils and arousal oils."

"Only, we hadn't gotten to use any of them yet," Lynette said. I turned them toward the door.

"Well, I'm sure you won't have any trouble finding someone to use them on," I said. "There's lots of guys out there."

"But we like you, Zack," Darlene said.

"And I like you, too, but it has been a long day."

I got them to the porch, and they stood there pouting.

"You owe us a rain check," Lynette said.

I smiled.

"And we're going to cash it in," Darlene said.

I smiled some more and kept on smiling until they walked away.

30

The next morning, Darcy Whitehall dispatched another big black Mercedes for us to take to Benton Town, but Alan wouldn't have anything to do with it. He insisted we go in his car—a battered Honda Accord missing two hubcaps.

Otee drove. I rode up front with him. In addition to the Browning in his waistband, Otee had brought along a long black rifle case that no doubt held what it had been designed to hold. It occupied the console and rested in my footwell. Alan took over the backseat, spread out papers from his briefcase, and started working on his laptop from the moment we were rolling.

Fifteen minutes from the resort and we were on a snaky mountain road that looked down on a clay-colored river. The mountainsides were green, green, green—a proliferation of silk cotton trees and gumbo limbos and tree ferns. Every now and then, a mongoose would dart from the underbrush and skitter across the blacktop.

Alan shut down his computer and closed his briefcase.

"So tell me about this thing we're going to," I asked him.

"Quarterly meeting of the Benton Town Co-op," said Alan. "It's a loose federation of church groups and schoolteachers and people from the community trying to take care of things that need taking care of. Electricity to all the homes. Running water. HIV-AIDs awareness programs. Meals for the elderly. And, of course, decent housing."

"Which is where you come in."

Alan nodded.

"Homes for the People has built nearly a dozen houses in Benton Town. We've had quite an impact on the quality of life there. But, as you'll see, there is still a great deal that needs to be done."

"Guess that makes you a pretty popular guy up there. You can count on the people of Benton Town to vote for you in the election?"

"Let's hope so," said Alan. "Of course, some will vote against me just because I'm PNP."

I was no expert on Jamaican politics, but I knew that PNP stood for the People's National Party, the ruling party, which had been in power since the late 1980s. The JLP, the Jamaican Labour Party, was its main opposition.

Party faithful of every ilk were zealous about promoting their allegiances, wearing T-shirts in party colors and taking advantage of any opportunity that presented itself to promote their cause. All across Jamaica, hand-scrawled posters covered telephone poles. Political slogans were emblazoned on stop signs. And since political parties seemed to sprout like weeds after a rain shower—the Jamaican Democratic Party (JDP), the National Democratic Movement (NDM), the United Party of Jamaica (UPJ)—it was an island splattered with acronyms.

"You got a good chance of getting elected?"

"I think so," said Alan. "Trelawny Northern generally goes PNP. But Kenya Oompong was born in the district and she's standing for election, too. So that could siphon off some of the vote."

"Who's Kenya Oompong?"

"Founder of Nanny's People United, the NPU, the one they call Nanny Two. A complete radical, a Marxist, but a smart woman. Brilliant, even. Went to the London School of Economics. Returned to Jamaica a few years ago and started organizing in the garrisons."

"Garrisons?"

"The worst neighborhoods of Kingston, places of awful poverty, places like Grant's Hill and Tivoli Gardens and Trench Town."

"Where Marley sang about."

"Yes. You know why they call it Trench Town?"

I shook my head.

"Because it has a ditch running right through the middle of it, a sewage ditch. Not a pretty place," said Alan. "Each of the garrisons has allegiance to a different political party. The gangs that run the garrisons also run the dope trade. The politicians get the police to lay off the gangs and the gangs deliver the vote."

"Sounds like Chicago in the good old days."

"We get the system we deserve, I guess. And it's not really in the interest of the politicians to change things."

"You talk about politicians like you aren't one of them," I said.

"Trying hard not to be," said Alan. "But Kenya Oompong and the NPU are trying just as hard to paint me as old guard, part of the privileged class."

"Not to burst your ideological bubble or anything, Alan, but your father is one of the wealthiest men in Jamaica. You *are* part of the privileged class."

He smiled.

"Money," he said. "It's such a goddam burden."

31

A few miles later we turned off the blacktop and onto a dirt road that twisted along a hillside planted in banana trees. Goats roamed with impunity, and Otee did an admirable job of dodging them while Alan and I talked.

Alan was an easy guy to like. Smart, self-deprecating, not a shred of arrogance about him, seemingly devoted to a life of public service. A rare young man, indeed.

"What makes you so sure the NPU isn't behind the bombs?" I asked him.

"It's just not their style," he said. "For all her faults, Kenya Oompong is not inclined toward violence. She started off by going into the garrisons, trying to get the gangs to put down their weapons and preaching reform. Almost cost her life. More than one garrison gang tried to do her in."

"What kind of reform is she preaching?"

"A lot of it is typical Marxist dogma. The working class must rise up and throw off the shackles of oppression. That kind of thing. But she couples it with a back-to-the-land spiel, a sort of New Age nationalism. Says that Jamaicans should be living off the bounty of the island, tending plots and raising livestock, instead of slaving at resorts and taking care of white foreigners. It's why they call themselves Nanny's People.

They're following the same route the Maroons did nearly three hundred years ago when they said to hell with the plantations and headed for the hills. And it's why they call her Nanny Two."

Otee let out a snort.

"Bet Nanny Two, she coochie don't shoot bullet," he said.

Alan laughed. He looked at me.

"Part of the legend of Nanny was that she had a secret weapon for fighting the British. As the story went, whenever the Brits launched an attack, Nanny would throw up her skirt and show them her vagina and stop them in their tracks. Then, while they were standing there gape-mouthed, she'd fire bullets out of it and cut them down."

"Pretty neat trick," I said.

"Kenya Oompong has some pretty neat tricks of her own. She knows how to rally a crowd and attract attention, that's for sure."

"She have a lot of followers?"

"More than most people ever thought the NPU would have. She staged some well-publicized demonstrations at a couple of resorts in Negril. Convinced several of the staff—kitchen help, housecleaners, maintenance crews—to quit their jobs and follow her to the hills. They squatted on property and claimed it as their own. That got the ball rolling and others joined up with the NPU. Now there are NPU settlements all over the place."

"I came across some squatters yesterday," I said. "In the hills above Falmouth, off Old Dutch Road by Fishkill Morass."

"Oh, really? What were you doing up there?"

"Just sight-seeing," I said. "You familiar with that area?"

"Not as well as I should be. It's in my district. Or, rather, what will be my district if I get elected. I need to pay a visit there."

He didn't give any indication of knowing about the land his father owned. And I didn't press the matter.

"Government doesn't do anything to stop people from squatting on the land?" I said.

Alan shook his head.

"Squatting is something of a tradition in Jamaica. According to the last statistics I saw, only nine percent of Jamaicans own their homes and forty-seven percent rent. The rest, as many as a million people, are squatters," said Alan.

"Must make for some nasty legal squabbles from time to time," I said.

"Oh, yes. Landowner wants to sell his property, the squatters can tie it up and stake a claim. Landowner most always ends up winning, but yes, it can get ugly," said Alan. "It's one reason why we started Homes for the People. Turn squatters into owners. Pride of ownership is a powerful thing."

The road got worse the farther we went, boulders occasionally blocking a portion of it and causing Otee to take precarious detours along nonexistent shoulders. It was treacherous going.

After twenty minutes we rounded a corner and Alan had Oteele stop the car.

"Just look at all that," Alan said. "Beautiful, isn't it?"

Beyond us spread a landscape of slender, jagged mountains, some of them looking like dunce caps, others like cathedral spires. The seismic upheavals that created them eons ago had also formed hundreds, even thousands, of small, isolated, bowl-shaped valleys that pockmarked the blanket of vegetation as far as we could see.

"Cockpit Country," I said.

Alan nodded.

"British had another name for it," he said. "Nanny and her people were always ambushing them up here, so they used to ride two to a horse, back-to-back. That way they could keep an eye out in all directions. Called it the 'Land of Look Behind.' "

"Gee, maybe I ought to sit on the bumper, watch our rear flank," I said.

Alan laughed.

But I couldn't help noticing that Otee had taken his hand off the wheel and let it rest on his rifle case.

32

The road ended in Benton Town, which wasn't so much a town as it was a broad scar at the base of a mountain—muddy streets and ramshackle stores and glassy-eyed men sitting on rum-shop steps.

It was about as downtrodden a place as I had ever been. The only exception was a horseshoe of new concrete-block houses set around a playground near the center of town.

There was nothing fancy about the houses. They all followed the same cookie cutter design with living room at the front, kitchen in the middle, two bedrooms in the back, but given the surroundings they might as well have been mansions.

They were painted different colors and the owners had done what they could to lend personal touches. Small gardens. Flower pots along the porch. Most of the backyards sported fifty-five-gallon drums turned into homemade jerk pits.

"This is some of our work," said Alan, pointing to the houses as Otee parked the car alongside the playground. "We'll soon have another dozen more."

Almost immediately, a group of kids began running toward the car.

"Mr. Alan, Mr. Alan," they squealed.

Alan leaned forward to Otee and said: "I don't want the children seeing your guns."

Otee said, "Get out, den, and me follow in da car."

I got out of the car with Alan and stood by him as the kids all got in their hugs. Alan spoke to a couple of them by name, asking about their parents.

Then he turned to me.

"We'll walk to the co-op hall from here," he said. "It's only a short way."

He set off down the street, children in tow. I followed a couple of steps behind, with Otee bringing up the rear in the Honda.

Every now and then, Alan would stop and exchange a few words with someone—an old woman doing her laundry in a washtub, a shopkeeper sweeping the steps of her store, a young man minding a vegetable stand. More children joined the others who had encircled Alan, reaching out for a chance to touch him.

Everyone recognized him, and everyone seemed glad to see him. Alan, for his part, seemed quite in his element. I couldn't imagine that the few hundred votes Benton Town might deliver would be so crucial that Alan Whitehall would devote much time here, but it was his campaign to run, not mine. I was just along to make sure nothing happened to him.

And as far as I could tell, the only threat came from being hugged to death by small children.

33

The crowd at the Benton Town Co-op Hall spilled onto the street. Inside, it was hot and stuffy and standing-room-only.

A podium sat in the middle of a low stage flanked by two tables set with pitchers of water and paper cups. Several men and women sat at the tables, wearing their Sunday best.

Alan made his way toward the stage greeting people as he went. I stuck as close to him as I could. He hopped up on stage. I hopped up with him. After he introduced me to the men and women at the tables—trustees of the Benton Town Co-op—I took up a position in the wings where I could watch the whole room. Otee had chosen to stay in the Honda and keep an eye on things outside. I could see him through a window by the backstage door.

It was obvious from the outset that we were in for a whole lot of speechifying. Each of the trustees took a turn at the podium, and nearly an hour passed before it came time for Alan's introduction. There was loud applause and cheers as he stepped to center stage, but it was interrupted by a commotion at the back of the hall.

All eyes turned to a tall, thickly built woman who was pushing her way through the crowd. She wore one of those African dashiki things, in a design of burnished yellow and fiery red.

Her skin was almost blue-black, and she towered over most of the men in the crowd, the red turban atop her head making her seem even taller.

A cadre of men and women wearing red-and-yellow T-shirts and red-and-yellow bandannas surrounded the tall woman in the turban, helping her wedge her way toward the stage. I recognized the bandannas. They were identical to the bandannas worn by the three boys who had been spray-painting NPU slogans on the wall at Libido the night I arrived.

"Dat Nanny Two," I heard a woman standing near me say.

Two of the co-op trustees, both of them big, burly men, jumped down from the stage to stop the advance of the newcomers. There was pushing and shoving and shouting as they faced off with the woman in the turban.

Others in the crowd joined in the fray. It was getting ugly. One of the bandanna-wearing women pointed a finger at Alan and shouted: "He PNP! He not for we!"

Others in her group took up the chant.

"He PNP! He not for we!"

I glanced outside and saw Otee trotting toward the backstage door, holding the rifle at his side. As I moved in to the podium, alongside Alan, the woman in the turban boomed: "We have a right to be here! We will not be denied!"

It put a hush on the room, and in the lull, Alan Whitehall seized the chance to speak.

"Please, please. Leave them be," he said. "She's right. They deserve to be here."

It eased some of the rancor in the crowd. Then Alan Whitehall looked directly at the woman in the turban.

"Kenya Oompong," he said. "We welcome you."

He offered her a slight bow. Kenya Oompong held his gaze for a moment, then closed her eyes and sharply turned her head away—that Caribbean sign of contempt known as giving someone the "cut-eye." No one in the crowd missed it.

"Now," said Alan, "if we might continue . . ."

He waited as the two trustees returned to their seats onstage. The atmosphere in the room was still prickly, but for the time being the situation was defused.

I moved back to my position in the wings. Otee had opened the backstage door and was standing just inside it.

"People of Benton Town," Alan began. "And honored guests."

Another bow to Kenya Oompong, only this time I detected a slight smile on his face, as if he knew his equanimity had won the moment. Kenya Oompong drew herself up. She folded her arms across her ample chest, defiant, as she prepared to listen to what Alan Whitehall had to say.

His speech lasted twenty minutes. He spoke with humor and with substance. The platitudes were few and well chosen. He spoke about the lessons of the past, the hard realities of the present, and the glorious promise of the future. All in all, it was as good a speech as I had ever heard a politician give. And that's not intended to damn by faint praise.

When it was over, applause once again rocked the hall. After it died, Alan looked at Kenya Oompong and said: "And now, should my worthy opponent wish to take the podium . . ."

The tall woman let out a snort.

"Cho!" she said. "Dat podium need airing out after you stink it up so. Me stand right here to say what me have to say. And me mek it short."

Her supporters nodded their heads, urging her on.

"Give a monkey plenty money and even monkey can build a house. But dat don't mean a man should sleep in it." She shot a look at Alan, then turned back to the crowd. "You 'member dis: When monkey wipe his arse him don't care where da leaf fall."

She spun on a heel and headed for the door. Her supporters followed her. And the crowd fell back to let them go.

34

Gee, that went well," I said as we rolled out of Benton Town on the bumpy dirt road. "But then, I've always had a soft spot for monkeys."

Alan Whitehall laughed.

"Could have been worse," he said. "I mean, by Jamaican standards that was pretty mild. People expect their politicians to call each other names. Part of the give-and-take."

"Like wit ol' Auntie-Man," said Otee.

"Yeah, like that," said Alan. He glanced my way, then back at the road. "Few years back, this barrister name of Ernest Pantemann stood for parliament in St. Ann's. He was JDP. And his opponent, from the PNP, twisted his name around, started calling him Auntie-Man."

"Auntie-Man?"

"Yes, same as calling him a sissy. That's an Auntie-Man," said Alan. "So Mr. Pantemann, he had to respond some way, you know? But what's he going to do? Make speeches denying he was an Auntie-Man? That just make the people laugh at him more.

"So what he did, he put up signs all over St. Ann's that said: 'PNP Can Go to Hell.' Just that, nothing else, just 'PNP Can Go to Hell.' It became his campaign slogan. Pretty soon everyone was saying it."

"He win?"

Alan shook his head.

"No, he lost. But people, they liked him for it. Showed he wouldn't step away from a fight."

We bounced along, putting Benton Town behind us. There was just another hour or two of daylight left. Thunderheads were forming above the mountains, threatening a storm.

We were nearing the cutoff where the dirt road met the blacktop when we spotted the white van. It shot out from behind an embankment, straddling the road and blocking our way. Otee hit the brakes and we skidded to a stop maybe thirty yards from the van as two men piled out of it, pointing pistols at our car.

Otee jammed the gear shift into reverse, but stopped as a gray Toyota pickup pulled in behind us. A man got out of it. He held a pistol, too. All three of the men wore red-and-yellow bandannas, tied off so only their eyes were showing.

They kept their distance, pistols leveled at the car.

"You, in da backseat, Whitehall! Get out!" yelled one of the men by the white van. "Get out now and we let da other two go."

"Dey ain't letting no one go," Otee said in a low voice. "Dey shoot us soon as they got him."

"I'm thinking you're right," I said.

I turned around to Alan. He looked remarkably calm, considering.

"Get down on the floorboard behind the seat," I said. "Keep your head low."

"What are you going to do?"

"Don't quite know yet. Think we're making it up as we go along."

Alan squeezed down on the floorboard, and I turned back to Otee. He was slowly unzipping the rifle case that sat on the console between us, one hand still on the wheel, his gaze fixed on the two men by the van.

"You can reach da gas pedal with your foot?" Otee asked me.

"Uh-huh."

"You gonna have to steer, too."

"I can do that."

The two men in front of us moved closer to our car.

"Get out, Whitehall! Now!" one of them yelled. He was waving his pistol, and then he fired it, a puff of dirt exploding in the road just in front of us.

After that everything happened in a blur: Otee let go of the steering wheel and pulled the rifle from its case. I reached for the wheel, slammed down on the gas pedal, and the Honda shot forward, fishtailing in the dirt. The two men leapt aside as we sped toward them. They fired, their shots wild and wide.

Otee leaned out the window with his rifle—a wicked-looking thing, brushed black steel with a banana clip. He squeezed off a volley. One of the men went down.

The Honda slid out of control toward the edge of the road and a hairy drop-off that led God knows where. I whipped the wheel and it straightened, plowing into the rear end of the van, knocking it aside and giving us just enough room to rumble past.

Otee fumbled to open the front door, and as I let my foot off the gas and found the brake, he rolled out of the car, onto the dirt road, unleashing another round of shots, more shots than I could count, as the Honda came to a stop. Then everything was quiet.

I looked behind us and saw two bodies in the road. The gray pickup truck was already speeding away, in the direction from which we'd come. Otee stood up and brushed himself off.

"You OK?" I asked Alan.

"Yeah," he said, unfolding himself from behind the seat.

Otee walked down the road toward the two bodies. We got out of the car and joined him.

Otee nudged the bodies with a foot. They didn't move. Otee's rifle had chewed them up pretty badly.

Two pistols lay by the bodies. Otee picked up one of them and looked at it.

"G39," he said. "Just like the ones got stolen from the guardhouse."

35

Three hours later we were in Mo Bay, sitting in Eustace Dunwood's office at the Jamaica Constabulary Force headquarters. I'd driven Alan in his car while Otee followed in the white van, the two bodies in the back. I'd tried not to look at the faces of the dead men when we'd loaded them. They were just kids, really, barely out of their teens. No IDs on either one of them.

Otee had argued against going to the police, saying it was just a waste of time. He was all for dragging the bodies off the road, rolling them down the side of the mountain, and us being on our merry way. But Alan and I had prevailed, and now we all sat on one side of Dunwood's desk as the inspector leaned back in his swivel chair.

"There'll be an investigation, of course, but based on what you've told me, I'm not recommending charges," he said. "You figure they were planning to take you hostage, Mr. Whitehall, and demand a ransom?"

"I don't know what their intentions were," Alan said. "But they knew I was in the car, and they were demanding that I get out and go with them."

Our statements about the shoot-out were sitting on Dunwood's desk. He rocked forward in his chair and looked at them.

"The two got shot, they were wearing NPU colors?"

"So was the third one, the one who got away," said Alan. "Red-and-yellow bandannas."

"Just like the other night," I said.

Dunwood cocked his head.

"The other night?"

I reminded him how we'd caught the group spray-painting slogans on the Libido wall.

"These two dead boys, could they have been with them?" said Dunwood.

Otee shook his head.

"Nah, ones the other night they just children; they run off scared. Ones today, they different. Nothing scared about them."

"Let me ask a dumb question," I said.

They all looked at me.

"Why would they advertise who they were?" I said. "Why would they be wearing those bandannas, something that would point a finger at the NPU? Doesn't make sense."

"No, it doesn't. Except in Jamaica," said Dunwood. "The way it works here, everything is politics. Even when it's not. You can't separate it. It's like wet on rain."

"But wouldn't they at least try to avoid throwing suspicion their way?"

"It's like this, Zack," Alan said. "Say some Kingston boys go into a grocery store, shoot the owner, and take all the money out of the drawer. Turns out the store owner supported the People's National Party, the PNP."

"The party you belong to," Zack said.

"Uh-huh. The majority party," Alan said. "So if the store owner was PNP, then who's automatically going to get the blame? The opposition party, the JLP, the Jamaica Labour Party."

"Even if it was just some guys walking into a store and robbing it only because they were low-life scum who wanted the money?"

"Even if," said Alan. "So next thing that happens, some JLP store it gets robbed and that gets blamed on the PNP. It just goes on and on, robbing and killing and calling it politics."

"But what if the store owner doesn't back any of the parties, doesn't have any opinion about politics?"

It brought snickers from all three of them.

Otee said, "Dis Jamaica, mon, everyone he got an opinion. Ain't no one sits on da damn fence like dey do where you come from. Here, everyone dey with one party or da other. And dey like to advertise it."

"The politicians are always making speeches condemning the gangs, saying they're against the violence, claiming their party has nothing to do with it," said Dunwood. "But at the same time they got their henchmen out on the street paying this gang for allegiance, promising another gang they'll do something for them. Politicians figure they got juice on the street then it gives them juice at the polls."

I looked at Alan Whitehall.

"You got henchmen out on the streets?"

He smiled.

"Just you and Otee," he said.

"But your party, the PNP, it pays off the gangs like Dunwood here says?"

"It's something I prefer not to know about," he said. "The system isn't perfect. I'm trying to do what I can to change it."

"Here's what it all boils down to, Mr. Chasteen," Eustace Dunwood said, "Kenya Oompong is Mr. Whitehall's opponent and the head of the NPU. Something happens to Mr. Whitehall and everyone is going to say the NPU was behind it."

"Still," I said, "why would the guys who stopped us on the road wear those bandannas? It just doesn't fit for me."

"Because the NPU is new on the scene. Trying to make a name for itself. Since they're going to get the blame no matter what, why not wear the colors, just go ahead and underline it?"

"Gives them some street cred," I said. "Makes them seem bold and badass."

"Exactly," said Dunwood. He looked at Alan Whitehall. "You want me to haul in Kenya Oompong, all of us sit down, ask her what she knows about this?"

"No," Alan said. "She'll just call a press conference, bring in the newspaper and the TV cameras, say she's being set up for something she didn't do. It would be like throwing fat on the fire."

Dunwood folded his arms across his chest and thought about it. Didn't seem to give him much pleasure.

"Guess all we can do is see how it plays out. Figure out who those two boys were, ask some questions, see where that white van came from. Get lucky, maybe we can find the third one, the one driving that Toyota truck." He looked at Otee. "You get me the serial numbers of the Glocks that were stolen and we'll compare them against the ones those two were carrying."

Otee nodded.

"I'll call you first thing in the morning," he said.

"One more thing," I said. "Them trying to hijack us up there on the road, grab Alan, do whatever they were going to do . . . what does that have to do with the bombs?"

No one said anything. Finally it was Alan who spoke.

"I really can't see how it's connected. I still don't think the NPU had anything to do with the bombs."

"I agree," said Dunwood. "Think we have two different things going on here. We got someone messing with Darcy Whitehall. And we got someone else messing with his son."

Dunwood stood. So did we. He stepped from behind his desk and opened his office door. As we left, he put a hand on Alan's shoulder.

"Like I told you, we'll do what we can. Still, you know how it goes once things like this get started. People want to get even, match things tit for tat. Best watch yourselves," he said.

36

It was almost 10 P.M. before we got back to Libido. We went straight to Darcy Whitehall's house to let him know what had happened.

"He's in his office, on the phone," said the security guard who'd been assigned to the house.

Call me insecure, but I had the distinct feeling Darcy Whitehall was avoiding me. Still, I couldn't let that get in the way of what needed to be done.

"Come on," I told Alan. "We're going to get your sister."

"What for?"

"I'll explain once we get down there," I said.

Otee went with us as we took a golf cart down the hill to Ali's house. The lights were on, and Ali was busy at her easel, working on a sketch when we knocked at the door. She spun around, surprised. She was wearing a black, floor-length gown with ruffles and sequins, something fit for a fancy ball.

"That's one of mother's gowns," Alan said.

Ali bristled at his words.

"I like to wear it sometimes when I'm working. I find it inspiring," she said. "If you don't mind."

"No, no, I just didn't know you had it, that's all," Alan said. "I thought all Mother's things had been . . ."

"What, thrown out? Burned? Destroyed? Purged from the face of the earth?"

Ali was dragging out the family laundry, and Alan was quite obviously embarrassed by it. He started to say something, but held back. He stepped onto the porch. Otee joined him.

I sat Ali down on the couch and told her about what had happened on the road back from Benton Town.

"Oh my God," she said when I was done. "Who were they?"

"Still trying to figure that out," I said. "Maybe NPU."

She clenched her jaw.

"My brother and his goddam politics. I don't care what he says, this whole thing—the bombs, Monk dying—it's all because of him. Isn't it?"

I didn't have the answer to that. I left her on the couch and went out on the porch.

"How many security guards does the resort have?" I asked Otee.

"Be something like forty to fifty, working eight-hour shifts," he said.

"We need to beef it up," I said. "I want you to call security, tell them there'll be twelve-hour shifts starting immediately. More patrols, no one just sitting around in the guardhouses. Then I want you to tell them to send four guards up to Mr. Whitehall's house as soon as they can get there."

"Dem boys gonna want extra pay," Otee said.

"Tell them they'll get it." I was playing fast and loose with Darcy Whitehall's money, but what could he do, fire me? "Just make sure they get someone up to Mr. Whitehall's house right now."

Otee went off to use the phone, and Ali stepped onto the porch to see what was up.

"I want you to get your things," I told her.

"What things?"

"Whatever it is you need to spend the night up in your father's house."

"I'm not spending the night up there," she said.

"Yes, you are. And you'll be staying up there until everything settles down," I said. "So will you, Alan. I want everyone in one place, not spread out all over the property. After what happened today, I want someone keeping an eye on all of you, all the time."

"There's no way I'm staying up there with . . ."

"Just go do it, Ali," Alan said, cutting her off.

She left in a huff.

"I apologize for my sister's behavior," Alan said. "Old wounds."

"Every family's got them."

"Yeah, but ours seem to run deeper than most."

Before he could offer any more than that, Otee returned from using the phone.

"Dey sending guards up to Mr. Whitehall's house right now. Want to know if dey can send up someone else with dem."

"Someone else?" I said.

"Yah, mon," said Otee. "Fellah from the embassy. Said it was important that he see you."

37

It took Ali longer than it should have to put her things together, her way of registering displeasure about the unwanted sleepover. Which meant Jay Skingle and the security guards had been waiting for us several minutes when we arrived at Darcy Whitehall's house. Skingle looked very official, from his dark suit and striped tie down to his peeved, screw-faced expression, his way of registering displeasure about us wasting his precious time.

I introduced Skingle to Ali and Alan, and then the two of them stepped inside with Otee and the guards while I spoke with Skingle in the driveway.

Skingle held a dull gray metal canister, about the size of a thermos jug. I had a pretty good idea what was in it.

"There was very little in the way of remains, shredded clothing, not much more," Skingle said. "Still, the family generally likes to have something. I wanted to get it to you so that you might proceed with the final arrangements at your earliest convenience."

He handed me the metal canister. Ashes to ashes, dust to dust. Gave me the chills. I didn't want to think about it.

"There were a couple other things," I said. "Monk's wallet, his Super Bowl ring."

"I assume that's still part of the investigation. I'll inquire about it and get back to you," he said. "I did take the liberty of notifying the Department of Veteran Affairs on the family's behalf. Mr. DeVane is eligible for interment at a national cemetery, should the family so desire. Do you know what they've decided?"

"Haven't had a chance to speak to anyone about it since yesterday," I said.

"It's really not a good idea to dawdle in matters such as these, Mr. Chasteen," he said. "I suggest you move forward with all due speed."

So young, and already so very pompous. The guy had a brilliant future doing government work.

"Just one more thing," said Skingle. "A formality."

He reached inside a coat pocket and pulled out some legal papers. We moved under a light by the front door of the house so we could see them better.

"I just want to look through these one more time, make sure everything is here," Skingle said.

There were several pages and he took his sweet time looking at them. Minutes passed. Seemed to me that he was the one who was dawdling, but what the heck did I know?

He handed the papers to me.

"Please read these over carefully," he said. "Then sign where I've indicated."

I read the papers, perhaps not as carefully as Skingle might have liked, but most of it was just boilerplate legalese and didn't bear a word-by-word inspection. A release form for Monk's remains. A "Statement of Death" issued by the Jamaican government.

"Make sure you show them that when you go through airport security," said Skingle. "That way they might not make you open up the canister."

I signed the papers. Skingle tucked them away.

"So," he said. "When's your flight out?"

"Don't have anything booked yet."

Skingle made a face. This simply would not do.

"I'll pull what strings I can and see if we can't get you something early tomorrow morning."

"Don't bother. I'll handle it."

"Well, please see that you do," he said. "By the way, it's really not necessary for you to return."

"Oh?"

"Believe me, there's nothing you can do. Just let my office and the Jamaican authorities do our jobs. I will personally keep you posted regarding our progress."

"Personally? You mean we can exchange home phone numbers and stuff like that?"

"No reason for you to make this difficult, Chasteen."

"You're right. So, personally speaking, what sort of progress have you and the authorities made so far?"

"You have to understand, these things take time," Skingle said.

"Something I've got plenty of. Might as well spend it here."

"I really don't think that's a good idea. Particularly if it leads to episodes like the one today up in the mountains. Jamaican-on-Jamaican crime is one thing, happens every day. But when a U.S. citizen is involved it is quite another. You can't imagine what sort of problems it has caused our office. It would have been even worse had you managed to get yourself killed."

"That really would have created a lot of extra paperwork for you, huh?"

Skingle narrowed his eyes. I think it meant he was trying to look tough. He didn't have the face for it.

"I don't appreciate your sarcasm, Mr. Chasteen."

"Somehow I'll find a way to live with that."

Skingle put a hand to his mouth and coughed, like some people do when they can't think of what to say.

"Well then," he said, straightening his tie, "I suppose I should be going."

"With all due speed," I said.

38

I like to flatter myself by thinking I'm a man of action and decisiveness, but at that particular moment, watching Jay Skingle walk away while I was cradling a canister that contained the meager remains of an old friend, I wasn't sure which way to go, or what to do. I needed to get back on track. I needed to come up with some kind of game plan, not just stand there immobile in the driveway. I started kicking things around in my head, hoping maybe that would jump-start me.

I wondered why Skingle was so anxious for me to leave Jamaica. I didn't have an answer for it, other than the fact that he didn't like me and I didn't like him. Little boy stuff. If we were in third grade we could have met each other on the playground after school and duked it out and probably wound up best friends. Nah, I take that back. Skingle was a born prick, nobody's best friend. I would have preferred to just beat the hell out of him and been done with it.

I wondered why Darcy Whitehall was acting the way he was. I felt sure he was holding out about something, something that might put matters into perspective, something that might explain why bombs were exploding and people were dying. I wanted to squeeze it out of him. But I didn't want to go sit inside his house. Too much sticky business, some weird family vibe. Best to let it air out, at least for the night.

I wondered about Monk. How had he managed to get hooked up with Darcy Whitehall in the first place? There were some big gaps in Monk's life, and more than a few indiscretions. What had led him here? Would those files in the dresser back at his cottage help explain anything?

I wondered about the two dead guys. Had they and their partner dreamed up the plan to waylay our car and snatch Alan? Or had someone else been behind it? If someone else, then what other sort of mayhem might they now be plotting? And would the shoot-out set off a round of political revenge that would get even uglier?

I wondered if there was anything that tied all this stuff together. From the skybox in Gainesville to the airport parking lot to the dirt road near Benton Town—how could it all possibly be related? I didn't see how it could.

Eustace Dunwood and Alan Whitehall were right. There were two separate things going on. Had to be. Because if they were wrong, if it really was all tied together, then whoever was behind it had more resources than any of us did, orchestrating acts of bedevilment and violence from Florida to Jamaica, acts that, even if they misfired, required a certain degree of logistical finesse and know-how. Just what the hell was going on?

Too damn many questions. My head was ready to explode. I needed something to settle me down.

Which was when I got to wondering about Barbara. I missed her, needed to talk to her. When things in my life fly out of control, as they'd been doing for the past three days, she has a way of putting them back in their proper orbit. She's my gravity.

But Barbara was in Berlin, and in Berlin it was, let's see, six hours ahead of us, only 5 A.M. A little too early to call. I needed to give it an hour or so, but I didn't want to just go sit in my cottage and wait.

And so I finally made a decision that got me moving again: I needed a drink, and I set out find one.

39

There were several nightclubs at Libido, and I picked the first one I came to—the Kama Sutra Lounge. A placard by the entrance announced that it was "Glitter & G-String Night" and everyone was dutifully observing the theme. Two guys walked in wearing jockey briefs adorned with sequins. It passed for conservative attire. The women with them wore just sequins.

I found an empty space at the end of the bar, put the metal canister down in front of me, and ordered a glass of rum. When it came I raised the glass and clinked it against the canister. Cheers, Monk, old pal. Why did you drag me into this?

The place was dark and done up in Oriental fashion, incense heavy in the air. Big murals on the walls showed men and women in various contorted positions based on the ancient practice of tantric sex. Private alcoves with gauzy curtains lined the room. Just as well it was dark. I didn't much care about seeing what sort of pairings the murals had inspired inside the alcoves.

I ordered another rum. I checked the time. Ten minutes since I had ordered the first one. At this rate I would polish off another four rums before it was time to call Barbara. Pace yourself, Zack-o.

The music was canned and it was some kind of trance/ambient/techno nonsense. What was taking place on the dance floor wasn't so much dancing as it was syncopated writhing. It was all very pseudo-tribal with much rubbing of bodies and no small amount of groping—foreplay before stepping off by twos and threes and fours and more to one of the private alcoves.

I was working on my third rum when Lynette and Darlene walked in, spotted me at the bar, and came over to join me. Both wore thong bikini bottoms, tiny T-shirts that barely covered their breasts, and spike heels. They had on some kind of sparkly makeup that made them glitter with specks of gold and silver.

"We just came from your place," said Lynette. "Thought we'd pay you a surprise visit, see if we could drag you out to have some fun."

"And here I am."

"Yes, here you are. And here we are," said Lynette. "You know what that means."

"Time to party!" said Darlene. She wiggled up against me.

"Only, you are so overdressed," said Lynette. "You ought to at least take off your shirt or something."

"Afraid I might catch a chill."

"Don't you worry, baby, I'll keep you warm," Lynette said, sliding close. She undid the top button on my shirt and snaked a hand inside.

"Oh, what a nice cocktail shaker," said Darlene, grabbing the canister. She shook it and started to unscrew the cap.

I pulled away from Lynette and took the canister from Darlene.

"Yeah," I said. "They sell them in the gift shop."

I tightened the canister's cap and put it back down on the bar.

"You know, your neighbor's really creepy, not very friendly at all," said Darlene.

"My neighbor?"

"Yeah, the guy who lives next door to your place. He was coming out when we were walking up and we asked if you were around. He just ignored us. Hurried off like we weren't even there."

"He was carrying this big old garbage bag," said Lynette. "Looked like he'd been cleaning house."

"Hmm," I said. Profundity masking for total bafflement is one of my strong suits.

Darlene slid close and rubbed a hip against mine. Lynette did the same thing on the other side. Then they started rubbing up against me in time with the music.

I drained the rum and grabbed the metal canister.

"Gotta go," I said.

"But we just got here," said Lynette. "Don't you want to party with us?"

"You know, I really didn't dress for the occasion. Feeling a little out of place," I said and headed for the door.

41

Whoever had gone through Monk's cottage had been neat about it. Nothing was out of place, but when I opened the bottom dresser drawer it was empty. Monk's files were gone.

I went to the phone, called the guardhouse by the main entrance, and when a man answered I asked him to check the logbook to see when Jay Skingle had signed out.

"Don't need to check," he said. "Watched him sign out about half an hour ago, then saw the two of them drive away."

"The two of them?"

"Uh-huh. That embassy man had a driver."

"You see what the driver looked like?"

"White fella. Slight. Not much to him."

"Nothing more than that?"

"He was inside the car."

"What did he do while Skingle came up to see me?"

The guard thought about it for a moment. Then he said: "Didn't keep a real close eye on him. After the embassy man came up to see you, the other one he parked way down at the far end of the parking lot, out of the light. Didn't see him again until they drove away."

I thanked him and hung up.

I tried to picture the guy who'd accompanied Skingle to the

police headquarters in Mo Bay. Slight, not much to him. Yeah, that was the guy.

Skingle had kept me busy with paperwork while his buddy pilfered Monk's place. What were the two of them up to? And what did Monk have that they wanted?

Two good questions, but before I could put my vast intellect to work on them, the phone began ringing in my cottage, and I ran next door to grab it.

41

"No, Aaron Hockelmann isn't nearly as awful as I expected," said Barbara. She was calling from her hotel in Berlin. "Still, I don't know that I intend to crawl in bed with him."

"You're speaking in a business sense, right?"

"Well, of course, darling. Not that I could even conceive of crawling in bed with him in any other sense. He's just much too . . ."

"Germanic?"

"Or Trumpish. Very full of himself. Boorish. Consumed by his own self-image. I can't imagine that he would be much fun in bed at all."

"Not that you've imagined it."

"Not that I have at all," said Barbara. "I've only been imagining you."

"Was it good for you?"

"Yes, but not as good as if you were here with me. Not as good at all."

"Are you in bed right now?"

"Yes, I am. Just woke up a few minutes ago and called you right off. Well, I called room service first. For coffee. But you were a very close second."

"Good to know," I said. "What are you wearing?"

"Excuse me?"

"Are you in a bathrobe or what?"

"No, I'm wearing my white silk pajamas. The ones you bought me at the Mandarin Oriental when we were down in Miami a few weeks back."

"Just the pajama top, right?"

"Yes, just the top. With panties."

"What color are the panties?"

There was a pause. Then Barbara said: "Zack, we aren't really going to do this, are we?"

"Do what?"

"Have phone sex."

"Is that what we were doing?"

"Well, it certainly seemed as if we were heading in that direction."

"You don't like phone sex?"

"Don't know, never tried it. But no, I don't think that I would like it very much at all. Seems rather desperate."

"Well, I am rather desperate. And on top of that I'm horny."

"Subliminate," said Barbara.

"Excuse me?"

"Suppress physical desire for as long as possible and, when it is finally satisfied, then it is ultimately more fulfilling."

"Nice theory on paper," I said. "But me, I've always been a firm believer in bonk-on-demand."

"Well, then," said Barbara, "perhaps I shall just have a slot installed on my forehead and you can pop in a quarter whenever you've got the urge."

"Make it a dime, toss in a dollar-bill changer, and you've got a deal."

We must have talked for an hour. I hoped Aaron Hockelmann was paying for the call. We talked about everything. I got her up to speed about where things were on my end, and she did the same. It was good medicine for both of us.

Finally, Barbara said: "Maybe the man from the embassy is right. Maybe it is time for you to go home."

"Not until this all gets worked out."

"Zack, it will all get worked out. With or without you."

"But there's no guarantee that it will get worked out the way I want it to get worked out."

"And which way is that?"

"The good guys win and the bad guys don't."

"Zack, dear, is it impossible for you to accept the fact that things sometimes just can't turn out the way you want them to?"

"Yeah, I'd say that's pretty much impossible for me to accept. Does that make me a control freak?"

"Yes, but a lovable one," she said. "So. Who are the good guys and who are the bad guys?"

"Ah, there's the rub," I said. "I'm pretty sure Alan Whitehall is a good guy. Even if he's a politician. Everyone else, I'm reserving judgment."

"Even Monk?"

"Monk's out of the picture. Doesn't matter."

"Still, it sounds as if you're not as keen on him as you once were. All that business about running out on his ex-wives, leaving them high and dry."

"Apparently, he was still married to one of them. Not that it slowed him down in the least."

From her end I could hear a doorbell ring.

"Oh, that's room service. Right back." When she returned she said: "Fifteen dollars for a pot of coffee. It's a scandal."

"Charge it to Aaron Hockelmann," I said.

"I intend to." I could hear her blowing on the coffee to cool it, taking a sip. Then she said: "I must agree, it does seem as if Darcy Whitehall is being rather circumspect about all this. Why do you suppose that is?"

"Beats me," I said. "All I know is that he's totally committed to his son and seeing to it that he gets elected to Parliament."

"And somewhat less committed to his daughter."

"Yes, there's a distance between them. Probably measurable in light-years."

"Which could explain why she took up with Monk. She can't please her father, but she can please the father figure."

"That's a psychological explanation. Could be there was just a mutual attraction and they wanted to fuck each other's brains out."

"My, but you do have fucking on your mind today, don't you?"

"Comes with the turf, only not my specific turf. I feel like I oughta be wearing a T-shirt with a big 'C' on it."

"For celibate?"

"Bingo."

"Well, if it becomes too great a burden for you to bear then I would surely understand if you were to submit to animal instinct."

"Like hell you would."

"You're right," said Barbara. "I'd claw your eyes out. Hers, too."

"You might have your hands full," I said. "There's two of them."

I told her about Lynette and Darlene.

"Doesn't sound as if I really have anything to worry about," said Barbara.

"You don't," I said. "But one question."

"Ask," she said.

"Are they black?"

"What?"

"The panties . . ."

42

When I arrived at Darcy Whitehall's house the next morning, three of the guards were spread out around the place. They carried rifles and wore the glum expressions of men who are engaged in something serious but are trying very hard not to look bored. The fourth guard was stationed by the front door. I stepped inside.

Otee sat at the kitchen counter, eating a plate of food, peas 'n rice it looked like, watching something on television. His Browning was on the countertop. I walked to the living room, where Alan sat in a chair working on his laptop.

"Where's your father?"

"He was heading out the door when I was getting up," he said. "Mentioned something about going to Mo Bay."

"He went alone?"

Alan shrugged.

"I don't know. Like I said, I was just getting up and . . ."

"Went by himself," Otee hollered from the kitchen. He appeared in the kitchen door, wiping his mouth with a napkin. "Tried to go with him, but he wouldn't hear it."

"Did he mention what he was doing in Mo Bay?"

"Or *who* he was doing?"

I hadn't heard Ali Whitehall walk up behind me from a hall that led to the sleeping quarters. She was barefoot and wearing a white terrycloth robe.

Alan ignored her.

"I'm assuming he had business to attend to," Alan said.

"What kind of business, did he mention that?"

"No, he didn't say. Father really doesn't discuss his business affairs with me."

"Nor his other affairs," said Ali.

Alan shot her a look.

"Ali, please," he said.

"Please what? Keep quiet about him and the way he runs around? That's what Mother did for all those years. And look where it got her."

Alan snapped shut his laptop and got up from the chair.

"If you'll excuse me, I think I'll work in my bedroom," he told me. "I have a speech scheduled tomorrow in Falmouth. Will that be a problem?"

I looked at Otee.

"Can you go with him?"

Otee nodded.

"We'll find someone else, too," I said.

"What about you?" Alan said.

"I'm planning on heading back to Florida."

"Not for good, I hope."

"Remains to be seen," I said.

I told them about Monk's memorial service. When I was done, Otee returned to the kitchen. Alan excused himself and stepped down the hall. Ali watched him go.

"He's in denial, always has been," said Ali. "He thinks our father is some kind of saint."

She plopped down on a couch. I took a chair beside it.

"Tell me about your mother," I said.

"Why?"

"Because I can't think of anything else to talk to you about. Because if I bring up your father or your brother I'm afraid you'll bite my head off. Because I don't want to talk about the weather. And because I'm trying to figure why you've got such a goddam chip on your shoulder."

Ali looked away. She curled her legs under her, ran a hand through her hair.

"My parents were together for eighteen years, but came a point and she just couldn't take it anymore."

"Take what?"

"Living here, the whole sordid scene. Father was much more a part of it all back then, mixing it up with the guests, carrying on just like they do. And when he wasn't cavorting with Miss Flavor-of-the-Day he was off somewhere tending to business. Or so he said. Anyway, he was never around," Ali said. "I think Mother just saw herself wilting on the vine.

"When they finally decided to split up—Alan was seventeen, I was almost eleven—they gave us the choice of living with whichever one of them we wanted. Alan chose Father, god knows why, probably because he was already plotting his political career back then. And I chose Mother. The two of them stayed here; Mother and I went off to live in London. And my father has never forgiven me for it."

She got up from the couch, walked to a bamboo armoire, and pulled a framed photograph from a shelf. She handed it to me and sat back down again.

"Taken shortly after they were married," she said.

It was an old Kodachrome and the colors had washed out, but the woman in the photo had a brilliance that years couldn't fade. Dark skin, an easy smile, big sad eyes. She wore a long blue gown with rhinestones on the bodice, and she was vamping for the camera, one hand cocked on a hip, the other fanning out the edge of her gown.

"She looks just like you," I said.

"Everyone says that."

"It's true. She's beautiful."

"The gown she's wearing in the picture, she designed that," said Ali.

"So that's where you get your talent."

"I'm nothing compared to her. She was amazing. Too bad

she never decided to do anything with it until it was too late."

"What happened?"

"You mean, how did she die?"

I nodded. She took a deep breath, a faraway look in her eyes.

"We were living in this tiny little flat, typical low-rent London because she refused to take anything from my father. Still, we were happy, you know? She was consumed with starting a career as a fashion designer, working insane hours, her sketches and fabric scattered everywhere. She knew lots of musicians—Father's contacts in the recording industry did help on that front—and the musicians knew lots of models, so some of them were always dropping by and trying things on. That got her some notice, a story in the *Times,* another one in the *Daily Mirror.* She had just opened a shop in Mayfair and was planning a spring show," said Ali. "Then one night she took a bunch of pills and didn't wake up."

"Accidental?"

"I doubt it," Ali said. "I mean, I don't know. It might have been. At first, I told myself that it had to be an accident, that she would never just choose to leave me. Then I convinced myself that she must have discovered she had cancer or something and didn't want to suffer. Finally, I just accepted the fact that she wanted to die."

"So that's when you decided to come back here to live with your father?"

She shook her head.

"I had no intention of coming back here. Ever. He came to London and got me."

"But that's got to count for something," I said. "Proof that he loves you."

"He really didn't have a choice," Ali said. "I was in jail."

I didn't say anything.

"Grand larceny. Drugs." She paused. "Some other things, too."

I didn't say anything.

"That was four years ago," she said. "He brought me back here, built a little house for me, and let me be. Out of sight, out of mind. Might as well still be in London."

"If you're so miserable, why don't you just leave?"

"I've thought about it," Ali said. "Monk and I had even made some plans. And then . . ."

Ali stood from the couch, forced a smile as she walked away.

"But now we're all under one roof, living happily ever after, eh?" she said. "Some fairy tale."

43

I spent the next hour on the phone at Darcy Whitehall's house, trying to find a flight back to Florida. After much finagling, I finally snagged a standby seat on Air Jamaica that left the next day at noon, with an evening connection to Tampa. I'd worry about finding a return flight on the other end.

The rest of the morning passed uneventfully. No bombs, no thugs with guns, nothing to spoil yet another gorgeous day in paradise. Alan stayed in his bedroom working. Ali stayed in her bedroom, doing whatever. And Darcy Whitehall stayed gone. There hadn't even been a phone call from him.

Otee brought me a copy of that morning's *Gleaner.* A front-page headline screamed: "Bloody Shoot-out Leaves Two Dead."

There was a photo of Alan Whitehall speaking at the co-op hall in Benton Town the day before. Another photo showed police unloading the two bodies from the white van at police headquarters.

The police had done some legwork since we'd met with Eustace Dunwood. They now had identities on the dead men. They were brothers—Neville Andrews, 20, and James Andrews, 22, both of Montego Bay. The newspaper had managed to dig up mug shots of the two that must have been taken when both were still in school. Neither one of them looked any more than fourteen in the photos, smiling, fresh-faced kids wearing white shirts and black ties.

The story quoted Eustace Dunwood as saying "while the suspects were wearing NPU colors, there is nothing at this time that connects them or their accomplice with the NPU."

That was followed by a quote from Kenya Oompong saying she did not know the dead men and suggested that the shooting was "part of an ongoing attempt by the People's National Party to discredit our cause and garner sympathy for the sham candidacy of Alan Whitehall, who is nothing more than a fetch-boy for foreign interests and progeny of one of the most vile exploiters of the Jamaican people."

Woman had a way with words, had to give her that. I could almost hear Oompong's thundering voice as she'd said it.

The story didn't identify Otee by name, saying only that "Whitehall's personal bodyguard returned fire from the assailants, killing them." It didn't identify me either, except to say that "a second bodyguard, a U.S. security expert hired by Whitehall's father, wealthy resort owner Darcy Whitehall, was also present at the altercation."

I put down the paper.

Otee said, "Story called you a security expert."

"Has a nice ring to it, don't you think?" I said. "Bet it'll scare off anyone else who thinks about messing with us, huh?"

"Shit," said Otee. "Be no end to the people want to mess with us now."

"You worried about that?"

"Be less worried if you worth a damn with a gun, mon."

In Darcy Whitehall's absence, Otee and I decided it would be a good idea to meet with the resort's executive staff—the general manager, the director of operations, and the director of guest relations—to map out a plan for making sure no one entered the resort grounds unless they were supposed to be there. We all sat down in the living room.

"Should we advise the guests about what is going on?" the general manager asked.

"What do they know already?" I said.

"They're oblivious," said the director of guest relations.

"Once they get here they couldn't care less about anything that goes on outside the resort walls. I'd be willing to bet that most of them know nothing about the bomb at the airport, much less about the shoot-out yesterday."

Consensus was that the resort would carry on as if nothing had happened. The only option was to level with the guests and start handing out refunds. That would have been fine with me, but I thought that decision should come from Darcy Whitehall. Where the hell was he anyway?

The chief of security, a heavyset former policeman named Glenroy Wilkes, said he'd need a dozen new hands in order to run full shifts around the clock, tighten the resort's perimeter, and keep extra men on guard at Darcy Whitehall's house. I told him to go ahead and hire them. And Otee said that as soon as the new guards arrived he would meet them at the main guardhouse to issue weapons.

After everyone else left, I was sitting alone in the living room when Ali Whitehall came in.

"I meant to ask earlier, but who was that man last night, the one who came to talk to you?" she said.

"He works for the U.S. Embassy. Skingle's his name. Why?"

"I've seen him before," she said. "With Monk."

"He told me he didn't know Monk."

"Well, he's lying then," said Ali. "I saw them together a couple of weeks ago."

"Where?"

"At this place, the Bird's Nest, about halfway between here and Montego Bay," she said. "My father was off-property for a few days, at one of the other resorts, and Monk and I had planned to spend the afternoon together at my place. I'd made him lunch and everything. But at the last moment he canceled on me, said something had come up and he couldn't make it. He wouldn't tell me what it was about, and, well, I was suspicious."

"Why?"

"I was jealous, you know? I thought he might be going to see another woman. Monk was a flirt. He was always hitting on women here at the resort, even after he and I hooked up. I knew he'd had a couple of flings with some of the girls on staff—one of the scuba instructors, a massage therapist at the spa—and I thought maybe he was up to something like that. He left in his car and I followed him. That guy was waiting for him in the parking lot. I saw them talking and then they walked inside together."

"You sure it was Skingle?"

"Positive. He was all dressed up, just like he was last night," she said. "What's with that guy anyway?"

"I don't know," I said.

But I was ready to find out.

44

I checked with Mr. Skingle and I'm afraid he is tied up for the better part of the afternoon, Mr. Chasteen," the secretary told me over the phone. "May I tell him what this is in reference to?"

She had a lovely voice. Jamaican, very sing-songy. I've been known to fall in love with women based simply on the sound of their voices over a telephone.

"Tell him it's in a reference to a two-by-four."

"A two-by-four?"

"Yes, the two-by-four that will be applied to the side of his head if he doesn't make time for me."

Was threatening bodily harm to the assistant consul for Homeland Security a federal offense? Screw it.

Besides, I thought I heard the secretary giggle before she put me on hold.

When she came back on, she said: "How does five-thirty sound?"

"Sounds like four and a half hours from now. Nothing sooner?"

"Afraid not."

"Then tell Mr. Skingle that I would be delighted to join him at five-thirty."

"Very good. I'll put you down," she said. "And, Mr. Chasteen?"

"Yes?"

"That two-by-four won't be necessary."

"Fine," I said. "But can I still bring along the ball peen hammer for his kneecaps?"

This time she laughed. A lovely laugh. Oh, Zack, you charmer, you.

I had an afternoon to kill. Otee and the security guards had things under control at Darcy Whitehall's house, which was still minus Darcy Whitehall. No need for me to get in the way.

What to do, what to do? Here I was, in the lap of sybaritic delight. So many seductive pleasures to choose from. A seaweed wrap at the Libido spa? Croquet-in-the-buff on the poolside lawn? Bikram yoga in my birthday suit?

I pulled Monk's "Ideal Executive Daybook" out of the backpack and flipped the pages until I came to what I was looking for.

****K.O.****
MARTHA BRAE
1019 CHRIST CHURCH LANE

The Mercedes was just sitting out there waiting for me. Nice afternoon for a drive.

45

On the road to Martha Brae, I got stuck behind a tour bus filled with would-be river rafters and had to put up the windows on the Mercedes to shut out the diesel fumes.

It was slow going, but every now and then I got a glimpse of the Martha Brae River, its gray-green waters oozing between the muddy banks. A procession of bamboo rafts bobbed down the river, gondolas gone tropo, each carrying two passengers reclining in chairs, while a guide steered the course with a long bamboo pole. Not a rip-roaring Class 5 thrill ride by any means, but an easy-does-it way to fulfill the minimum daily vacation requirement for getting close to nature.

The town of Martha Brae straddled the river. I found Christ Church easy enough, a stalwart Anglican fortress just off the market square, and followed Christ Church Lane a couple of blocks until I came to a cozy little white-frame house with a green slate roof and yellow trim. A picket fence enclosed the yard with an arbor gate bearing a homemade address marker announcing that it was 1019.

OK, I'd found it, now what?

I parked across the street, got out of the car, and walked toward the house. A giant mango tree stood on one side of the house, a breadfruit tree on the other, their branches touching in the middle and keeping the roof well shaded. A profusion of purple-flowered vines entwined the porch columns.

A garage apartment sat behind the house, considerably newer than the main dwelling but painted to match it. No car in the garage.

I was reaching for the gate when the dog lunged out from under the house, a big black and tan and snarling thing, some Jamaican riff on a Rottweiler. It leapt for the gate and I leapt back, a chain thwarting the beast's intent just inches before it had me. The dog strained against the chain, standing on its back legs, quite nearly as tall as me, barking and slinging slobber.

"Hesh up!"

A woman stepped out of the house and onto the porch. She was an old woman, a big old woman, not fat so much as she was just plain massive. A bright blue dress went to her ankles, a white apron over the dress, white hair pulled tight to her head with a hairnet. She held a wooden cane in each hand, and she planted them in front of her on the porch, propping herself up as she peered out toward the gate, squinting from the shade of the porch into the sun.

The dog kept barking.

"Hesh up!" the old woman yelled. "You done your job. Go on back. Go!"

The dog gave me one last malevolent look, then returned to the cool dirt under the porch, sighing as it circled and lay down. The old woman kept squinting in my direction, looking from side to side.

"Who you?" she said. "Talk at me!"

"I'm Zack Chasteen, ma'am," I said, and she zeroed in on me. Then her eyes wandered. She was blind.

"You a white man?" she said.

"Uh-huh. Yes, ma'am."

"What you want?"

She had me there. I didn't know what I wanted. And I was thinking I should maybe just slink quietly back to the car and drive away when she said: "You that same white man was out here before, snooping around?"

"No, ma'am," I said. "When was that?"

"Few weeks back. I was off to church. One of the neighbors seen him. I told my daughter about it. She the one got me this dog."

"Some dog," I said.

"What you want?"

I've always found that when dealing with old women, especially big old blind women with big mean dogs, honesty is the absolute best policy.

"I'm trying to find who killed my friend," I said.

"What friend's that?"

So I told her the story about the bomb at the airport. She'd heard about it on television. And I told her about finding Monk's daybook with her address in it.

"Don't know why my house would be in some dead white man's book," she said.

"Neither do I, ma'am. That's what I'm trying to find out."

She was looking straight at me now.

"It hot out there?"

"Yes, ma'am, it's real hot."

"Well, come sit up in the shade of the porch," she said.

I reached for the gate. The dog growled.

"Hesh up, Tiny," the woman said.

46

She told me to sit down while she went inside the house. I planted myself in one of the rocking chairs. She came back out a few minutes later with a glass of water and handed it to me.

She took the chair beside me, placed a hand on my arm, squeezed it, then worked her way up to my shoulder, across to my chest, then back to my arm. She kept her hand there.

"You stout," she said.

"Yes, ma'am," I said. "I've heard that."

"Stout man's a good man. Stout woman, too."

I sipped the water and rocked in the chair.

"You seen our river?" she said.

"Yes, ma'am. Saw it on the way in. Nice river."

"Nicest river in all Jamaica. You know the story of its name?"

"No, ma'am, I don't."

"Long time ago, before they brought the first slaves here even, back during the Spanish, there was this Indian princess, this Arawak, and her name was Martha Brae."

"So there really was a Martha Brae?"

"Oh yeah, and she was something. She knew the secret of the river, knew where it kept its gold."

"Gold?"

"Uh-huh, this river used to have a cave filled with gold and Martha Brae she was the only one knew how to find it. The Spanish they came marching in and they grabbed Martha Brae and they told her she had to show them the cave of gold. So she took them straight to it. And soon as they got inside the cave, while those Spanish were busy looking at all the gold, Martha Brae she said her words."

"What words?"

"Her secret words, powerful words, words that changed the course of that river so it threw a big boulder up to seal the mouth of that cave and locked them all inside."

"Martha Brae, too?"

"Uh-huh, she died right there with 'em, just so those Spanish couldn't carry away all that gold."

"Quite a woman that Martha Brae."

"Yes, she was. Strong woman. That's why I named my daughter after her. That's her place in the back, although she's hardly ever here."

"Your daughter's named Martha, too?"

The old woman nodded.

"Her middle name, but she doesn't go by it. She goes by her first name—Kenya."

"Kenya Oompong?" I said.

The initials in the daybook—K.O. Man, how thick could I be?

The old woman turned her head my way.

"Why, yes. Our surname be Freeman, but Kenya she took on the name Oompong, because that's what some of our people were called. They were Maroons," the old woman said. "You know Kenya?"

"Not exactly," I said. "But I know who she is."

"Then you know all about the NPU."

"Yes, ma'am," I said. "I do."

"She's a fighter, Kenya. Stirring things up. Might not get elected, most probably won't, but she's making a name for herself."

"She's doing that," I said.

I drank the rest of the water. We rocked quietly for a while.

"Let me ask you a question," I said. "This white man who

was here a few weeks ago, did your neighbor get a good look at him?"

"Not much of one. It was night. I was off to church, singing in the choir. That's what I do on Wednesday nights."

"Did your neighbor say he was a big man, you know, a stout man like me?"

The old woman shook her head.

"Oh no, said he was a slight fellow, not much to him at all, like a shadow coming out of my yard, getting in his car and driving away."

"Anything missing from your house?"

"No, uh-uh. I called Kenya and she drove all the way up here and looked around and she couldn't find anything missing either. That's when she went out and got me that dog. I call him Tiny."

"Yes, ma'am. That Tiny's a real fine dog," I said.

47

When someone says they work at the U.S. Embassy it conjures visions of a stately building where diplomats and dignitaries mingle, a handsome edifice with a big flag flying outside and an aura of grandeur, even in this buttoned-down era of international terrorism. While Uncle Sam has an embassy like that in Kingston, the Department of Homeland Security suboffice in Montego Bay was not the sort of place that caused the heart to swell or inspired spontaneous renditions of "God Bless America." Johnny Cash's "Fulsom Prison Blues" would have been more appropriate.

It sat in an industrial zone next to the airport, and it looked exactly like what it was—a cluster of nondescript concrete-block buildings that had been given drab coats of beige paint and encircled with enough electrified fence and concertina wire to outfit a couple of maximum-security state penitentiaries. Marines with rifles guarded the entrance.

I parked the Mercedes, walked up to the guardhouse, and stated my business. The Marine inside made a phone call. He hung up and said: "He can see you now, sir. Building B, Room nine." He pinned a visitor's badge on my shirt. The gates opened, and I followed a sidewalk to Building B.

Inside, there was a large waiting room. A dozen or so people, mostly Jamaicans by my guess, were filling out various applications, probably for visas of one sort or another.

Ever since the aftermath of 9-11, the Department of Homeland Security had been in charge of what used to be the Immigration and Naturalization Service. Critics of the system said it was part of a larger plan, hatched by xenophobic conservatives, to seal our borders to people of color. Supporters said it was a first line of defense in the war against terrorism.

At that moment I didn't much care about the political implications; I just wanted to get some answers from Jay Skingle. I hung a left down a hall and came to a reception desk outside a suite of offices. The woman at the desk looked up and smiled.

"You must be Mr. Chasteen," she said.

She was older than her voice had sounded on the phone, a bit more substantial, too, but no hardship to look at.

"I am he."

"I see you came empty-handed," she said.

"I bring only my boyish charm. That marine outside made me check my good looks."

She smiled.

"Ah, that explains it," she said. "Mr. Skingle can see you now."

She got up from her desk and I followed her down the hall. She was a pleasure to follow. She knocked lightly on a door, then opened it and nodded me in.

Skingle was sitting behind a desk, talking on the phone. He waved me to a chair and kept on talking. The secretary gave me another smile and shut the door.

I sat down in the chair and looked around the room. A few pictures on the wall—Skingle glad-handing it with other guys in suits, a signed photo of him with the current president. His college diploma. Princeton. The date on it was ten years ago. Skingle was older than he looked. Yet he was still just an assistant consul. Guy definitely wasn't on the foreign service fast track.

Skingle hung up the phone, and before he could say anything, I said: "Where's your buddy?"

"My buddy?"

"Yeah, the guy who was with you the night of the airport

bombing, the guy who drove you to Libido last night, the guy who stole Monk DeVane's files."

"I don't know what you're talking about."

"Cut the crap, Skingle. Someone saw your guy leaving Monk DeVane's cottage carrying a black garbage bag. I got there a little after that and all Monk's files were gone. Ray Charles could connect those dots."

Skingle didn't say anything.

"Plus you lied to me, saying you didn't know Monk. You met him at a place called the Bird's Nest a couple of weeks ago."

"Who told you that?"

"Doesn't matter," I said. "All that really matters is that when it comes to credibility, yours is shot."

Skingle made a tent of his fingers and put them under his chin, studying me. I'd read somewhere that if you want to gain leverage in a conversation then you should subtly mimic the body language of the other person. So I made a temple of my fingers and put them under my chin and studied Skingle back. I don't know if it gained me any leverage, but Skingle got up from his chair and turned his back on me, looking out a window.

When he turned around, he said: "OK, I'll level with you. But I must have your guarantee that nothing I tell you leaves this office."

"That was good," I said. "Sounded like right out of the movies."

"Do I have that guarantee or not, Mr. Chasteen?"

"Sure," I said, "I'll play."

Skingle put his hands behind his back, paced in front of the window. The guy was all about dramatic effect. Finally, he said: "Certain of Mr. DeVane's effects are now under review by this office."

"Why?"

"Sorry, that's classified."

"Wow, you really know all the lines." I got up from my chair. "Who's your boss?"

Skingle looked startled.

"Excuse me?"

"Who's your boss? I want to see him."

"It's a her."

"Fine. Let's go see her."

"Why?"

"So she can explain why the U.S. government is sneaking around taking things that belonged to one of its citizens—of late, deceased—and which now belong to his rightful heirs. And if she can't explain, then I'll get the name of her boss and I won't stop until someone tells me something."

When I hop on my high horse I give it a good ride. Skingle thought it over. It looked as if it pained him.

"OK," he said. "I'll tell you what I can."

"Ah, the voice of reason."

He sat back down. I did, too.

Then Skingle said: "Mr. DeVane worked for us."

It was my turn to look startled. Skingle appeared to enjoy it.

"For the Department of Homeland Security?"

"Not directly. It's a joint investigation, involving the resources of several departments."

"An investigation of what?" I said.

"I really can't go into any of the specifics. I've already told you more than you should know."

Skingle leaned back in his chair. I sat there trying to process everything. It was a lot to process.

"Does this involve the NPU?" I said.

"Really, Mr. Chasteen, I've said all that I can possibly say. To reveal anything further would be to jeopardize the integrity of a plan that has taken months and months to put in place. And it would hinder our attempts to bring whoever killed Monk DeVane to justice," Skingle said.

"Do you know who did it?"

"I think we're closing in on it, yes," said Skingle. "That is why I suggest you return to Florida and let us do what we have to do. Once again, may I assist with your flight arrangements?"

I shook my head.

"Taken care of," I said. "I leave tomorrow."

"Excellent," said Skingle.

He stood. I stood.

Meeting over.

48

When I got back to Libido I checked in briefly at Darcy Whitehall's house. Darcy Whitehall still hadn't made an appearance.

"He left a message earlier," said Alan. "He'll be staying over the night in Mo Bay. That's all I know."

"Everything good here?"

"As good as house arrest can be," Alan said. "At least I'm getting plenty of work done."

"Your sister still in a funk?"

"She's being Ali. Thought I'd try to talk to her."

"Do the big-brother thing?"

"Doesn't really work on her," he said. "If we can just spend five minutes in the same room without getting into an argument, I'll consider it progress."

I went back to the cottage. I sat on the porch for a while. The tobacco seeds and salt that Otee had spread a couple nights earlier were still there, doing their job, keeping the duppies away.

I went inside. I sat on the couch for a while. I watched the ceiling fan turn, listened to the refrigerator hum.

I was hungry. The buffet at the resort's beachside restaurant went on until midnight. I didn't want to deal with the whole scene. Still, that didn't make me any less hungry.

The phone rang. I answered it. It was Barbara calling from Berlin.

"What time is it there?" I asked.

"Almost three A.M. We went out clubbing."

"Baby seals?"

"Cute," she said. "We hit the Scheunenviertel district. Aaron and some of his friends."

"You sound a little drunk," I said.

"I am. A little. But I can still pronounce Scheunenviertel. We had fun."

"Hmmm," I said.

"How about you?"

"I'm not drunk. And I'm not having fun."

"Does it take one to have the other?"

"No. Sometimes. I don't know."

"Zack, what's wrong?" she said.

"Nothing."

"Bullshit."

"Just at loose ends, that's all. Darcy Whitehall's run off somewhere. Monk DeVane was working for the feds. I almost got mauled by a bigass dog. I'm hungry. I'm beginning to wonder just what in hell I'm doing here. And I miss you."

"Me, too."

"You, too, what?"

"I miss you," she said. "And I'm beginning to wonder just what in hell I'm doing here."

"Thought you were having fun."

"Oh, I am. Kinda. Not really. Oh, not at all," she said. "Should have stayed at home."

"Why?"

"It's a control thing, you wouldn't understand."

"Meaning?"

"Meaning you never have to worry about being in control of what's going on around you because you are in control no matter where you are."

"Believe me, I'm in control of nothing that's going on around me right now. I can't seem to get a handle on anything."

"But you will. You'll find a way. Because that's who you are.

You can plop down anywhere and you're still the same Zack. You've got everything you need within you. You're that army of one, like in those commercials they run to get kids to sign up for the military."

"Stupid commercials."

"Yes, but that's you through and through. You're self-contained. You define yourself. Me, I need my office, my people, the phone ringing all the time, this emergency to deal with, that fire to put out. It tells me who I am, and I'm feeling a little cut off from all that here, and I'm out of my element and, yes, I'm a little drunk."

"Don't you think that's what Hockelmann had in mind?"

"What, getting me drunk?"

"No, taking you out of your element, putting you on his turf. Getting you drunk was just a bonus."

"Oh yes, that's absolutely what he had in mind. I knew it when he suggested I get on his stupid jet and fly over here with him. I knew it was just a power thing. It's just that I thought I could cope with it better than I seem able to."

"So what you're saying is that, basically, you are a control freak and you can't stand letting someone else be in charge of things and calling all the shots."

"Yes, that's it exactly. I make no bones about it. Only when I'm with you my whole control neurosis shuts off and I don't feel that need to . . ."

"Boss people around?"

"Yes, that. What do you think that means, Zack?"

"I think it means you're having some real misgiving about selling Orb to Aaron Hockelmann."

"Oh, I know that. I've already made my mind up. I can't possibly do it, no matter how much money he throws at me and, believe me, he is throwing a lot," Barbara said. "But what about the other part, Zack? Why is it that I'm not like that when I'm with you?"

I didn't say anything.

"Zack?"

"Yes?"

"Why is that?"

"I don't know exactly."

"Me either. But it's that way, isn't it? We go good together, don't we?"

"Yes," I said. "We do."

49

My standby flight was at noon, so I got up early, went for a long walk, hit the Libido breakfast buffet, dropped by Darcy Whitehall's house—he was still gone, Ali and Alan were still in bed—and was on the A1 to Montego Bay before 9 A.M.

They'd reopened the airport to traffic, and I found a spot under covered parking to leave the Mercedes for a couple of days. Then I went through immigration and security and sat in the Air Jamaica terminal for more than an hour only to learn there wouldn't be a seat for me on the noon flight. The only guaranteed seating was on a 7:30 P.M. flight to Miami. I took it.

No way I was going to sit in the terminal until then. So I did the whole immigration and customs thing again, got the Mercedes out of parking, and thought about the best way to kill an afternoon. I thought about eating, but I didn't want to eat. I thought about drinking, but I didn't want to drink. That didn't leave much to do but drive, so I drove.

I followed the Queen's Road to a butt-puckering, four-lane roundabout and let it spit me out where it wanted. I wound up on a road that followed the gentle curve of the broad harbor and I looked out on the water.

Three hundred years earlier the Spanish were drawn to this

point of land by the large number of wild pigs that roamed the shore. They killed the pigs and rendered the fat to lard, or *manteeca,* "pig's butter," as they called it. On some early British maps, the area was even called Lard Bay, but most stuck with manteeca, and over the years that mutated into Montego, which had a lyricism not normally associated with swine.

As I neared the crunch of shops and so-called craft markets known as Gloucester Avenue, I made the obvious observation: things really hadn't changed all that much over the years, at least in the sense that vast numbers of porkers still roamed the shore, only now they were known as tourists, most of them fat, happy Americans recently disgorged from cruise ships or on furlough from all-inclusive resorts. And the locals were busy rendering them into cash flow.

Cheap beads, hair braids, and wood carvings; snorkeling trips, fishing trips, sunset cruises; ganja, cocaine, more ganja— Gloucester Avenue had the highest concentration of hawkers, hagglers, and touts of just about anywhere in the Caribbean. And given the natural Jamaican propensity for confrontation— a direct result, many claimed, of Jamaica being on the receiving end of slave ships that pulled their primary cargo from the ranks of Ashanti warriors—the tourists walked in tight little groups, some of them clutching each other with the nervous eyes of wary prey.

I couldn't blame the locals for their aggressive pursuit of business, not if it meant a ticket out of the tin-shack ghettos in the hills above Montego Bay. Prying bucks from tourists yielded richer results than selling yams on a blanket at the vegetable market. And I couldn't blame the tourists for being repulsed by the whole scene. Most of the stuff for sale was crap, and some of the people selling it were really scary.

Faced with all this, Kenya Oompong's tirades against cattle-call tourism made a certain kind of sense. Maybe if this were my home, I'd be just as outraged and militant as she was. Maybe I'd join Nanny's People, spray-paint invectives on resort walls, harass the fetch-boys of foreign interests, and head for a better life in the hills. It wasn't an altogether unreasonable reaction to what was surely an unpalatable set of circumstances.

The only downside: I wouldn't look good in a red-and-yellow bandanna.

Which got me to thinking: What was I going to wear to Monk's memorial service?

The only clothes I had were the ones on my back—khaki shorts, a blue polo—both way too big and borrowed. With the change in flights, I wouldn't have time to buy anything in Miami, where I was now going to have to spend the night, or in Tampa, where I was going to have to get off the plane, rent a car, and drive straight to the memorial service. It was scheduled to take place at the national cemetery in Bushnell, a small town just north of Tampa. I couldn't show up looking the way I looked.

I found a parking lot where the attendant seemed slightly trustworthy, or at least she did after I gave her ten dollars with the promise of ten more if the Mercedes was still there when I got back. I left the metal canister sitting in the front seat, although Monk would have probably loved walking around Gloucester Avenue, and I took with me the backpack containing the few other things I had—a toothbrush, a clean T-shirt and the black daybook I'd taken from Monk's dresser.

I headed up the avenue and cut into the first shopping mall I came to, a three-story warren of shops, one of which turned out to carry some fairly presentable sportswear. I bought a long-sleeved black silk shirt, some tan silk pants, and a pair of black loafers. It wasn't a funereal ensemble by any means, but it was fairly dignified in an island kind of way and it would have to do.

Point of fact: I can run boats across open water without charts and get exactly to where I'm going, but put me in a shopping mall and I get all turned around. I couldn't find the way I came in, and when I stepped out it was on the backside of the mall and I didn't recognize anything. I started walking in what seemed like the right direction, but stopped after a couple of blocks when it became clear I was going the wrong way.

I looked up at a street sign: Dover Road. I knew that name from somewhere. I reached into the backpack, pulled out Monk's black daybook, and flipped to the final entry.

****EQUINOX INVESTMENTS****
314 DOVER RD MB

It was only a couple of blocks away. What the hell.

50

There wasn't a sign that said Equinox Investments outside the building at 314 Dover Road. But there was something even better parked on the street: Darcy Whitehall's black Mercedes, recognizable by his initials monogrammed in gold on the front doors.

How freaking fortuitous.

The building wasn't much to look at, six stories of glass and concrete that could have been anywhere. I walked into the lobby, which was occupied by the building's main tenant, Great Nation Bank. Lines were long and the tellers were busy. A directory listed Equinox Investments in Suite 601. I took an elevator to the top floor and got out.

Suite 601 was the only office on the sixth floor. A small, tasteful brass plaque on one of the polished teak double doors gave the company name. I opened the doors and stepped into a small reception area. Nothing fancy, but much nicer than the rest of the building would have led me to believe: muted lighting, soft textured carpet, contemporary furniture, nice art on the walls.

A pretty young woman wearing black reading glasses and a navy blue suit sat behind a polished teak console that served as the reception desk. Another set of double doors was behind her.

The pretty young woman looked down her glasses at me and said: "May I help you?"

"Yes, I have an appointment later today with Darcy Whitehall. I was walking by, saw his car out front, and thought I might just pop in and catch him, save us both a little time. Could you tell him I'd like to see him if he's not too busy?"

The woman studied me for a long moment. I gave her my friendliest "aw-shucks" grin. Somehow she managed not to melt.

"And you are?"

"Zack Chasteen."

"One moment, Mr. Chasteen, and I will see if Mr. Whitehall is available."

She stood and went through the double teak doors. I nosed around the reception area. There wasn't much to see. No magazines on the table. And the art on the walls really wasn't as good as it had appeared at first. Just prints in fancy frames.

After about five minutes, the young woman returned.

"I'm sorry," she said, "but it seems as if Mr. Whitehall is not on the premises at this time."

"Oh, shoot, that's too bad," I said. "Is he with Mr., uh, Mr. . . ."

"Mr. Arzghanian?"

"Yes, is he with him?"

"I would assume so, yes."

"And they went to . . . ?"

"I'm afraid I don't know that."

"And they'll be back . . . ?"

"I'm afraid I don't know that either."

"Oh well," I said. "It was worth a shot."

The young woman nodded.

"Is there a message?" she said.

"No, no message," I said. "But do you happen to have any company brochures?"

"Excuse me?"

"You know, something that tells me a little bit about Equinox Investments, an annual report, anything like that. Mr. Whitehall has spoken so highly of your company that I'd like to learn a little more about it for myself."

The young woman shook her head.

"No, Mr. Chasteen," she said. "I'm afraid we don't have anything like that at all."

"Hmm, that's too bad. Because they'd be nice to have. You might want to mention that to Mr. Afghanistan."

"Arzghanian," she said.

"Him, too," I said.

I rode the elevator down to the first floor and tried to figure out what I'd just accomplished. I knew slightly more than when I'd arrived. I knew that Darcy Whitehall had been there and was scheduled to come back. Or maybe he really was there and just didn't want to see me. I knew that he was most likely with Mr. Arzghanian, whoever he was. I knew that while Equinox Investments didn't balk at throwing around money for expensive office furniture, it cheaped out when it came to printing up a few measly company brochures. Not much on public image.

I also knew that the pretty young woman looked quite fetching in her navy blue suit with just a hint of cleavage and a nice pair of legs to go with it. But that was neither here nor there. Hell, maybe it was all neither here nor there.

Still, there had to be some reason why Monk had made a note about Equinox Investments in his daybook, just as there had to be a reason why Equinox Investments was buying the piece of land off Old Dutch Road from Darcy Whitehall for a whole lot more than it was worth.

51

I made it back to Miami just in time to check into my room at the MIA Hotel then catch dinner at the sushi bar in the concourse lobby. The place was getting ready to close, and I was the last one left sitting at the bar, holding down a stool that gave me a primo view of people coming and going in the terminal.

I was sipping a Kirin Ichiban and working on my first course, a spicy bowl of ika sansai, when a short stocky guy with a briefcase came in from the concourse, walked all the way around the bar, and sat down next to me.

I nodded at him. He nodded at me. The sushi chef came over and said to the guy: "Sorry, we close now."

"No problem," said the guy. "I'll just sit here and watch my friend eat."

He turned in his stool to look at me. I looked at him. He had close-cropped hair, bushy eyebrows, and a nose that sat off kilter in his chunky face. My age, maybe a little older. He was wearing a suit, a cheap one, and a white polyester shirt with the tie loosened.

"I know you?"

The guy ignored my question. He looked at the bowl of ika sansai.

"What the hell is that?"

"Marinated squid salad," I said. "Pretty good."

The guy made a face, shuddered. Then he smiled.

"Hey, you hear the one about the squid who walks into a jazz club?"

I didn't say anything. I went back to eating my ika sansai. But the guy was not to be denied.

"Bartender tries to kick the squid out and the squid says: 'My good man, I'll have you know that I'm a very talented musician.' Couple of musicians sitting at the bar overhear him, and one of them says: 'Oh, yeah? Well, I've got a guitar right here. And fifty bucks says you can't play it.' He slaps a fifty-dollar bill on the bar, pulls a guitar out of a case, and hands it to the squid. Seconds later, the squid is wailing on the guitar. It's like Jimmy Fuckin' Hendrix. He puts down the guitar and collects the fifty dollars.

"Second guy says: 'I got fifty bucks says you can't play my trumpet.' He puts his money down, pulls out a trumpet, and seconds later the squid is playing hell out of it, like Louis Fuckin' Armstrong. Squid collects another fifty bucks.

"Then the bartender looks at the squid and says: 'I got something for you.' Bartender goes into a back room, comes out a few minutes later, and he's carrying a bagpipe. Bartender puts his money down and hands the bagpipe to the squid. The squid looks at the bagpipe. He turns it over and inspects it from every possible position.

"Bartender says: 'What's a matter? Aren't you gonna play it?'

" 'Play it, hell,' says the squid. 'I'm gonna fuck the damn thing soon as I can figure out how to take off its pajamas.' "

The guy grinned at me.

"Pretty good one, huh?"

"First time I heard it, it was an octopus."

"Yeah, I guess that'd work, too. What you think looks more like a bagpipe, an octopus or a squid?"

"I'd have to go with the octopus."

"Yeah, maybe you're right. Next time I tell it, I'll change it around."

The sushi chef arrived with my main course and set it down in front of me. I'd asked him to surprise me and he'd outdone himself. There were sweet shrimp, three big ones with the heads still on, perched up on their tails like little pink crustacean puppies begging for a treat. There was marbled tuna belly—two thick blood-red pieces—and pink albacore, sliced paper thin and reassembled to look like a rosebud. The centerpiece was a small mound of yellowtail dappled with salmon roe and displayed between two generous slices of smoked freshwater eel, glazed with fermented molasses, which were meant to be dessert.

"Ah, *arigatu gozaimasu*," I said, and offered a little bow.

"*Doita shimashite*," said the chef, with a bow of his own.

"Exactly odo, Quasimodo," said the guy.

"That Japanese?" I asked him.

"No, it's a line from a song by John Prine. Kinda like 'No shit, Sherlock.' Alliterative, ya know?" said the guy. "I just said it to hold up my end of the conversation."

I picked up my chopsticks and went to work, starting in on the yellowtail. The guy rested an elbow on the counter, put his head on his hand, watching me. I was attacking the sweet shrimp when he said: "So let me ask you, Zack, you eat much sushi down in Jamaica?"

I stopped eating. The guy was grinning big-time now.

"You're sitting there wondering, who the fuck is this guy, how does he know me, and how the fuck does he know I just flew in from Jamaica. Am I right, Zack?"

"Yeah," I said. "That's exactly what I'm wondering."

He opened his wallet, got out a business card, and put it on the counter in front of me. I read it without picking it up. The gold embossed logo said: "United States Drug Enforcement Agency." Under that it said: "Lanny Cumbaa, Special Agent."

The guy stood, grabbed his briefcase, and slapped my shoulder.

"They got a bar on the top floor, Zack. I'll be up there when you're done," he said. "I sit here watching you eat, I'm gonna toss my guts."

52

Lanny Cumbaa was saying, "You know how tough it is to make money running a resort in the Caribbean, anywhere for that matter?"

"Not my field of expertise," I said.

"Well, it's mine," said Lanny Cumbaa. "And you can't fucking make a dime, that's how tough it is. The overhead those places have? Shit, they bleed money. That's why so many of 'em get set on spin-dry."

"Spin-dry?"

"Laundered money, Zack. Got all kinds of dirty dollars going through those resorts. It's a royal bitch to keep track of it all."

"Thought the DEA just worried about drugs."

"Shit's all connected, Zack. Follow the money, find the drugs. Delivery and dispersal, two sides of the same operation."

A waitress brought our second round. Another beer for me. Bourbon and seven for Cumbaa. We were sitting in highback chairs in a darkish corner of the Top of Port lounge, looking out on the twinkly lights that lined the runway, every now and then a big jet touching down or taking off.

"So, what you're saying is, Darcy Whitehall, he's laundering money through Libido," I said.

"No, I'm not saying that," said Cumbaa. "What I'm saying

is, he used to. Twenty years ago, when he built that first fuck-palace of his, the one you're staying at, that was all his money, on the legit, money he'd made in the music business.

"But the resort biz, it was more than he bargained for, way more. Inside of a year and Whitehall was ready to go belly-up. Enter Freddie Arzghanian."

I pretended like the name didn't mean anything to me. It didn't take a whole lot of pretending.

"This Arzghanian, he's in the drug business?"

"No, he's in the money business. Works out of Mo Bay, but he has what you might call a global enterprise. Drug guys come to him with their money and he invests it for them so that it comes back smelling fresh and clean. So anyway, Arzghanian offers to partner up with Darcy Whitehall and suddenly everything is beautiful. All the bills are paid. Rooms are filled, guests are happy, everyone's getting laid. Meanwhile, money's going out the back door, sixty cents on the dollar, boomeranging back to Freddie Arzghanian, and for him that's better than getting laid.

"A few years later, Whitehall decides he wants to expand, and Freddie he is way into that because he's got money coming at him from every direction and needs somewhere to wash it. Build a Libido in the Bahamas? No problem. Build another one in St. Lucia? Love it. It's like little money-laundering franchises set up all through the Caribbean."

"So Arzghanian, he's pretty big as far as money launderers go?"

"No, Zack, he's not big. He's fucking giant. He's King Shit, man. Baddest of the bad and all that. Sooner or later everything goes through Freddie Arzghanian." Cumbaa stopped talking and looked past me. His face dropped. He leaned toward me and lowered his voice. "You see that bartender over there, Zack, the one watching us?"

I turned around. The bartender turned away, started washing some glasses.

"He works for Freddie Arzghanian. I'm keeping an eye on him, making sure he doesn't pull a gun and pop us."

Cumbaa studied my expression. Then he reached over and gave my cheek a friendly pat.

"I'm fucking with you, Zack. Fucking with you." He sipped his bourbon. "But Freddie Arzghanian, he's got guys like that all over the place, and they'll do shit, major shit, no questions asked."

"Like plant a fake bomb in a skybox?"

Cumbaa nodded.

"Just to get Darcy Whitehall's attention," he said.

"Or blow up a car in an airport parking lot."

"To make him shit his pants."

"But why? If Arzghanian already has Darcy Whitehall in his pocket, why does he need to do all that?"

"Oh-oh-oh, I forgot to tell you," Cumbaa said. "Sorry, but I left out some important shit. I drink a couple bourbons and my brain goes soft. Vodka, gin, it doesn't affect me like that. Bourbon though . . ."

Cumbaa drained his drink. He signaled the waitress, and she brought refills. The lights kept twinkling out on the runway.

"See, four or five years ago, something funny happens," said Cumbaa. "Darcy Whitehall gets religion."

"What do you mean?"

"I mean, suddenly, out of the blue, Darcy Whitehall decides he doesn't want to do business anymore with Freddie Arzghanian. He wants to go clean."

"Which isn't so easy."

"Which is im-fucking-possible. Except, for some reason, maybe because they been pals so long, Arzghanian cuts Whitehall some slack. Maybe thinks he'll hang himself with it and come crawling back and he'll get into him even deeper. But a funny thing happens: Whitehall makes it work. He's borrowed a shitload of money from legitimate sources, and he's mortgaged to the proverbial hilt, but he's turning a profit on the up-and-up. Not a giant profit, but respectable. Turns out, he's a decent goddam businessman and he really doesn't need Freddie Arzghanian."

Cumbaa sipped bourbon and smacked his lips. I looked at

my glass of beer. I didn't want any more of it. I was all beered out. I was trying to decide if I should move to rum.

Cumbaa said, "But suddenly the worm turns. Suddenly something is up with Darcy Whitehall. Suddenly he needs money and he needs it bad and he is cozying up to Freddie Arzghanian. It looks like they're in business again."

"How do you know all this?"

"Hey, we know. We know all kinds of shit." Cumbaa sat back in his chair, stretched out his legs. "We know, for instance, that a U.S. citizen by the name of Zachary Taylor Chasteen came into possession of one hundred forty pounds of gold bullion last year, sold it to a dealer in Miami, and has yet to pay taxes on the profit, which was somewhere near two million dollars."

I didn't say anything. Cumbaa smiled.

"Hey, don't go dark on me, Zack. I'm prepared to work with you here. You brought in a creep, you're entitled to a little something."

"That creep cost me two years in prison for something I didn't do."

"Yeah, yeah. You got screwed, it sucked, life's unfair. But like I said, I'm willing to work with you here. Tit for tat. You help me, I help you."

I didn't say anything.

Cumbaa drained his bourbon, set the glass down on the table.

"You got a card?" he said.

"No card."

"So what's your cell-phone number?"

"No cell phone."

"You're shitting me."

I shrugged.

"OK, jeez, here's what I'm gonna do." He opened the brief-case, rummaged around, and pulled out a cell phone. He handed it to me. "It's old-school Nokia but it works. Got it on an inter-national plan, courtesy of Uncle Sam. Here, got this, too."

Cumbaa pulled an AC adapter and a charger from his brief-case.

"Now you don't got no fucking excuse if I call you and you

say the fucking phone lost its juice, know what I mean? I'm on the last flight to San Juan, then I'll be in Mo Bay day after tomorrow. We'll talk, OK?"

He got up, grabbed his briefcase, gave me a slap on the back.

He said, "And all the money you got, Chasteen? I'm letting you pick up the tab."

53

It was a pretty good turnout for Monk's memorial service, maybe a hundred of us in the chapel at the Florida National Cemetery in Bushnell. I sat beside Rina Murray, who had driven up from Tampa with Monk's wife, Annie, and the two children. The little boy, Donnie, named after his dad, was four; the little girl, Taylor, three. Both cute as could be.

We sang a couple of hymns, and the chaplain said some prayers and made a few generic remarks about Monk and how he was such a fine man who had served his country well. While the chaplain was talking, little Donnie blurted out: "My daddy played football!" It got laughs out of everyone, and drew more than a few tears.

A few of Monk's friends got up and told stories on him, but I wasn't one of them. When the service was over, we all filed outside and walked down a path to the "Veterans Memory Garden." There was a nice breeze moving through the pine trees, as pleasant as a day like that could be. The chaplain said a few more prayers, then Annie took the metal canister and placed it inside a vault that already had a brass plaque with Monk's name on it.

An army bugler played taps, and a representative from the AmVets presented Annie with an American flag. As he was handing it to her, Donnie raised a hand to his forehead in a salute. Little Taylor copied her big brother. People were misting up like crazy, and I was one of them.

Some of Monk's army buddies had reserved a room at the AmVets post, with a buffet and a bar. Most everyone dropped by for a while.

I stood around talking with a guy named Clint who had driven down from Toccoa, Georgia. He and Monk had known each other when they were stationed together at Fort Sill, Oklahoma.

"Home of the 61st Ordnance Division," Clint said. "We were a wild bunch, I'll tell you. Had to relieve all that pressure somehow, blow off the steam, you know? Hell, one time, me and Monk and this fellow named Scotty Connigan . . ." He stopped. "You know Connigan?"

"No, sure don't."

Clint looked around the crowd.

"I'm surprised Scotty Connigan isn't here. He and Monk were pretty tight, although they were opposite as day and night, Monk so big and outgoing, Scotty Connigan this skinny little guy, hardly ever said two words. Anyway, this one time, a bunch us . . ."

I half listened as Clint told a long story that involved stealing a jeep from Fort Sill and then driving around the nearby town of Lawton trying to pick up girls.

Clint said, "You ask me, the prettiest girls in the world, they come from Lawton, Oklahoma."

When he was done I moved across the room and talked a bit with Annie and the kids. She was a shy, pretty woman who'd been through her share of hell in the last couple of years. She'd met Monk in Sarasota and been dazzled by his big personality, his house on the bay, his big plans for the future.

"He had this idea for selling time-shares in a fleet of fancy yachts at marinas all over the world. He was getting investors and buying boats, and then everything just kind of fizzled out," Annie said.

They'd sold the house on the bay and moved to a smaller place outside of Brandon. There was a bankruptcy, which staved off creditors for a little while, but then Monk began racking up other debts and everything just kept piling up on them.

"I knew Monk had done some work for the government in the past, but he didn't like to discuss it. Joked that it was one of those 'if-I-tell-you-then-I-gotta-kill-you' kind of things. But he started talking about getting in touch with some people he used to work with, and I had a feeling that's what it was all about," Annie said. "Then he came home one day, said he had a lead on a good job and was flying out that afternoon. Said he couldn't tell me all the details, but that it was going to be something good. That was four months ago, the last I heard from him. I didn't even know he was in Jamaica, until I got the call that, well, you know."

The children were getting antsy. The little girl started to cry.

Annie said: "They're ready for their naps. I need to see if there's a place where they can lay down for a while."

She stepped away, and Rina Murray joined me. The years had treated her well. She was wearing a black dress, but the way she filled it out was anything but somber. Her smile was just as big and real as it ever was. Monk had been a damn fool to leave her.

I said, "The other day, after I talked to you, they found Monk's Super Bowl ring at the bomb site."

"You bring it with you? I know that little boy and girl of his would like to have it, something to remember him by."

"It's still with the investigators, but I'll make sure to get it when they're done."

Rina smiled a sad smile.

She said, "You know, they won the Super Bowl the year after we got married, the year Monk got traded from the Saints."

"I remember. It was my last year with the Dolphins."

"Gosh, he was proud of that ring. Even had our initials engraved on it, inside the band." She was quiet for a moment. "They were some good years. Guess I was as happy then as I've ever been. When Monk was good he was very good."

"And when he was bad?"

"Aw hell, even when he was bad he wasn't awful, Zack. He tried, you know? Only nothing he did ever seemed to click. And he just didn't have that sticking-around gene in him. That stay-faithful gene either."

She let out a sigh, said: "You had a chance to go through all his papers yet?"

"No, not yet," I said. I didn't want to tell her that they had been stolen from his cottage and confiscated by the U.S. government.

"I'm really hoping there's some kind of life insurance policy. That poor Annie has gotta have something," Rina said. "Her mom and dad are both bedridden. She's looking after them and the kids, got next to nothing coming in except some social security, barely pays the bills. I gave her a little something, thought I'd quietly ask around some of the people here today, see if I can't get a few of them to chip in a little, too."

I had plenty of cash on me and I gave most of it to Rina. Said I'd see about lining Annie up with something more once I had a chance to go through all of Monk's papers.

Rina gave me a kiss and a hug. Then she stepped back and looked at me.

"How come you're not married yet?" she said.

"Been saving myself for the right woman," I said.

"You need to stop saving and start investing," she said. "Life's too short, Zack. It's way too goddam short."

54

The rental-car place in Tampa had issued me a Mustang, a red one, a retro model with a scooped hood and racing stripes. Not my style, but it was fast, and just a little more than an hour after getting on I-75 near Bushnell and pointing north, I was in Gainesville.

I stopped at the stadium. There was a lost-and-found department, but the woman in charge of it told me she didn't think anyone had turned in a first-edition signed copy of *A House for Mr. Biswas* after the stadium was evacuated on Saturday.

"I'd have remembered a book; no one ever brings a book to a ballgame," the woman said.

"It was kind of a special book," I said.

"Honey, the clean-up crews probably just chucked it," the woman said. "But you're welcome to take a look around."

I spent the next half hour rummaging through all kinds of wayward stuff—ponchos, handbags, binocular cases, backpacks—but no *Mr. Biswas*. I'd been hoping to surprise Barbara with it, but no deal. Damn.

On the way out of town, I swung by the Alachua County Sheriff's Department. Captain Kilgore was in. He invited me back to his office.

"We had to turn everything over to the feds after what happened down in Jamaica," Kilgore said. "They're working to see if there's some kind of connection."

"You can tell that, even after things get all blown to hell?"

"Oh yeah, there's most always something, little piece of this or that. Building a bomb's like leaving a fingerprint. Something unique about every one of them."

"What about the one in the skybox?"

"Well, I can tell you this: It was a damn elaborate dud. One of those LOL designs."

"LOL?"

"Layer on layer. Made to look like one thing, winds up being something else. Whoever put it together was a pro. It was almost like he was showing off," said Kilgore. "All that time Mr. Whitehall was sitting in that chair, afraid to move, we thought we were dealing with something had an ADP."

"ADP?"

"Anti-disturbance penalty. You fuck with it, you move, you try to open it, and it goes off. Only, turns out it wasn't like that. Darcy Whitehall could have stood up from that chair and nothing would have happened," said Kilgore. "We found an SCR."

"Hmmm," I said.

"You know what that is?"

"Got no idea," I said. "Just trying to pretend like I knew something for a change. Didn't want to look dumb."

"Hard being you."

"Yeah," I said. "A constant struggle."

"SCR stands for silicon-controlled rectifier," said Kilgore. "Like in a garage-door opener. Got a remote gadget on one end that sends out an electrical impulse and it completes the circuit on the other end."

"And kablowie."

"And kablowie," said Kilgore. "Or in this case, just a bunch of squibs that stunk up the skybox and made our eyes water. And whoever did it was sitting back laughing at us."

"You mean, they were right there in the stadium?"

"No, not necessarily. They could have been anywhere. Some SCRs have a longer range than others. Rig it up right with a cell phone and you can detonate it from the other side of the world, provided you got a decent carrier. But chances are, whoever did it, they were fairly close by, just to make sure," said Kilgore. "You want some coffee?"

"Yeah," I said. "Black."

He went down the hall to get some. When he came back we sat there, blowing on the coffee, cooling it off, talking about football. The Gators had another soft weekend coming up at home, against Wyoming, then it was the real deal, Tennessee. The Vols were preseason No. 1 in both the AP and the *USA Today* polls. They were opening up that weekend against Fresno State, and to bet on them you'd have to give twenty-seven points.

"What about videotape in the skybox?" I said. "Stadium security get anything on that?"

"Nada," Kilgore said. "Turns out the only cameras on skybox level are out in the halls, nothing inside the boxes themselves. Think it's because a lot of high rollers use the skyboxes to entertain politicians and none of them want any of that on tape, lest it come back and bite them in the ass. But someone else is working on that, and it's probably been kicked up to the feds, too. I'll ask around, though. I'd like to know myself."

The coffee wasn't bad, and it had cooled off just about enough where I could enjoy it. I wrote down my contact info on a sheet of paper, gave it to Kilgore, and asked him to give me a holler if anything else popped up that he thought I should know.

"Will do," he said. "And Zack?"

"What?"

"I expect you to do likewise."

55

I was back at my house in LaDonna by five o'clock. I walked down to the boathouse and looked out on the lagoon. There was a falling tide, and I would have liked nothing better than to have grabbed a rod and reel and headed out in the Hewes to make some casts under the edge of the mangroves where the water runs deep and cool and the reds like to hang on summer days when you can't find them on the flats. Would have liked nothing better, but . . :

I turned around and walked to the house. I could make it to Orlando International by seven, maybe catch something that would get me back to Jamaica that night. There was no real urgency; I could just as easily wait until tomorrow, but I was sensing something that felt strangely like momentum and, since I had little else going for me, I thought maybe I shouldn't squander it. Needed to keep moving.

I went to my bedroom and opened the closet. I started throwing shirts and shorts into a bag. Not a good approach to packing. So I got out a bigger bag and transferred everything to it. I'd have to check luggage, but what the heck. It would be nice to wear clothes that fit me for a change.

I was sitting on the bag, fighting with the zipper, when I

heard steps in the hall and looked up to see Karly Altman standing in the doorway.

"Whoa, this is weird," she said.

"What? You've never seen a grown man wrestling a suitcase before?"

"No, not that. It's just . . ." She stopped, laughed to herself. "This morning we were sitting down to eat breakfast when Boggy, just out of the blue, said: 'Zack comes.' And now here you are. Spooky."

"That's Boggy."

"You swear you didn't call him and tell him you were on your way?"

"Yeah, right. You know Boggy doesn't answer telephones. Or even talk on them unless he has to."

"Well, ever since then he's been acting sort of strange," Karly said. "He wouldn't eat what I made for breakfast. Or for lunch, but he went out and picked all this stuff from that little garden of his—I recognized liverwort and dandelion, but not much else—and he made something out of it. Then he drank at least a gallon of water. It must have made him sick because I heard him outside and it sounded like he was throwing up."

"He's not sick. He's cleansing himself. It's a Taino thing."

"But why would he be cleansing himself?"

"That's probably something you should talk to him about."

She shook her head, smiled.

"He never ceases to amaze me."

"Makes two of us," I said. "Say, you mind holding this end of the bag while I pull on the zipper?"

She knelt down to help me out. We didn't make much progress.

Karly said, "I really didn't expect you back so soon."

"Me, neither."

She obviously hadn't heard anything about what was going on down in Jamaica.

"Well," she said, "I'm pleased to report that the palm world is abuzz about your carossier. With your permission, I'd like to have a little gathering here in a couple of weeks. Some of my associates from Fairchild want to come up and see this for themselves. Thought I might also invite some friends from IPS."

"That the International Palm Society?"

"I'm impressed. You're learning the lingo."

"It's been a big day for me and acronyms," I said. "LOL. ADP. SCR. All kinds of interesting crap."

Karly looked at me.

"Zack, what on earth are you talking about?"

So I filled her in on everything, and when I was done she said: "Omigod, I had no idea. We haven't watched TV or looked at a newspaper since you left. I feel so removed from everything here. It's nice."

"Yeah," I said. "Wish I could stick around and enjoy it."

The back door slammed and there were footsteps in the hall. Karly said: "I'll be right back."

I heard her talking just outside the bedroom door. The other voice was Boggy's.

I got rid of some clothes, kept yanking on the zipper, finally got the bag closed and dragged it into the hall.

Karly had just finished giving Boggy a hug. He turned and looked at me. He travels light. Everything he needed was wrapped tight inside a cotton hammock that doubles as his go-bag. It was slung over a shoulder.

He said, "I am ready to go, Guamikeni."

Just like I knew he would be.

56

It was after midnight when Boggy and I arrived at Libido. We dropped off our bags at the cottage. I washed up while Boggy hung his hammock on the porch. Then we went to Darcy Whitehall's house and checked in with Otee.

"Everything cool, mon. Mr. Whitehall come back yesterday. Not go nowhere since," said Otee.

"What about Ali and Alan? Everything OK?"

Otee nodded.

"Dey all dem sleeping now. Got four fresh guards just arrived for a new shift."

Otee was eyeing Boggy with a wariness that I hadn't seen in him before. I introduced them.

"Otee's the one I told you about, the one who put the salt and tobacco seeds on the cottage porch to keep the duppies away," I said.

Boggy gave him a nod. Otee gave him one back, but he edged away, keeping a distance.

Boggy said, "I am sure it has worked well, the salt and the tobacco. It is powerful medicine to frighten away the spirits." He turned to me. "Zachary, have you seen the duppy of your friend, Mr. Monk DeVane?"

I was already feeling pretty punchy from the day I'd put in, so Boggy's question only added to my sense of disconnectedness. Last thing I needed was to stand there and listen to ghost stories. Still, over the years I have learned to put a lid on my skepticism and respect Boggy's Tainocentric view of the cosmos, a view in which the spirits seem always close at hand.

"Nope, no duppies," I said. "My life has been amazingly duppy-free."

Boggy looked at Otee.

"If you do not mind, please come back with us to the cottage."

"What you want, mon?" said Otee.

"I will show you when we get there," said Boggy. "Also, a container for the salt and the tobacco seeds. Do you have something special that you keep such things in?"

"Yah, mon. I got my special pouches," said Otee, patting a pants pocket. "Keep dem with me always."

"Good," said Boggy. "Let us go. Now."

57

"You want me to do what, mon?"

"Please, remove the salt and the tobacco seeds from around the cottage," said Boggy.

We were standing on the cottage porch. I was dead on my feet. And I was pretty much in Otee's camp on this one. If Boggy wanted that stuff gone, he oughta just get rid of it himself.

Otee said, "Why you want me do that?"

Boggy took a moment to answer, as if he were picking the right words.

"You and me, we have different ways with the spirits. In Hispaniola, where I come from, we seek answers from the dead, we do not wish to drive them away."

"So you invite duppy to come visit you?"

Boggy nodded.

"If they wish, yes," he said.

"Dat foolishness, mon. Duppy nothin' but trouble."

"Sometimes yes, sometimes no. But I need you to take away the salt and the tobacco."

Otee bristled, jabbed a finger at Boggy.

"Cho, mon, why you not just sweep it away yourself? I look like ya house niggah?"

But no sooner were the words out of his mouth than Otee

jumped back and slammed against the porch railing, almost as if Boggy had shoved him. His eyes went wide, his mouth dropped. I don't know if it was possible for Otee to ever truly look scared, but this was close to it.

When Boggy spoke, he spoke softly.

"You have your medicine, I have my mine," he said. "For my medicine to do its work you must remove yours. That is the way."

Otee looked at me and said: "You got broom in da cottage?"

I found a broom in the kitchen closet and brought it to him. Otee started in with a vengeance on the salt and tobacco seeds, sweeping it across the porch and toward some bushes, but Boggy reached out and stopped him.

"No, no, not like that. Go slow. Think about why you placed it here, how it did its job, and why now you are taking it away," he said. "You must carefully sweep each into a pile and put it in your pouch and remove it from here."

Otee did as he was told. Boggy stepped solemnly aside, watching silently as Otee began to sweep with deliberate purpose, and the whole process, which had seemed at first little more than housecleaning, began to take on the air of ritual.

A few minutes later the salt sat in one pile, the tobacco seeds in another. Otee swept each pile into a dustpan then dumped them carefully into separate leather pouches, making sure not to leave so much as a single particle behind on the porch. He pulled the drawstrings tight on the pouches and held them up for Boggy to see.

"Where I take this now?" Otee said.

"Salt to sea, seed to field," said Boggy.

"OK den, I do dat."

Boggy offered a slight bow, then turned and stepped inside the cottage.

"Look," I told Otee, "I apologize for Boggy. He gets a little carried away sometimes."

"S'alright, mon. Him know what him know. Him throw da heat on me."

"He did what?"

"You saw it wit your own eyes. Him throw da heat on me. Dat's why I jump back from him like dat."

"What do you mean he threw heat?"

"I mean it shot outta him, mon, like a bolt. Something smack me right here." He rubbed his chest. "Him got heat and him know how to throw it. Him a man you not cross."

Boggy returned to the porch carrying a cloth sack. He reached into the sack and pulled out a mat of woven palmetto, rolled it out on the deck, and sat down on it. He pulled other things from the bag and placed them in front of him on the mat: a stone mortar and pestle; a small tray, carved from burnished hardwood, with the head of a dog and the tail of an alligator; a six-inch-long piece of bone, hollow and skinnier than a soda straw; and a half dozen small pouches of his own. The pouches were woven from bright threads, like the kind you see in Mexican blankets, and adorned with feathers and beads.

Boggy opened the pouches. He took a pinch of something from each of them—seeds, dried leaves, pieces of bark—put it in the mortar, and ground it until it became a fine powder. Then he put the powder on the small wooden tray.

"What you call dat?" asked Otee.

"It is the cohoba," said Boggy.

"It a sacrament, like ganja?"

"Yes, like that."

"Dat what make the duppy come?"

Boggy nodded. He picked up the hollow piece of bone and held it between the palms of his hands, rolling it back and forth. He closed his eyes and his lips began to move, but we could not make out the words.

I turned to Otee.

"I've seen him do this before. He's been getting ready all day, purging his body, cleansing himself," I said. "This is when he likes to be left alone."

Otee looked around. The night seemed to have grown darker, the air still. It was quiet as quiet could be.

"Yah, I tink now a good time to go, mon," said Otee.

He backed off the porch and hurried away.

Boggy stopped rolling the piece of bone, his eyes still shut, his lips still moving. I headed across the porch to the cottage door, turning just before I stepped inside to see him hold one end of the bone to his nose and bend down toward the powder on the small wooden tray.

58

I couldn't have been asleep for more than an hour when the gunfire erupted—a volley of shots shattering the night. It came from somewhere near the resort entrance.

By the time I threw on clothes and rushed onto the porch, the shooting had stopped. Boggy sat on the mat, hands folded in his lap, eyes closed. If the gunshots hadn't roused him, then no good me trying.

I raced down a path to the main guardhouse. A commotion was coming from the other side of the wall, out by the highway. The gates were open, and I ran past them to see half a dozen guards standing in a circle about a hundred yards away, between the resort wall and the road.

When I reached them I saw the two men on the ground. One wasn't moving. The other was moaning, a leg covered in blood.

Glenroy Wilkes, the chief security guard, knelt beside them, attending to the wound in the man's leg. The man screamed, beating his fists on the damp grass.

"Gonna be alright," Wilkes said, trying to calm the man down. "We get you to the hospital."

A Libido van rumbled up alongside us. Wilkes and the guards loaded the two men into the van and it sped away, in the direction of Mo Bay.

I hung back as Wilkes spent a few minutes speaking with the other guards. When he was done, he came over to talk to me.

"Bucket of bad fish this is, mon," he said. "That one, he'll be alright. But that other one, he ain't gonna make it. He got a wife and two daughtas. This no good at all."

"What happened?"

"The two of them, they were walking the perimeter, and they were back there by the entrance, when they saw this fella with a paint can, writing on the wall, way down this end. They hollered at him, but he keep at it, so they start out after him and just when they get close, the fella he take off running across the road to a truck parked right over there behind the trees." Wilkes pointed to a stand of cedars on the other side of the road. "Then this other fella raise up out the back of the truck and start shooting."

"So he was sitting there waiting for them?"

"Yeah, mon, dey ambush 'em. Tomkins—he the one got it in the leg—he fell right off. But Tully, he the other one, he got off some shots until they got him, too. Then the truck, it took off."

"Anyone get a good look at the truck?"

"Other guards, they come out, saw it, too, said it was a gray truck. No more than that."

"The other day, on the way back from Benton Town, when they tried to grab Alan, the guy who drove off, he was in a gray truck. A Toyota."

"Yah, I know," Wilkes said. "Probably only about five thousand gray trucks on this island. Gonna make it real easy to find."

"If it was the same guy."

"That, too," said Wilkes.

"You check out the other side of the road yet, where the truck was parked?"

Wilkes shook his head.

"Not yet," he said. "Let's go see."

We crossed the road and padded around in the tamped-down grass. Other than tire tracks and a scattering of gravel where the truck had spun out onto the road, there wasn't anything to see. Then Wilkes spotted something a few yards into the bushes and went after it. He came up holding a rifle. It was just like the one Otee had used when we'd been waylaid on the road from Benton Town.

"Now ain't this something. AR-15. Same as the ones got stolen from the main guardhouse a while back." He held it close, trying to get a better look at it. "Can't tell if the serial numbers been ground down. Get it inside and check it under the light."

"It a pretty common rifle?"

"Yeah, they all around," said Wilkes. "But it's a whole lot of rifle to leave on the side of the road."

"Unless they didn't want to get caught with it."

"Even then," Wilkes said. "It's like throwing away money. Whole lot of money."

We headed back across the road to the resort grounds, and it was then I saw what had been written on the wall. The graffiti from a few days earlier had been painted over, but this new one was still fresh and wet and shiny.

"NPU say no to dirty money!" it read.

59

I sometimes read stories about guys, very disciplined, hard-ass guys, who go to bed, tell themselves that they will wake up at 5:14 A.M. or something and then at precisely that time their eyes pop open and they leap out of bed, ready to get on with their hard-ass days. After going with Wilkes to the guardhouse—the serial number on the AR-15 indeed matched one of those that had been stolen—I made my way back to the cottage. I checked on Boggy—he was still off in cohobaland—and crawled between the sheets. I set my interior clock for a 7 A.M. Zack-to-Zack wake-up call and called it a night.

I dreamed about Barbara. Details aren't important, but it was a very fulfilling dream. Do guys who are married ever dream about making love with their wives? And at what point exactly does the woman of your dreams stop being, quite literally, the woman of your dreams? Questions that make a grown man require lots of sleep.

Anyway, somewhere around 9 A.M. my brain gave me a nudge and said: "Yo, Zack buddy, I think maybe it's time you dragged your ass out of bed."

A front had moved in, and it was raining, a steady drizzle that gave no sign of letting up. I went out on the porch. No

Boggy. All his things were tied up in a bundle by the door. Who knew what he was up to. Whatever, I wasn't worried about him.

It was one of those days that, under different circumstances, I would happily spend in a comfortable chair just watching the rain come down, a day perfectly suited for putting off the inevitable; the inevitable in this case being a little show-and-tell session with Darcy Whitehall. I needed to show up at his house and make him tell me what was going on.

I pulled some clothes out of my bag and put them on. The pants were a little snug, so I found another pair and put them on. No better. Maybe I'd just gotten used to wearing Monk's too-big clothes. Yeah, that was it. I couldn't possibly be putting on weight.

I looked at my profile in the bathroom mirror. OK, so maybe I was getting a little thick. But nothing some daily crunches and a little jogging couldn't fix. Soon as this current mess got straightened out, I'd work on it. Immediate solution—undo the button on my pants and wear my shirt out. State of denial for the expanding man.

I tried getting through to Barbara, landed in her voice mail, and left a stupid rambling message that got cut off before I finished. I hung up, and as soon as I did I heard a phone start to ring. It was coming from my duffel bag. And then I remembered—the cell phone that Lanny Cumbaa had given me. I got it on the fifth ring.

"Yo, Zack, I was afraid you were blowing me off," said Cumbaa. "Let's do lunch. Only none of that sushi shit."

It was Lanny Cumbaa, calling as promised. Or warned.

"I need to take care of some things," I said.

"Like what kind of things?"

"We had a shooting here last night. I need to get a handle on that. Two of the guards were injured, one of them pretty bad."

"Yeah, so bad that he's dead," said Cumbaa. "It's all over the TV and the radio. You got a shitstorm brewing is what you got. We need to talk."

"Right now, I'm on my way to see Darcy Whitehall."

"About what?"

"About the shitstorm."

"Well, you talk to him and then you talk to me," said Cumbaa. "Because listen, Zack, I got a proposition for you."

"Gee, too bad you can't see my face right now."

"Why's that?"

"Because I don't look the least bit surprised."

"You're a real smart-ass, Chasteen."

"You bring out the best in me."

"Yeah, I'm good like that. I got people skills. I got much better people skills, say, than the IRS does. I know how to work toward a mutually beneficial resolution, know what I mean? The IRS, all it knows how to do is take people's money. Or throw them in jail. Or both. You shouldn't lose sight of that."

"Don't worry, I have excellent vision. Where do you want to meet?"

"You know the Bird's Nest?"

The same place where Ali Whitehall had seen Monk meeting with Jay Skingle, the day she'd followed him.

"Yeah, I know it."

"Be there at noon," Cumbaa said.

60

Alan Whitehall met me in the foyer of his father's house.

"It's not a good time now," he said.

"Why's that?"

"We're having a family meeting."

Behind him I could see Darcy and Ali in the living room. Ali sat in a chair, Darcy on the ottoman beside it. He held both her hands in his. She was crying.

"This a good thing?" I said.

Alan nodded.

"Yeah, I think so. Long overdue. A lot getting said that needs to be said. Especially between the two of them."

"OK, then, I'll come back," I said. "Is Otee around here?"

"No, he left maybe an hour ago with your friend."

"With Boggy?"

"Yes, short fellow with long black hair, looks Indian. He came by here this morning and introduced himself," said Alan. "What's his story?"

"A long one," I said. "Another time."

"Anyway, he said he needed to see Otee. Then the two of them headed off together."

"They say where?"

"No, but I figured it must have something to do with what happened last night."

"What's your take on last night?"

Alan shook his head.

"Can't make sense out of something like that. TV's already calling it a revenge shooting, so that's how it's going to play no matter what," he said.

"You see what they spray-painted on the wall out front, about dirty money?"

Alan nodded. "Had a shot of it on television," he said.

"What's that all about?"

"No idea," he said. "No idea at all."

"You sure about that?"

He looked hard at me, held my gaze.

"Yes, quite sure."

"Then maybe it's something you need to take up at your family meeting."

Alan shot a look to the living room. Ali had gotten up from her chair and was standing by the sliding glass doors, looking across the porch to the water. The day was gray and the sea was, too. Darcy stood to join her, draping an arm around her shoulder, giving her a hug.

Alan eyed me guardedly.

"Exactly what are you saying?" he asked me.

"I'm saying maybe you need to ask your father if he knows anything about dirty money."

Alan looked away. He didn't say anything.

"You're not a stupid guy," I said. "You've heard things."

I gave it a moment. Alan nodded his head slowly.

"Yeah, I've heard things," he said.

He still wouldn't look at me.

"I'm going to eat lunch," I said. "I'll be back in a while."

61

It was a thirty-minute drive to the Bird's Nest, and about twenty minutes into it I realized I was being followed.

White Range Rover, fairly new one, with a grille rail, Altezza lights, and titanium racks. Nice set of wheels. It had been behind me when I pulled off to get gas at a National station near Waverley Hall. Then, in a roundabout just before I got to Falmouth, it slipped behind me again. Two guys, white guys, sitting up front. Couldn't tell much more than that.

The Bird's Nest sat all by itself on a stretch of road just west of Falmouth, a rambling wooden structure tacked precariously onto the limestone cliffs. I drove past it. About half a mile down the road, I pulled into a Stop & Shop store and watched the white Range Rover keep going.

I went inside the store, bought a pattie, and sat in the car eating it. The drizzle was slowing now, the clouds breaking. It was a pretty good pattie, the crust flaky, the shredded beef not all dried out like some of them get, with a little fire to it, but not too much, and just a hint of cardamom. I finished eating it, brushed off the crumbs, then circled back to the Bird's Nest and parked near the entrance.

I was early and the Bird's Nest was just opening for business. The woman who greeted me inside the door said I could sit anywhere, and I chose a table in a corner at the far side of the front room. The prime tables were outside on several small decks connected by catwalks on the face of the cliffs. Scenic as hell, but my table gave me a view of the front door, and I sat down and studied the menu. Some curries, some jerk, some fish, some sandwiches. All priced in accordance with the view.

A waitress brought me water, and I told her I was waiting for someone to join me. I drank some water. I enjoyed the view. Then I got up and headed for the door.

"Forgot something in my car, be right back," I told the hostess.

Outside, I fumbled around in the car, pretending to look for whatever it was I hadn't really forgotten. The white Range Rover was angled in at the other end of the parking lot, pointing out and ready to go. The two guys were sitting in it.

I went back inside the Bird's Nest, drank more water, enjoyed more view, and thought about the guys in the Range Rover. It didn't get me anywhere.

The place began to fill up. A mix of tourists and locals. The tourists sat outside, the locals took the tables around me.

There was music coming from the speakers—Peter Tosh, "Once Bitten." Then it was "African" and "No Sympathy." Good stuff, tough and edgy. There were times when Peter Tosh sounded better than Marley. This was one of them.

I looked at the menu. Curry. Yeah, I'd probably get some curry. Although maybe I ought to go with something light, in honor of the unfastened button on my pants. A salad, I'd get a salad. But there weren't any salads on the menu. That was good, because I wanted curry.

I was watching the front door when Jay Skingle stepped inside. His buddy was with him, the skinny guy with the hatchet face, the one who had taken Monk's files. They didn't see me. The hostess sat them in a booth by the door.

Well, well, well . . .

Two guys waiting for me in the parking lot. Two guys who

knew me in a booth by the door. A DEA guy with a proposition on his way to join me.

So many guys, so little Zack.

Peter Tosh with "Coming in Hot."

Yep, some kinda interesting lunch this was shaping up to be.

62

Lanny Cumbaa arrived shortly after noon. He didn't pay any attention to the hostess. He looked to his right and saw Skingle and the skinny guy sitting in the booth. The skinny guy looked up and saw Cumbaa. The two of them knew each other, no doubt about it, both of them surprised to see the other one, and covering it up quickly.

Cumbaa turned the other way, spotted me, and waved. He walked across the room. While he was walking I saw the skinny guy say something to Jay Skingle, and Skingle leaned out of the booth and saw me sitting in the corner. I pretended like I didn't notice.

Cumbaa was carrying a briefcase. He stashed it under the table and said: "How about you let me sit where you're sitting."

"What for?"

"Because I don't like my back to a room, OK?"

"Who are you, Wild Bill Hickok?"

"Funny, Chasteen, just move, alright?"

"I'm comfortable where I'm at," I said. "Besides, I want to keep an eye on your pals."

It threw Cumbaa, but he tried not to let it show.

"What're you talking about?"

"The two guys in the booth by the door. You know them."

Cumbaa gnawed his lip, didn't say anything. He pulled out a chair and scooted it around the table so he had a sideways view of the room. He picked up a menu, pretended to study it.

"Yeah, I know one of them," he said. "He works for the DEA out of San Juan. But it's not like you walk in a place, you see a guy like that, you get all chummy, know what I mean? Can't know what the setup might be. Particularly with a guy like Connigan. He's into some down-low shit."

"Who?"

"Connigan. Scotty Connigan. That's the guy's name," said Cumbaa.

He looked at the menu.

Scotty Connigan. Monk DeVane's best friend from his army days, the two of them stole a bus, the one who hadn't made it to Monk's memorial service.

Some coincidence. Too bad I didn't believe in coincidences.

Cumbaa said, "So what you getting to eat anyway? They got good cheeseburgers here. I always get the cheeseburger. Helluva view, isn't it? Glad that fucking rain stopped."

The waitress arrived. Cumbaa got a cheeseburger. I got curried goat.

"So," said Cumbaa. "You want to hear my proposition?"

I nodded.

Annie DeVane at the memorial service saying Monk had done some work for the government in the past, talked about getting in touch with some old friends. Scotty Connigan. The 61st Ordnance Division at Fort Sill. All of it swimming around . . .

"It helps, you pay attention," Cumbaa said.

63

The proposition was about what I figured it would be. Cumbaa repeated his suspicion that after years of running a clean business, Darcy Whitehall was cozying up to Freddie Arzghanian again, looking to increase his cash flow by moving things out the back door. My job: put the pressure on Whitehall, get him to roll, then let Cumbaa sniff the money trail until he got the goods on Arzghanian.

"And what's the payoff for you, Zack, that what you want to know?"

"I've got a pretty good idea already."

"You get to keep breathing fresh air, not that stale shit runs through the AC in one of those federal lockups, got a smell all its own," said Cumbaa. "You know that smell I'm talking about, don't you, Zack?"

I didn't say anything.

Cumbaa reached across the table, slapped me on a shoulder.

"So put on your happy face, Zack. Life goes on. Ob-La-Di, Ob-La-Da. A sweet deal, you ask me."

I said, "You want to put it in writing?"

"You outta your fucking mind?"

We finished our food. The curry goat was decent, not tough like it sometimes is. Still, I left a lot on the plate. Wasn't like me.

Across the restaurant, Skingle and Scotty Connigan left their booth and headed for the door. Cumbaa turned and watched them. They never looked our way.

"Cute couple," said Cumbaa. "Wonder who the other guy is."

I didn't say anything.

Cumbaa turned back to face me.

"So," he said. "You got questions?"

"Yeah," I said. "Why do you think Darcy Whitehall all of a sudden needs money?"

Cumbaa shrugged.

"Who knows? Talk is he wants to expand that airline of his, maybe get into the cruise-ship business. Cruise ships got casinos. Freddie Arzghanian would love a taste of that," Cumbaa said. "Or maybe I got it wrong. Maybe Whitehall doesn't really want the money, but Freddie Arzghanian is missing the little partnership they used to have and is tightening the screws to get it going again. Hence, the bomb in the skybox just to scare the fuck out of Whitehall. Hence, the bomb in the van that blew up your friend to scare the fuck out of Whitehall some more and let him know Freddie's serious. Hence, a lot of fucking shit."

"Not often you hear someone use hence and fuck in the same sentence."

"I got a golden tongue, what the fuck can I say? All I know is, Whitehall and Arzghanian, they're working something," Cumbaa said. "Take a look at this."

He reached under the table, fumbled through his briefcase, and came out holding a sheet of paper. He handed it to me. It was a copy of a legal ad from the *Gleaner*. The same legal ad the woman had shown me at the office of deeds and surveys in Falmouth, the one detailing the "Notice to Sell" for the land off Old Dutch Road.

Cumbaa said, "Interesting, huh? Says here that Whitehall is selling this land to Freddie Arzghanian. What I want is to take a ride and eyeball that property for myself, see if it's really worth anything. Something tells me it's not. Something tells me it's just a way for Arzghanian to start feeding Whitehall money again."

I handed him the legal ad. I sat there looking at him.

Cumbaa said, "What is it?"

It all comes down to taking chances on people. Some you trust, some you don't. You make a gut choice, then you go with it. My gut was telling me that I could trust Lanny Cumbaa, even if he was threatening to lower the boom on me if I didn't throw in with him. Besides, I was in serious need of an ally. It was going to have to be him.

"Some things I need to tell you," I said.

I told him how I'd seen the same legal ad, had checked out the property, pegged it to be worthless, and come to the same conclusion that he had: Whitehall and Arzghanian were working some kind of deal. I told him that Monk DeVane had a friend named Scotty Connigan and there weren't enough Scotty Connigans in the world for them not to be one and the same. I told him how Connigan had taken Monk's files from the cottage and delivered them to Jay Skingle. And I told him how Skingle had, under considerable duress, admitted to me that Monk was working for them.

When I was done, Cumbaa slumped back in his chair and chewed it over.

"Well, fuck me," he said.

I said, "So what I'm thinking is, maybe Skingle and Connigan are working something on Whitehall and Arzghanian, and it cancels what you've got going and you don't have a proposition for me after all, huh?"

"Two hands scratching the same nut sack. Wouldn't be the first time, fucking government work," Cumbaa said. "You say this Skingle guy is with Homeland Security?"

I nodded.

"Makes sense. Homeland Security, that's where all the cowboys are these days. They want to stir some shit, they stir it, no questions asked, whatever it takes. Fuck the oversight, just let 'er rip. Scotty Connigan, he'd fit right in."

"So why don't you make some calls, see what's what, who's doing who?" I said.

"Doesn't work like that," Cumbaa said. "It's not like there's an answer man you go to with all the questions. You got to be careful who you ask. Got all kind of allegiances and shit like that. Especially once you throw in another agency. And even more especially when the agency is Homeland Security."

He sat there thinking. I sat there watching him think, doing some thinking of my own. It was a galvanizing spectacle, I'm sure.

"What makes you think I could get Darcy Whitehall to roll?" I said. "I've got nothing to use on him."

"Ah, my friend, that's where you're wrong," Cumbaa said.

He reached under the table and fumbled through the briefcase again. This time he came out holding one of those accordion folders, thick with paper. He handed it to me.

"For your reading pleasure. If the DEA handed out a prize for literature this would fucking be it. Took me the past two years to put it together and it's some beautiful shit. Lot of numbers, lot of names—shows exactly how Whitehall sent money out the back door to shell companies, phony accounts and all that. Only thing it doesn't show is where the money was coming from. Got nothing here that can directly connect Freddie Arzghanian to anything. Still, there's more than enough to put Whitehall away long past the time when he can enjoy all that pussy comes to stay at his resorts," said Cumbaa. "Which reminds me, you getting laid?"

I didn't say anything.

"I'll take that for a yes. You lucky bastard. Maybe a little bit down the road, we get this thing set on cruise control, I can drop by the resort and the two of us we can do some sportfucking, waddya say?"

I opened the file, scanned some of the pages, pretended like I understood what I was looking at. Then I closed it and put it back on the table.

I said, "So you've got files like this on other resorts Arzghanian funnels money through?"

Cumbaa nodded.

"Probably a dozen of them. I've been a busy boy. Your tax dollars at work," Cumbaa said. "Oh yeah, that's right. You're a little behind on that front, aren't you, Zack?"

He grinned at me.

I said, "Have you confronted any of the others with what you've found?"

Cumbaa shook his head.

"No, Whitehall's the first one outta the box. He's got the highest profile, the most to lose. Figured I'd start with him first."

"So why don't you just go straight to Whitehall, lay it all out for him yourself?"

Cumbaa made a face.

"What, I look like I got a death wish or something? I gotta be Mr. Low Profile in all of this. Mr. Invisible. Darcy Whitehall tells Freddie Arzghanian that the DEA is on his tail and I'm dead meat, you know what I mean?"

"So I get to be the meat?"

"Yeah, you're the meat, Zack. Prime, select, grade-A meat. Doing a great service to your country. And to yourself. Win-win all the way around."

"And all I have to do is show Darcy Whitehall this file and use it to leverage the information that will bring down Freddie Arzghanian?"

"Yep, that's all you gotta do. Not like it's heavy lifting or anything."

"It's blackmail."

"Yeah, it is. Pretty cool, huh? First you, then him. It worked on you, and you know why it's gonna work on him?"

"Why?"

"Because what's the most important thing in Darcy Whitehall's life right now? This is an easy question, Zack. Don't think too hard about it."

"Seeing to it that Alan Whitehall gets elected to parliament."

"Bingo."

Cumba picked up the file.

"And what happens if word gets out to the newspapers or to that crazy bitch Alan Whitehall's running against, what's her name, Oompah-pah-pah . . ."

"Kenya Oompong."

"Yeah, her. She's just Castro with tits, you ask me. We got

the goods on her, too, which is why, deep down in its heart of hearts, your government very much wants to see Alan Whitehall get elected, Zack."

"He's a good man," I said.

"Yeah, whatever, who gives a fuck," said Cumbaa. "But what if word gets out that Darcy Whitehall is nothing but a money-laundering scumbag. Or worse, what happens if we swoop in and Darcy Whitehall goes to jail? What happens then?"

Cumbaa let the file drop on the table.

"Ka-fucking-thud," Cumbaa said. "It all comes tumbling down."

The waitress put our check on the table. We both sat there looking at it. Then Cumbaa looked at me.

"You gonna get that?" he said.

"I bought the drinks in Miami."

"Yeah, but see, the way I figure it, we're still kinda in the dating phase and you need to impress me so I'll put out for you."

I got out some cash, covered the check with it.

"I need you to put out right now," I said.

"Oh, Zack," Cumbaa said. "I love it when you talk that way."

I told him about the guys sitting outside in the parking lot, the ones in the Range Rover. I told him what I wanted him to do.

"Man, oh, man," said Cumbaa. "I love this kinda shit."

64

I walked out of the Bird's Nest and got into the Mercedes. The white Range Rover was still sitting on the other side of the parking lot. I could see a guy behind the wheel.

I put the key in the ignition and turned it, and in that instant I thought: Bomb. They followed me just so they could plant a bomb.

But nothing happened. The engine kicked over. I headed for the exit. And that's when the guy sat up in the backseat.

"Turn right," he said. "To Mo Bay."

There was an accent of some kind, I couldn't quite place it. Middle Eastern, maybe. I looked in the rearview mirror. The guy pretty much filled it up. Dark hair, dark eyes, the kind of beard you shave it and an hour later it needs shaving again. He was leaning back in the seat now, chewing gum. It made his jaw muscles ripple. If the jaw muscles were any indication of the rest of him then I was looking at some heavy-duty talent.

I turned right onto the highway and adjusted the rearview mirror. The Range Rover was right behind us. And I could see Lanny Cumbaa coming out of the Bird's Nest, strolling across the parking lot, taking his own sweet time to get to his car.

I said, "Man, this is such a cliché."

I met the guy's eyes in the mirror. He didn't say anything.

I said, "I mean, how many times have you seen a movie where someone gets in a car and then someone who's been hiding in the car sits up behind them?"

The guy chewed his gum, looked out the window.

"Yeah," he said. "You think it couldn't really happen. And then it does. You should have locked your car."

"Shoulda-coulda-woulda," I said. "Story of my life."

I checked the rearview. A green Honda was hanging back a little ways from the Range Rover. Maybe that was Cumbaa.

"Leaving your car unlocked, that solved many problems," the guy said. "We thought maybe we were going to have to grab you, put you in our car."

"You really think you could do that?"

Our eyes met in the mirror.

He said, "I think maybe you would make it difficult."

"You bet your ass I would."

The guy looked out the window. He rolled his neck to one side. It popped. He rolled it to the other side. It popped again. These muscle guys.

I said, "Thing is, in the movies, guy sits up in the backseat he usually sticks a gun to the other guy's head."

The guy kept looking out the window.

"I've got one of those," he said.

"So what happens next?"

"So what happens next is you keep driving. And you give me the file."

"What file?"

"The file given to you by the man in the restaurant."

I picked up the file from the seat and handed it to him.

We didn't talk much after that. I flipped on the radio, the guy in the backseat didn't tell me to flip it off. There was music. Then there was news. The news was about the shooting at Libido the night before. One dead, one wounded, suspects still at large. Then came the voice of Kenya Oompong denying any NPU connection to the shooting. Then the reporter was saying that Darcy Whitehall had been unavailable for comment. Yeah, I knew all about that. I flipped the radio off.

When we got to Mo Bay, the guy told me to turn left to bypass all the traffic on Gloucester Avenue, then right on Dover Road. I'd figured that's where we were going. Every now and then it's nice to be right.

"Stop here," he said when we got to 314 Dover Road.

The Range Rover stopped behind us. No sign of Lanny Cumbaa.

"Signs say no parking," I said.

"It will be OK," the guy said. "Trust me."

65

You picture someone named Freddie and you see this guy, maybe a block-shaped little guy, with flashy clothes, rough around the edges and a boisterous way of doing business. Freddie Arzghanian was not that kind of Freddie.

He was Andy Garcia, like Andy Garcia in *Ocean's Eleven*—great suit, hair that looked like he had a personal stylist on retainer, no laugh lines around his cold dark eyes. He was younger than I figured he would be, early forties, and he sat waiting for me on the other side of his desk. The desk was a slab of polished onyx cut in some free-form design, made it look like a shiny black amoeba. It was very cool.

So was Freddie Arzghanian. He watched me enter his office with the two guys who had been following me snug tight on either side. They were a matched set. The one who'd been in the backseat of my car handed Arzghanian the file that Lanny Cumbaa had given me. Arzghanian nodded the two guys to step back and they flanked the closed door. Then he nodded me to a chair by the desk. I sat down in it.

Arzghanian spent a few moments flipping through the file. Then he closed it and sat there studying me. I studied him back. It was a very thrilling moment.

Finally Arzghanian said, "Why did you come here the other day?"

"Got lost, stopped in to ask directions. Your receptionist was very helpful. She deserves a raise."

"Please, Mr. Chasteen, I haven't the time for this."

"Neither do I. I'll be going now."

I got up from the chair and turned for the door. The two guys moved to block my way.

I pointed at the one who'd been in my backseat, the gum chewer.

"I'm coming for you first. Then you," I said to the other one. "So if the two of you want to figure out a strategy to avoid getting your asses kicked then now's the time."

They both flipped back their jackets, put hands on their pistols. Helluva strategy.

"Sit back down, Mr. Chasteen," Arzghanian said.

Seemed like a reasonable option. I sat back down.

"Why did you come here the other day?" Arzghanian said.

"I was trying to figure out the connection between you and Darcy Whitehall."

Arzghanian looked me dead in the eyes, his face a perfect mask.

"Continue," he said.

"And I'm trying to figure out who killed my friend."

"You think these two things are somehow related?"

"Don't know. You tell me."

Arzghanian eased back in his chair. He folded his hands, propped his chin on them, and looked at me.

"If I were to say, yes, that I killed your friend, then what would you do?"

"Haven't worked that part out yet," I said. "I'm thinking I can probably jump across that fancy desk of yours and grab you before the two goons have a chance to pull their guns. After that it's anyone's guess."

Arzghanian smiled. At least I think it was a smile. His lips narrowed and turned up on the ends like lips do when people smile. Then again, maybe he was just doing face exercises, stretching his muscles, trying to avoid that middle-age sag.

Behind me, I could hear the two goons move in a little closer. Good to know I had them on the defensive.

Arzghanian said, "Perhaps your time is better spent asking what your friend was really doing working for Darcy Whitehall."

"I already know the answer to that. Monk was working for the feds."

"And for what purpose, do you suppose?"

"Hey, just a wild guess here, but I'm thinking it had something to do with money laundering. I mean, that's your business, isn't it?"

Arzghanian did that thing with his lips again. It wasn't so much a smile as it was a snarl.

"I am just a simple banker," he said.

"Smooth line," I said. "Bet you've used it before."

Arzghanian shrugged.

He said, "What about you, Mr. Chasteen?"

"What do you mean, what about me?"

"Do you work for the feds, too?"

"Why would you think that?"

"You come here to help your friend. He dies. You take over where he left off. Plus, you just had lunch with this man." He opened his desk drawer, pulled out a file, and slid it across the desk to me. I looked at it. Lanny Cumbaa's photo was paper-clipped to the outside.

Arzghanian said, "Mr. Cumbaa has been nosing into my affairs for years. He is very persistent." He tapped the thick accordion file Cumbaa had given me. "And his work is very thorough. I have seen it before. Has he recruited you to work for the DEA?"

"Yeah, matter of fact, he has," I said. "Care to hear my job description?"

"Please, if you'd be so kind."

"I'm supposed to use that file to squeeze Darcy Whitehall and get him to give up the goods on you. Then the feds swoop down, arrest you, and the world is a better place."

"Simple as that?"

"A piece of cake," I said. "So why don't you just let me borrow your phone and I'll call them right now and tell them I've got you cornered. Then you can confess to everything, and it'll save us both a lot of trouble."

This time Arzghanian did something with his lips that was more smile than snarl. He sat there, studying me. I studied him back. There we were, the two of us, and a couple of goons by the door, delighting in each other's company.

Arzghanian said, "You are a very interesting man, Mr. Chasteen."

"Gee, I find you pretty fascinating, too."

"What I mean is, I admire your directness. I would not expect you to be so open about your motive, especially when it is one that could so easily get you killed. Not that I would ever entertain such an idea, of course."

"Oh gosh, I know you wouldn't, Freddie." I gave my best coon-eating-shit-off-a-toothbrush grin. "So, seeing as how I've been direct with you, and you've decided not to kill me, I need you to be direct with me. What kind of jam has Darcy Whitehall gotten himself into?"

Arzghanian thought it over for a moment. Then he said, "All I can tell you is that he recently came to me saying that he needed a loan."

"For how much?"

"Please, Mr. Chasteen, that is banker-client privilege. Very confidential."

I put a finger to my temple.

"I'm thinking of a number, Freddie, and it's, let's see, it's five million dollars. Five million dollars U.S. The amount you're going to pay for that piece of property off Old Dutch Road."

It got raised eyebrows from Arzghanian. But nothing else.

"Public record, saw the legal ads," I said. "Plus, I took a drive up there to check out the property for myself. You're getting screwed, you don't mind me saying so. Plus, there's a bunch of squatters living up there. Pain in the ass to move them off."

Arzghanian made a face.

"The legal ad, it was Darcy's idea, not mine. He wanted it all to be on the up-and-up, nothing under the table."

"Doesn't sound like the way you two have typically done business in the past," I said.

Arzghanian shrugged.

"No, he did not want the old way," Arzghanian said. "Unfortunately, there are certain regulations involved with the way my bank does business. There really is no such thing as a simple loan."

"The way your bank works, you loan someone money and you own them, control the way they do business."

"A crude way to look at it," Arzghanian said. "I prefer to think that we are partners. At first, when Darcy approached me about the loan, about me buying that piece of property, it was with the understanding that we would resume our partnership. So he placed the legal ads and prepared papers for a standard real estate transaction. But he began to have misgivings when I spelled out certain terms of the loan."

"What terms exactly?"

"I'm afraid that's proprietary information, Mr. Chasteen. But five million dollars is a lot of money, and so the terms were, let's say, rather rigid regarding my expectations for resuming our partnership," said Arzghanian. "And that is why the deal fell through."

"So you aren't buying that property after all?"

Arzghanian shook his head.

"No, I am not. We came to that decision the other day when Darcy was here at my office, the day you visited. As you know, Darcy is preoccupied with getting his son elected to parliament. As well he should be. Alan Whitehall is an exceptional young man."

"Agreed," I said.

"Which, unfortunately, put Darcy in the position of having to decide whether to resume our partnership or maintain a clean break for appearance sake, for Alan's sake. In the end, he decided to make the break and withdraw his offer to sell the property. It was all very amicable, I assure you. Darcy is a friend. I tried to help him find other funding options through more, shall we say, traditional venues. That is why he was here in Mo Bay for two days. Sadly, we were unable to secure him any funding to that end."

"So he still needs five million dollars?"

Arzghanian nodded.

"Yes. And from all that I can gather he needs it quite soon."

"Why does he need it?" I said.

Arzghanian shrugged.

"I can't be sure. He hasn't shared the details with me. Only that he needs the money."

"But you have your suspicions, don't you?"

"Yes, I do. Whoever is behind this, they plague me as well."

"So, who is it?"

Arzghanian cocked his head and looked me. He took a long time answering.

Finally, he said, "How much loyalty do you have to your government, Mr. Chasteen?"

"I'm an American. Scratch me and I'll bleed red, white, and blue."

"That doesn't really answer my question. Perhaps I should rephrase it," said Arzghanian. "How much do you trust your government and the people who work for it?"

"I'm willing to give most of them the benefit of the doubt," I said.

"Not exactly a ringing endorsement."

"Considering some of the things that have happened to me in the not-so-distant past, it's the best I can do," I said. "But my ambivalence is equal opportunity. I'm willing to give you the benefit of the doubt, too."

"Fair enough," said Arzghanian.

He looked past me, to the goons by the door.

"Ramin, Hamil, you may leave us now, while we talk man to man," he said. "I do not think Mr. Chasteen intends to grab me."

The two left the room and shut the door.

"Ramin and Hamil?" I said.

"My sister's sons. We are Lebanese originally. Ramin it means gentle, and Hamil is for compassionate. Very poor choices of names," Arzghanian said. "You would not have made it across the desk."

Two hours later, I stepped out of the building at 314 Dover Road. The black Mercedes was out front, right where I'd left it. I got in and wound my way out of Montego Bay, back toward Libido. I heard the cell phone ringing. It had fallen onto the floorboard. I let it ring.

I was on The Queen's Road, past the airport, when the green Honda zoomed up from behind, its horn honking, the headlights flashing off and on.

I pulled over on the shoulder. Lanny Cumbaa hopped out of the Honda, came running up to my window, spewing profanity before he even got there: "Holy fucking shit, man. I saw where those two guys were taking you and I thought you were fucking dead. Freddie Fucking Arzghanian. Holy fucking shit."

"You really need to invest in a thesaurus," I said. "Get in the car."

Cumbaa hopped in the passenger's side, got himself settled, admired the Mercedes.

"Sweet ride," he said.

I said, "You know, I really appreciate it how, you being so worried and all, you sent in the cavalry and came to the rescue when I was in there with Freddie Arzghanian."

"Cavalry? What cavalry? You're looking at the fucking cavalry. And what am I going to do, put the life of a federal agent on the line just for some low-life informant?"

Cumbaa grinned. He said, "What part of that do you resent? The low-life part? Or the informant part?"

"That what I am now? An informant?"

"Well, yeah, that's what you do, Zack. That's how you save your ass from the IRS. So inform me, why don't you?"

I told him some of what he needed to know. It took a while. When I was done, Cumbaa wasn't nearly as puffed up as he'd been when I'd started.

"Jeez-o-fucking-Pete," he said. "There's always rumors within the agency about shit like this going on. You trust Freddie Arzghanian on it?"

"No reason not to."

"You mean, besides the fact he's Freddie Arzghanian."

"Besides that," I said. "You think he's got it right? You think someone you work with could be causing problems for Darcy Whitehall?"

"You mean, like shaking him down?"

"Yeah, like that."

"Like I said, there's always rumors. Mostly it works the other way—some scumbag offering one of our guys a shitload of money and our guy taking it. That kinda thing happens. But this here, it's a whole different thing. It's, you know, more proactive."

We talked. Cumbaa told me a little bit about how things worked on his end. Then I told him how I saw it all playing out on my end.

When I was done, Cumbaa said, "So you and Freddie Arzghanian, the two of you hatched this plan, huh?"

"It's just the beginning of a plan," I said. "Still needs some work, still needs a few things to fall in place."

"No shit, it does." Cumbaa blew out air, rubbed his head with his hands. "Things are happening too fast, I gotta think. Gotta get out and walk around."

"So do it."

He did.

I sat there, fiddling with the seat controls, got it to recline.

Cumbaa was right about the Mercedes. It was a sweet ride. Not my style, but still a sweet ride. Cumbaa was right about the way things were happening, too. Fast, much too fast. I leaned back in the seat and thought about how I could make all the things happen the way I wanted them to.

A few minutes later Cumbaa got back in the car.

He said, "So I guess what I need to know is, who are you working for? Me? Or Freddie Arzghanian?"

"Neither of you," I said. "We're equal partners in this thing. It works out, we all get a little something."

"Only I don't get Freddie Arzghanian."

"Did you really think you were going to?"

"Hell yes, I did. I was gonna be a hero."

"You're still gonna be a hero, Cumbaa."

"Yeah, but a different kind of hero."

"A hero all the same."

Cumbaa shrugged, said: "So what do you get out of it, Chasteen?"

"You mean, besides the everlasting gratitude of the U.S. government?"

"Yeah, like I'm sure that makes your heart go pitter-patter," said Cumbaa. "Look, I can't promise the IRS won't come after you."

"No, but you can promise that you won't sic them on me."

Cumbaa nodded.

"Yeah, I can do that easy enough." Cumbaa studied me for a moment, said: "So you got a side deal going with Arzghanian?"

I didn't say anything.

"Because you'd be crazy if you didn't, that's all I'm saying."

I didn't say anything.

Cumbaa said: "How much?"

I didn't say anything.

"OK, fuck you very much. That's your business," he said. "So what I got to do now, I got to contact my supervisor, run this by him, see about getting some backup in here for when this goes down."

"No," I said.

Cumbaa looked at me.

"What do you mean, no?"

"I mean, you don't contact anyone at your office. Trust no one you work with. At least for the time being. For obvious reasons."

Cumbaa thought about it. He knew I was right. He scrunched his lip, chewing on it, looking at me.

"That makes me very fucking uncomfortable."

"Paybacks are hell, huh?"

Cumbaa shook his head, started to say something, stopped. He looked out the car window. Then he looked back at me.

"I have to tell you, Chasteen, you are one ballsy mother-fucker."

"That mean you're in?"

"Yeah, asshole. I'm in."

drove their back to where they lived? Or used

67

When I got back to Libido I swung by my cottage before heading up to Darcy Whitehall's house. I went into the bedroom, started working the phone and eventually connected with an international operator who found a main number for Fort Sill, Oklahoma. Two calls later and I knew what I needed to know.

When I stepped out of the cottage, Otee and Boggy were sitting on the front porch.

"Thought the two of you had deserted me. Where you been?"

"Been talking to the mother of those dead boys, the two I had to shoot on the road out of Benton Town. It was his idea," Otee said, nodding at Boggy. "Me, I didn't want to go see her, but him say we had to do it."

Boggy's eyes were tinged with red, but other than that he showed no apparent ill effects as a result of his cohoba-induced trance the evening before.

"They came to me last night," said Boggy.

"Who came to you?"

"The spirits of those two who died. They were lost. They wanted to go home," said Boggy. "And so we took them there."

"What, you just opened the car door, told them to hop in, and drove them back to where they lived? Or used to live? You in the spirit-transporting business these days, Boggy? You make them wear seat belts?"

Boggy didn't say anything. He's accustomed to me unleashing a minor rant whenever he starts talking about communicating with the spirits. If he wants to sit around and snort cohoba, fine, we all have our vices. God knows, I love my rum. And I like where it gets me. Nothing wrong with getting a good buzz on, but that's all it amounts to. No need to attach anything more to it than that. All that stuff about connecting with the other side? Unh-uh. It begins to wear thin after a while.

Otee said, "Him come get me early this morning and say we need to find where them two dead boys lived. I remembered their names from the paper and so we drove into Mo Bay, asked around. Soon enough we found their mother's house. She live up on Camp Hill."

"You tell her you were the one who shot her sons?" I said.

Otee shook his head.

"No, I didn't tell her that. I let him do most the talking. And he found out much."

Boggy said, "Those two who died were her oldest. The woman, she was filled with much sorrow."

"Yeah, well, I'm afraid I don't have much sympathy. Not after what they did," I said. "She happen to mention how her sons came to get mixed up with the NPU?"

"That just it," said Otee. "Them mother, she say them not NPU. They always been PNP. Just like her. Them just doing what them did for the money. She say another one of her sons, a young one, just thirteen, him get paid, too. And guess what him get paid to do?"

"Paint NPU slogans on the Libido wall?"

Otee nodded.

"Yeah, him and some him friends. Getting paid good, too. One hundred dollars U.S. every time they do it."

"She say who paid them to do that?"

Otee shook his head.

"No, say she didn't know. But she say that younger son of

hers, the one thirteen, he'll be back at her house this evening. Said we come back she make sure he talk to us then."

"What about the police? Do they know about this?"

"No," Otee said. "She said they come by but she wouldn't talk to them. Afraid they'd take her younger son away and lock him up. Me, I didn't think she was going to talk to us either. Stood there at her door, she not wanting to let us in. But then Boggy, he set her down and talked with her soft-soft. Then she was crying. And then she was talking, telling us everything."

I looked at Boggy. His face was as neutral as neutral could be. I knew he bore me no ill will for having unloaded on him a few moments earlier. While I'd never buy into that whole speaking-with-the-spirits thing, I didn't begrudge him the fact that it sometimes got us where we needed to get.

"So, Mr. Silver-Tongued Shaman, what exactly did you say to this woman to get her to talk to you?"

"I told her that I had spoken with her sons, and that she no longer had to worry," said Boggy. "I told her they were standing right there with her and that they had found peace."

Otee shivered as Boggy spoke.

"I tell you true, mon, there was something in that room with us when he was saying all that," said Otee. "Hair was standing up on my arms. This cool draft come blowing through the house while it hot as all hell outside. Me want to run out of there, but me no can make me legs move. Me hope like hell them two duppies at peace."

68

"I should have come clean about everything from the start, when the phone calls first started," said Darcy Whitehall. "But I didn't trust the police. I didn't trust anyone. I thought I could handle it myself, make it all go away."

We sat in the living room at Whitehall's house—Whitehall on the sofa with Ali and Alan on either side, me in a rattan chair, facing them. Their morning soul session had yielded results—a family détente, an easing of whatever ill will had been between them, mostly on Ali's front. She leaned against her father, her hand in his.

I felt like the Grand Inquisitor. I'd been hammering Whitehall with questions from the moment I'd arrived.

At first he'd been defiant, telling me I had no business meddling in his affairs. But then I showed him the accordion file that Cumbaa had given me at the Bird's Nest, the one that provided a money trail for the years he'd been fronting for Freddie Arzghanian.

Whitehall skimmed through the file. Then he excused himself, stepped into his den. He returned a few moments later, holding a file of his own. I looked it over. The pages were identical to the ones Cumbaa had given me.

"It was the first contact they made with me. I found it sitting atop my desk one morning, as if it had materialized overnight. Believe me, it got my attention immediately," said Whitehall. "It's quite devastating to see something you've labored so hard to keep secret laid out in black and white, and in such detail. I felt like the whole world had come crashing down on me."

Whitehall shuddered, took a deep breath. Ali patted his knee. He put his hand on hers. I let the moment play out.

"When Margaret died—that's Alan and Ali's mother, my wife—it was a wake-up call. It was like I'd been living in a fog and it took something like that to bring me back to my senses."

He looked at Ali.

"I'm sorry," he said. "For everything."

"I know, we've been through that," Ali said. "You don't have to tell me again."

She smiled at him, sadly, sweetly.

Whitehall looked at me.

"I went to London to get Ali, and as soon as we returned I went straight to Freddie Arzghanian and told him I wanted out."

"What was his reaction?"

Whitehall shrugged.

"Freddie was Freddie. He gave me that cold hard look of his and said we had an arrangement, one that was irrevocable. But I'd made up my mind. I cut off the pipeline coming in, and I cut it off going out. I got financing, at no small cost I can tell you, and got the operation over the hump. I cut, I trimmed, and I didn't solve problems simply by throwing money at them. In the end, we turned the corner. But all the time, I was watching the door, thinking that Freddie Arzghanian would be coming after me."

"Why didn't he?"

Whitehall shrugged.

"Don't know, really. Point of honor, perhaps. I went to him face-to-face, dealt with him on the up-and-up. For all his foibles, felonious though they might be, Freddie plays straight with those with whom he does business. And he expects that in return," Whitehall said. "Plus, I think I might have humbled him somewhat with my remittance."

"Remittance?"

Whitehall nodded.

"Yes, that was *my* point of honor. Over the years that I did business with Freddie, I kept a loose running tally of exactly how much the resorts had benefited from his transfusions. A sizable amount, to be sure, but after I factored in certain operational costs—I was very generous on my side of the equation—I came up with a specific dollar amount that I felt I owed him. Somewhat less than Freddie might think I owed him but still a very considerable sum, mind you. I took that figure, put it under a proper amortization schedule, applied an interest rate to it—again, quite generous on my side—and began sending monthly checks to Freddie. All very kosher, of course, applying that sum to my business costs and using it as a deduction against corporate income tax. I've been sending Freddie Arzghanian checks on the fifteenth of each month, going on five years now. That's my remittance. All at my own doing."

"What was Freddie's response to that?"

"Don't know. He's never mentioned it. But I tell you this much: he's cashed every damn one of those checks."

It gave us all a chance to laugh.

Whitehall said, "I looked at the books the other day. One hundred forty more payments, not quite twelve years, and I'm all cozy with him. Deal even." He picked up the file he'd brought from his den, shook it. "So when this arrived, yes, it set me on a pretty good spin."

"Who'd you think was behind it?"

"I didn't know. At first, I thought it could have been Freddie actually, just doing something to keep the hooks in. Then I got the first phone call."

"When was that?"

"Same day the file arrived, a bit more than a month ago," he said.

"Monk was already here then, right?"

"Oh yes," said Whitehall. "He was here for several weeks before all this got started."

"How did he come to be here?" I said. "How did the two of you connect?"

"It was through the U.S. Embassy, actually," said Whitehall.

"They sponsored a two-day gathering to discuss what action we resort owners in Jamaica were taking to protect guests against violence and threats of international terrorism. We were invited to attend. Actually, it was rather more than an invitation. It was more like, 'If you intend to keep having paying guests from the U.S. fill your rooms then you damn well better attend.'

"So I went. The whole affair was rather ho-hum, though it did involve a bit of the scare treatment, giving us the idea that these terrorist sorts are lurking all about, ready to have a go at us at any moment. The embassy had brought in a couple of security consultants for the occasion. Monk was one of them. Some chap from the embassy staff introduced me to him."

"The guy who introduced you to Monk, you remember his name?"

Whitehall shook his head.

"No, but he was a rather fresh-faced fellow, eager and well turned out, the very image of a diplomat," Whitehall said. "He worked for your Homeland Security department, I do remember that."

I caught Ali's eye. We were thinking the same thing: Jay Skingle.

I said, "And you hired Monk shortly after that?"

Whitehall nodded.

"Yes, but first he spent some time here at the resort, giving it a thorough inspection, then submitting a report on what our weak spots were, securitywise. I was reasonably impressed. I mean, it wasn't something I didn't altogether know, but I certainly wanted to have the U.S. Embassy seal of approval, so I offered Monk a six-month contract. It helped that his salary was subsidized."

"What do you mean subsidized?"

"I was told I wouldn't have to pay him his standard rate because your government was footing the bill for half of it. Made it an attractive proposition, really. I would have been a fool not to hire him."

69

I sat back in my chair, sifting through the pieces. The sun was a half-hour gone and the sky was sucking up the afterglow.

Ali asked if anyone wanted coffee. We all said yes, and she stepped into the kitchen to make it.

"Take me through the phone calls," I asked Whitehall.

"There've been, let's see, six of them," he said. "As I mentioned, the first one came the same day I discovered the file on my desk."

"And you couldn't identify the voice?"

Whitehall shook his head.

"No, it sounded artificial, electronically generated, something not really human. But it was a man, definitely a man."

Alan said, "They were probably using one of those voice-scrambler devices. You can buy them online for next to nothing."

"What did the man say?" I asked Whitehall.

"He asked if I had received the gift. He called the file a gift. I kept asking who he was and he got angry, said I was not to ask any questions. He said many people would like to receive such a gift, a document that contained so much information—the newspapers, the police, Alan's political opponents, the U.S. government—but I had the opportunity to make sure no one would ever see it except me. He named his price—five million U.S. dollars. I told him to go piss in his pocket. And he hung up."

"Did you tell anyone about the call?"

"No one."

"Why not go to the police?"

Whitehall gave me a look, didn't even bother to answer.

I said, "And you didn't say anything to Monk about it?"

"No."

"Why not?"

"It was something personal, directed at me, nothing that would jeopardize the safety of the guests," Whitehall said. "I would have had to reveal many things to him that I did not want to reveal. I wasn't prepared to do that. Besides, I was keenly aware that Monk had connections with your government and, while I've done my best to tidy up the operation, the closet is something of a mess."

"Did you ever suspect that Monk might be reporting to someone at the embassy about his work here?"

"Why yes, of course. Indeed, I considered it a distinct likelihood. After all, there was no subterfuge about the fact that he was on their payroll, too."

"OK, let me ask you this: Is there any chance that Monk might have been the one making those calls?"

It threw Whitehall for a loop. Alan, too. Whitehall mulled it over before saying, "No, not a chance of that. He was sitting right where you are sitting when the second call came."

"When was that?"

"The day after the first one. Alan, you were sitting here with us, as I recall."

"Yes," Alan said. "I remember the phone rang. You took it in your den."

"What did the caller say this time?"

Whitehall thought about it for a moment.

"He said: 'Have you decided to accept the gift in the spirit in which it was given?' I told him he could go screw himself. And a few other choice remarks. Then I hung up. And I returned here to the living room."

"And you didn't mention that phone call to Monk?"

"No, not at all. Nor to Alan. Although I presume both of them might have heard me shouting into the phone. I was rather worked up about it."

Alan smiled.

"Yes," he said. "We did hear that. I remember saying something to Monk about how you must have been having a fight with one of your girlfriends."

Whitehall looked at him, with mock offense.

"Son, you know very well that I would never speak to one of my lady acquaintances in such a manner. Besides, I never fight with them. Nor they with me."

He looked at me.

"I remember that call distinctly because not five minutes after I hung up came the explosion in the maintenance building."

I recalled driving past the burned rubble of the building in the golf cart with Otee on the evening I'd arrived at Libido.

"I thought it was a fire," I said.

"An explosion, then a fire."

"I didn't know it was related to any threats."

"Nor did anyone else. But, bright fellow that I am, I made the connection immediately."

"And it happened just like that, right after the phone call?"

"Just like that," Whitehall said. "I hung up the phone, came back here, sat down, and—kaboom."

"And Monk was sitting right here when it happened?"

"Yes. We all jumped up and ran to the balcony. We could see the building ablaze from here."

"You find any evidence what might have caused it?"

Whitehall shook his head.

"We were doing everything we could just to put out the fire and make sure it didn't spread. Luckily it was far enough removed from the rest of the resort that it didn't even register with the guests," Whitehall said.

"What about the third call?" I said.

"Came later that night, after I returned to the house. The man said, 'You've seen what we can do. Has this changed your mind?' I told him, yes, I was prepared to negotiate. He said there was nothing to negotiate, the price was firm, five million dollars. Said if I didn't come up with the money then Alan's political career was over and I'd be in jail. I told him it could take some time for me to gather that sum of money, and he said he'd give me two weeks," Whitehall said. "I hung up with him and immediately called Freddie Arzghanian and made an appointment to meet him later that day. That's when I proposed selling him the property off Old Dutch Road."

"But you didn't tell Arzghanian that someone was blackmailing you because of your dealings with him?"

"No, I didn't want Freddie to know the details because, well frankly, I was scared. I was afraid that if Freddie knew about that file then he would see me as a liability, and Freddie has a way of, shall we say, reducing his liabilities," Whitehall said. "So I just told him I needed the money and proposed selling him the property as a way of creating a framework for the transfer."

"Didn't Arzghanian realize he was paying way too much money for that property?"

"Of course he did," said Whitehall. "But it didn't matter. The deal wasn't really about the land; it was about me getting the money and Freddie having an opening for running his pipeline through Libido again."

"How long until the next call came?"

"Two weeks exactly, just like he'd promised," Whitehall said. "I told him I was still working on all the logistics and that I needed more time. He accused me of stalling, said time was running out. Then we left for Florida and there was that incident in the skybox."

"And you heard from him after that?"

"Oh yes, indeed, right way. Came on my cell phone as we were walking to the car outside the stadium. That voice again, the man asking if they had succeeded in getting my attention. I clicked off the phone without saying a word, didn't want to discuss matters right there in front of everyone." Whitehall paused, let out air. "I've beaten myself up about it ever since. Perhaps, if I'd just stepped away and spoken to the bastard, told him that I was doing everything within my power to make things work, we could have avoided that horrific scene at the airport. And Monk would still be alive."

"Not your fault. I think that was bound to happen no matter what," I said.

"Oh, really?" Whitehall said, "What makes you think that?"

"Just a feeling in my gut. Can't put words on it yet," I said. "Then, what, you got the next call right after the bomb at the airport?"

Whitehall shook his head.

"No, that was the odd thing about it. All the other times, the calls came almost immediately after the incident, but after the airport they didn't get in touch for almost two days. I kept waiting and waiting, but it didn't come until the evening of what happened on the road from Benton Town, when Otee had to shoot those two men. This time the man on the phone was angry, said he was getting tired of waiting. He said I had two days to get the money. Then he hung up. I left first thing the next morning to go meet with Freddie Arzghanian again."

"And Arzghanian was ready to give you the money then?"

"Oh, yes, he had it all gathered together in neat stacks in two duffel bags."

"So," I said, "this may sound like a stupid question, but why didn't you just take it?"

"I was ready to, believe me. But then Freddie began laying out all the conditions that came with the money. And I just couldn't accept them. It would have meant returning to the way things were with him before and I had vowed not to do that. I had worked too hard, trying to make things right, and I needed at least the semblance of propriety. Both for my own shredded sense of dignity and for Alan's sake." He looked at Alan. "I'm sorry for my past, son, sorry that it's come to haunt you."

"We'll get beyond it," Alan said. "You did what you had to do."

I said, "So let me guess. You got another call this morning, about the two guards who were shot last night?"

Whitehall nodded.

"He thought he was being funny. He asked if I had seen the writing on the wall. Meaning, what they'd written about dirty money, as well, I suppose, as what the future might hold if I didn't get the money."

"Did he give you any idea when he would be back in touch?"

Whitehall shook his head.

We sat there for a moment. Whitehall looked drained, exhausted. So did Alan for that matter.

That's when we heard Ali in the kitchen.

"Omigod!" She appeared in the doorway, waving us to join her. "You've got to come see this."

70

The TV on the kitchen counter showed some old footage of Kenya Oompong pounding a podium as she gave a speech. At the bottom of the screen, a red banner headline screamed: "Police Seek Bombing Suspect."

Ali turned up the volume.

". . . are searching for her in connection with last week's bombing that killed four people at Sangster International Airport," the announcer said. "Oompong is also a suspect in recent violence directed against Alan Whitehall, her opponent in the upcoming parliamentary elections."

Then a new image appeared. This one showed police escorting someone else I recognized.

"According to investigators, a large stash of stolen weapons, incendiary devices, and other bomb-related material was discovered hidden beneath the home of Oompong's mother, Mrs. Ida Freeman, of Martha Brae."

The old woman struggled with her canes, a policeman on each arm helping her up a flight of steps at what looked to be the Jamaica Constabulary Force headquarters in Montego Bay.

"Police say they were alerted to the whereabouts of the weapons by an anonymous phone call," the announcer said. "The weapons matched those stolen from the Libido Resort several weeks ago. And investigators say the bomb-making paraphernalia could have been used to detonate an explosion similar to the one at the airport."

Then it was back to the footage of Kenya Oompong.

"Oompong eluded police when they attempted to arrest her after a political rally near the town of Buckley. Her whereabouts is presently unknown."

Another story came on, something about the upcoming World Federation of Cricket tournament. Ali turned off the TV.

"Finally," she said, "an end to this madness."

She went to her father, leaned against him. He put an arm around her.

Ali said, "It's over. Now, all they have to do is catch her."

Alan was still trying to absorb the news about Kenya Oompong.

"I was so wrong about her," he said. "I can't believe she was behind all this."

"She wasn't," I said. "She's been set up."

They all looked at me.

"By whom?" said Alan.

"By the same guys who are trying to blackmail your father."

As if on cue, Darcy Whitehall's cell phone rang. He stared at it. A second ring. A third. Then he flipped it open, said hello.

He looked at me.

It's him, Whitehall mouthed.

"Yes, I heard," said Whitehall. "We just got finished watching it on TV."

He listened.

"Yes," said Whitehall. "I understand."

Whitehall put away his phone.

"Tomorrow," Whitehall said. "He told me that if I did not have the money ready to give them by tomorrow, then the police would soon be coming after me, too."

He pulled out a chair by the kitchen table and collapsed in it. Ali and Alan stepped to his side, comforting him.

"I tried to make it right. But there's nothing more I can do." He looked up at his children. "I didn't want it to end like this."

"It's not gonna end like this," I said.

They all looked at me.

"Do you know something we don't?" Whitehall said.

"Yeah," I said. "Matter of fact, I do."

71

So I told them what I knew. And what I knew was mostly what Freddie Arzghanian had told me in his office when we'd had our little man-to-man talk. It went something like this:

Over the past year or so, at least three resort owners with whom Arzghanian did business—two on Barbados, another on St. Lucia—had been skimming from proceeds that Arzghanian expected to receive. Money laundering isn't governed by the tidiest of accounting procedures, and Arzghanian allowed for a little fudging along the way, but things had gotten way out of hand.

When Arzghanian, along with Ramin and Hamil, his gentle and compassionate nephews, confronted the wayward associates, all three had crumbled. And all told the same story: they had been threatened with public disclosure of their misdeeds, and almost certain jail time, if they didn't pony up the hush money.

"None of them had to come up with nearly as much as they're asking from you," I told Whitehall. "We're talking a few hundred thousand in each of their cases. Still, as you can imagine, Freddie's not real excited about these guys stepping in and becoming his silent partners everywhere he does business. He's anxious to remove them from the equation."

We were sitting around the kitchen table, sipping the coffee

Ali had made. It was a strong brew, sure to keep me up half the night. That was OK. The way this night was shaping up, I was gonna need all the buzz I could get.

"Are you sure these are the same guys?" Alan said.

"Pretty sure," I said. "In every case, they've made first contact with their targets the same way they did with your father. By surprising them with a file, a very incriminating file, like the file your father found on his desk."

"Which is identical to that file you brought here today," Whitehall said.

"Page for page," I said. "Given to me by the guy who did the research, put it all together."

Whitehall said, "And that would be . . . ?"

"His name's not important. He works for the DEA."

"Does he have any theories on how these other people might have obtained the files that they've been using?"

I nodded.

"The files exist on a DEA database, shared by any number of field agents who can review them or add information as they gather it. For anyone with access, it would have been a simple matter to make copies."

I finished my coffee. Ali poured me another cup.

Alan said, "So why did your contact at the DEA give you the file detailing my father's transactions over the years?"

"He wanted me to use it to reel your father in, so he could help the DEA get the goods on Freddie Arzghanian."

"In other words," said Whitehall, "he wanted you to blackmail me, just like these other guys are trying to."

I nodded.

"A more honorable goal maybe, but yeah, that's pretty much what it amounts to."

Whitehall said, "And you would have done that?"

"It never got to that point. Because Freddie Arzghanian put another offer on the table."

"What's his offer?"

"To make available his resources to catch whoever is trying to bring you down."

"His resources?"

"His money. Five million dollars of it. What they're asking for."

Whitehall shook his head.

"I told you, just as I told him, I won't take the money," he said. "I'm done with Freddie Arzghanian."

"It's not a deal between you and Freddie," I said. "It's between Freddie and me."

"You and Freddie?"

I nodded.

"And the DEA," I said. "It would be to their great advantage to catch these guys, too."

"No strings attached on my end?"

"Nope, all you have to do is sit right here, answer the phone when they call, and we take care of the rest."

Whitehall eased back on the couch, thinking it over. He said: "Alright then, I can see what Freddie gets out of it. But what about you? Why do you want to risk something like that?"

"A friend of mine is dead. I want to catch whoever did it," I said. "Now there's also the matter of an old blind woman sitting in jail for something she had nothing to do with. And her daughter is still on the run."

Alan said, "So you're saying the same people who are blackmailing my father also set up Kenya Oompong?"

"Yes, that's what I'm saying."

Ali let out a sigh, said: "What about Monk? He was in on it, too?"

"That's my guess. He was down on his luck, needed the money."

"But why would they kill him?" Ali said.

"I don't know," I said. "But believe me, that's the first question I intend to ask the two of them."

"The two of them?" Whitehall said.

I nodded.

"Scotty Connigan and Jay Skingle," I said. "Skingle you know. He's the one who works for the U.S. Embassy, connected you with Monk. Guess they thought it would help to have someone on the inside, someone who was good with bombs."

Which pretty much dropped the Big One on our conversation. The three of them sat there in stunned silence.

It was Whitehall who finally spoke: "You're saying that Monk planted the bombs?"

"Two of them I'm fairly sure about—the one that blew up the maintenance building, and the one in the skybox. I'm also willing to bet that Monk stole the weapons from the main guardhouse and got them to Skingle and Connigan. They, in turn, passed them along to the people they hired to waylay us on the road from Benton Town and to whoever it was that shot the two guards last night. They even instructed the ones last night to leave the rifle behind, knowing that it could eventually be tied to Kenya Oompong."

"So," said Alan, "they were making it look like it was all about politics when it was really about the money."

"Right. They even hired a bunch of kids to spray-paint NPU slogans on the Libido wall, just to underline it," I said. "Otee and Boggy have located one of them. We're supposed to have a little talk with him later on tonight."

No one spoke for a moment. It was a whole lot to take in.

Then Whitehall said: "Back to the bombs. What evidence do you have that Monk had anything to do with that?"

"Nothing solid," I said. "Only that he and Scotty Connigan served together in the army, the 61st Ordnance Division."

It got blank looks all around.

"Didn't mean anything to me the first time I heard it either. But it stuck with me and I made a couple calls before I came over here this evening. Finally got in touch with someone at the 61st Ordnance Division, stationed at Fort Sill, Oklahoma. Turns out, its full name is the 61st Ordnance Division EOD. Any guesses on what the EOD stands for?"

Nothing from any of them.

"Explosive Ordnance Disposal," I said. "Monk DeVane and Scotty Connigan both served in the army's bomb squad."

72

It was nearly nine o'clock when we arrived at Camp Hill, a hardscrabble assortment of shanties on the outskirts of Montego Bay. We'd left Otee at Libido, where he could keep an eye on the Whitehall clan. Besides, he'd been none too anxious to return to the tin-roofed shack where a slender woman now stood in the doorway, watching us as we approached. Boggy had told me her name was Altycia Andrews.

She looked me up and down. Then she looked at Boggy.

She said, "You didn't tell me no white man be comin' wit you."

"This is my friend, Zachary," Boggy said. "He is only white on the outside. Inside he is a dark man."

I don't know where he got that, don't know where he gets most of the stuff he comes up with, but the woman softened a little. There wasn't a front door, just a dirty blanket where a door should be. She held it aside as we stepped past, into her one-room home.

It was as clean and tidy as a place like that could be. The hard clay floor showed signs of a recent sweeping. The stench wasn't as bad as it had been outside, masked partly by fumes from a kerosene lantern that hung from the ceiling and partly by the souring smell of wet clothes that hung on a rack at the back of the room.

Altycia Andrews stood by a table where votive candles illuminated two photos of her dead sons. They were the same photos that had appeared in the *Gleaner.* Neville Andrews and James Andrews. Their funeral had been two days earlier. There were some flowers in vases around the table, most of them wilted now. And between the photos was a small pile of money, Jamaican dollars in various denominations, a sympathy offering from friends and neighbors, just a little something to help Altycia Andrews ease the pain.

I could see how the place might have spooked Otee when he visited earlier with Boggy. Nothing was registering on my personal duppy meter. But then, I'm just not tuned that way. Still, there was definitely something in that house, something that seemed to thicken the air and carry a weight of its own. Sorrow. A whole lot of sorrow. It showed on the face of Altycia Andrews, her cheeks hollow, her eyes weary and downcast. And it showed on the face of the boy who sat on an overturned washtub in a corner of the room.

Altycia nodded at him, said: "This be Terrance, my baby. Ask him what you need to ask."

The undertone being, ask him what you need to ask and then be gone.

Boggy reached out, took one of the woman's hands and held it between both of his. She looked startled but she didn't pull away. He kept holding her hands, speaking softly to her, as I stepped across the room and knelt by Terrance.

He was trying hard not to look scared, his eyes darting from his mother back to me. He was just beginning to fill out, to lose the little boy in him, to hop the fast track to manhood. For kids like him, in places like this, there was little in between.

"Nothing's going to happen to you for talking to me, Terrance. I promise you that."

The boy didn't say anything. He stuck out his chin, defiant, and cut his eyes away.

"Someone gave you money to paint those NPU slogans," I said. "Who was it?"

The boy shot a look at his mother. She said, "Go on. You tell de man what you know."

The boy glanced at me, then dropped his head.

"Cuddy Banks," he said.

"Who?"

The boy didn't say anything. He kept looking at the floor.

His mother said, "He talking about Cuddy Banks. Cuddy be friends with Neville and James. Da two of dem dey be running with Cuddy all da time, be staying with him. Only Cuddy, he didn't show to the funeral."

I drew closer to the boy and hunched down so he couldn't avoid looking at me.

"How many times did Cuddy Banks give you money?"

The boy didn't say anything, but he held up two fingers.

"Twice?"

He nodded.

"How did it work? Did Cuddy round up you and some of your friends, show you where he wanted you to write things with the spray paint, and after that he'd give you money?"

The boy nodded.

He said, "He give us NPU gonzi, tol' us to wear it."

"Gonzi?"

Altycia Andrews said, "Gonzi, dat what dey call da party colors. NPU got its gonzi. PNP got its. You wear da gonzi, show who ya be for."

Terrance stood. He turned over the washtub to reveal a pile of clothes. He sorted through them until he found what he was looking for—a red-and-yellow bandanna. He held it up for me to see.

"So that was you and your friends by the wall at Libido last week when we came rolling up in the car."

Terrance nodded.

"Where was Cuddy Banks?"

"He be waiting for us down the road."

"You the one who threw the rock at the windshield?"

Terrance took a moment, then nodded again.

"Nice shot," I said.

I smiled. The boy relaxed a little.

He said, "I gave dat money to me muthah. She have to give it back?"

"No, your mother can keep the money," I said. "But what else can you tell me about Cuddy Banks, Terrance? Who gave him the money to give to you? You know who he was working for?"

Terrance shook his head.

"Your brothers never talked to you about that, never said why they were doing what they were doing?"

Terrance looked at the floor, spoke low: "Yah, dey talked about dat some."

"What did they say?"

"Dey say Cuddy Banks he knew some people who had a mountain a money, kept it locked up in a house in da hills. Me bruddas and Cuddy dey all da time talking about how dey gonna get da money from deez people, be rich forever."

"You know where we can find Cuddy Banks, Terrance?"

The boy cut a look at his mother. She gave him a nod.

"He stay just up the road," Terrance said.

73

We drew our share of looks, walking through Camp Hill—a thirteen-year-old black boy leading a short, round Taino shaman and a tall white-on-the-outside man. Rain had set in, a steady drizzle, and few people were on the street. Mean-looking men watched us from rum shops. Sullen souls eyed us from the doorways of their shacks. Camp Hill was not the sort of place where one might reasonably consider opening a Welcome Wagon franchise.

The rain came down harder. Terrance grabbed a cardboard box from the side of the street, tore its corners, flattened it, and held it over his head, trying to keep dry. Boggy produced a poncho from his satchel and put it on. I got wet.

As we rounded a corner and headed down a muddy street, three young men edged out from the shadows, moving in our direction, malice written all over them. Boggy leveled a look their way. The three stopped dead in their tracks, then backed off. Hell, maybe Boggy really could throw heat. It was no time for being a skeptic about such things.

My stomach growled. It seemed like days since lunch at the Bird's Nest, when I'd been unable to finish all my curried goat. What I wouldn't have given for the leftovers. My stomach growled again, this time loud enough for Boggy to hear.

"Been a long damn day," I said.

"You have much night left, Zachary."

"Yeah, many miles to go before I sleep and all that. But I'm starting to fade."

Boggy reached a hand under the poncho, into his satchel, and came out holding something about the size and shape of a carrot, only it was white with smudges of dirt. A root of some kind. He wiped it off, snapped it in two, and gave the larger portion to me.

"Chew on this," he said. "A little bit now, a little bit later as you need it."

He nibbled on his end of the root, then stuffed it away.

"What is it?" I said.

"Taino call it Ama Aji. I know it from Hispaniola, where it grows near waterfalls. I found this at the resort, near that false river where the naked people ride. A strange place for Ama Aji, but there it was."

"What does it do?"

"It does what it is supposed to do, Zachary. As do we all."

"Yeah, yeah, cut the horseshit. What I mean is—it's not going to make me slip off into some trance and see things, is it?"

"No," said Boggy. "Ama Aji it is not like that. The old Taino, from long ago, they would chew it when they had to make long journeys and could not take time to sleep. It will make sure that you do not fade."

I took a small bite of the root and chewed it slowly as we continued down the street, navigating past table-sized potholes as we went. The taste was bitter, but not unpleasant, with a finish of cloves and pepper. Might go well with a hearty zin or a big rioja. I took another bite and tucked it away, my tongue beginning to tingle.

Terrance turned down a street, narrower and even gloomier than the others. At the end of the street, slightly removed from a cul-de-sac, sat a ratty plywood-and-clapboard house. The front door was closed and a low amber light glowed through a sheet of thick plastic that served as a window.

A small black sedan, a Honda it looked like, was parked in the cul-de-sac. And under a blue tarpaulin that served as a carport sat a gray Toyota pickup. Couldn't be sure it was the same gray Toyota pickup that had waylaid us on the road from Benton Town, but there it sat.

Terrance stopped and pointed at the house.

"Dat Cuddy place," he said.

I looked at Boggy.

"So what now?" I said, only it came out sounding funny, like I was drunk. My tongue wasn't working the way I was used to it working. It was numb and seemed to occupy my entire mouth. Must have been the damn Ama Aji. A moment's panic as I envisioned my throat swelling shut, unable to swallow, choking . . .

Bam-bam!

Two gunshots sounded from the house.

Then two more—*bam-bam*!

I grabbed Terrance by the arm and darted behind a pile of rubbish heaped in front of another shack. Boggy ran to the other side of the street, taking cover behind a junked car.

Beside me, Terrance wiggled from my grasp. I didn't realize how hard I'd been squeezing his bony arm.

I peeked over the top of the rubbish pile and saw the front door of the house open. Out walked a slender figure, his head ducked down against the rain, holding something under his raincoat, something that looked like a shotgun. He got into the Honda, cranked it, and eased away from the house.

As the car drove past, I caught just enough of the man's profile to ID him, and then I saw Boggy moving toward the house.

"Stay right here," I told Terrance.

I caught up with Boggy by the front door. We stepped inside, stopping as we saw the two bodies on the floor. I don't know which one of them was Cuddy Banks, don't know that anyone could have recognized either of the two men. The scene would have kept a team of blood splatter technicians busy for hours. I'd seen all I needed to see, and I backed out the door. So did Boggy.

He said, "The one who left in the car, he is the friend of Monk DeVane?"

"Yeah, Scotty Connigan, Monk's old army buddy," I said. "I'm guessing that second body in there belongs to whoever it was helped Cuddy Banks shoot those two guards at Libido last night. Connigan probably came here under the guise of paying them, but decided to cover the trail instead."

We collected Terrance and hurried away, none of us speaking until we were back at Terrance's house. His mother watched us from the doorway as we stood by my car.

"Sorry you had to be there for that," I told Terrance.

The boy looked scared.

"That man, he be coming after me, too?"

I hadn't considered that. Didn't think it was a likelihood. Still . . .

Boggy said, "I'll stay here for the night. Just to watch things."

Terrance seemed to like that idea. He stepped toward his house.

"You sure about this?" I asked Boggy.

He nodded.

"Yes," he said. "I am not so much worried about that man Connigan. But the boy, I think there is more that he can tell us."

74

I was totally wired by the time I got back to Libido. And it wasn't just a result of seeing two bodies lying dead on the floor. The Ama Aji was working a number on me.

I was wide awake, had all the energy in the world. Stimulation presented itself on another front, too. There's no delicate way to explain it, except to say: I had an erection that would not quit, a hard-on that kept on keeping on. It had presented itself shortly after I got in the Mercedes at Camp Hill and was still with me an hour later when I rolled up to my cottage.

Some guys pay good money for such results, and as much as I appreciated the stand-up performance—indeed, my member seemed to have taken on a life of its own—I couldn't put it to good use, and I was getting a little tired of it. Nothing I hate worse than a show-off.

I took off my clothes, got in the shower, and kept it on cold, the showerhead aimed directly at its target. Three minutes of shivering and grinding teeth, and my manhood was still at full mast.

I lay down on the bed, but that didn't work because I couldn't take my eyes off it. Damn thing was grinning, mocking me. A terrible, terrible waste. I tried rolling onto my stomach, but that was, well, painful.

So I got out of bed and stepped into a pair of shorts. They

were snug enough already—Christ, I was putting on the pounds—but I finally got myself squeezed in, zipped up without injury, then slipped into a long baggy T-shirt that provided some camouflage for my personal, portable tent pole.

A nice brisk walk in the evening air, that's what I had in mind. I was hoping exertion would lead to exhaustion and with that a return to a less aroused state.

I set out down a path that wound its way to the beach. I walked ten minutes in one direction, all the way to the promontory upon which sat Alan Whitehall's house. Then I turned around and walked in the other direction, all the way to Ali's house. The rain had stopped, and the moon was poking out from behind the clouds. I looked down at my shorts. I was poking out, too.

I cut back through the resort, staying well clear of the bars and nightclubs, eventually finding myself at a swimming pool in a far corner of the property. The pool had a hot tub attached, a halo of steam above it.

Maybe it was just a matter of relaxing, I thought. What the cold water hadn't wilted, maybe the warm water would soothe into submission.

There was no one else around. I took off the T-shirt and eased into the hot tub, inching lower and lower, until my chin was just above the water. I felt myself wind down a notch. I closed my eyes, leaned back, rested my head on the edge of the hot tub.

Ahhh . . .

And that's when I felt the chain collar slip over my head and go tight around my neck.

I jerked forward, and something jerked me back. I flailed behind, grabbing a leash attached to the collar. It was one of those choke collars, like they use in dog obedience school, no way to get out of it when it was pulled tight.

"Heel, boy!"

Darlene looked down at me, leash in one hand and a whip—a *whip?*—in the other. She wore thigh-high leather boots, leather panties, and a sleeveless leather vest that she hadn't bothered to button, with nothing on underneath.

Lynette stood beside her, decked out in an identical outfit. At the end of her leash, a brass stud collar around his neck, stood a lanky young fellow in a black Speedo. His skin was shiny and smooth, like he'd been shaved of all body hair and rubbed down with baby oil.

Lynette looked at the guy. She gave her whip a snap.

"Rex, sit," she said. And the guy rested on his haunches, panting, his tongue dangling from a corner of his mouth as he mooned his eyes at her, looking like he enjoyed it. It was some kind of sick, I'm telling you.

Darlene eased off the leash a bit and grinned at me.

"We been out looking for you," she said. "Don't you know it's Pet Night?"

"Sorry," I said, "I've been out of the loop."

"Well, now that I've got you collared that means you officially belong to me and have to do everything I tell you to do. And if you don't behave, I am going to punish you. Now heel, boy," she said and gave the leash a mighty tug.

I climbed out of the hot tub and stood dripping on the pool deck. The trauma of the moment had not nullified the effects of the Ama Aji. Wet shorts made my predicament all the more apparent.

"Whoa," said Darlene. "A good man is hard to find."

"I think it's the other way around," said Lynette.

"Whatever," said Darlene. "You won't be hearing me say, 'Down, boy.'"

Lynette snapped her whip and yanked her leash and Rex, or whatever his name was, leapt up and let out a bark. I kept a wary eye on him, lest he start sniffing my butt.

"We've got ourselves a couple of pedigreed studs," Darlene said to Lynette. "Think we ought to head down to Club Libido and make them do tricks for the crowd? They're handing out prizes for Best in Show."

Lynette looked at me, said: "You could be a real contender in the pointer group."

I smiled. They smiled. Then I gave the leash a yank and it jerked free from Darlene's grip.

Darlene snapped her whip at me.

"Bad dog!" she said.

And I took off running toward my cottage, cutting a path through the foliage. I couldn't get the collar off, but I gathered up the leash so I wouldn't trip over it as I hurdled a heliconia and made my escape.

There was no way they were going to catch me, but they were faster than I gave them credit for. And I could hear Rex, letting out howls like a hound on scent.

I was at the cottage steps when headlights lit the road and a car horn blared. I turned to see a taxi swerve, narrowly missing the pack on my tail as they emerged from the bushes. Darlene had busted free of her leather vest and was waving it overhead as she whooped and hollered, her boobs bouncing to beat the band.

The taxi cut between me and them and came to a stop. A back door opened and someone got out.

It was Barbara.

She looked at me. I looked at her.

"Nice leash," she said.

75

There are many reasons why I love Barbara Pickering. And just one of them is that after seeing what she saw—about as incriminating a scene as I can imagine without being caught in the actual act—she didn't get back in the taxi and drive away.

After unloading her luggage—being temporarily paralyzed on the cottage steps, I wasn't any help—she paid the driver and sent him off. Then she turned to Darlene and Lynette and said: "You must be the two Zack told me about."

"And you must be the girlfriend," Darlene said.

Barbara smiled.

God bless women. They possess an innate knack for slicing through bullshit and immediately assessing the rank and order of things. It's an intuitive gift. And to their everlasting credit, Darlene and Lynette immediately assessed that Barbara far outranked them and they needed to put their things in order.

"It's not what it looks like," said Lynette. "He was running away from us."

"So I saw," Barbara said.

"We didn't do anything, I swear to God, he wouldn't let us," said Darlene. "I don't think he even likes us. We have been after him and after him, but he won't have nothing to do with us. First, I thought he might be gay, but . . ."

Barbara put up a hand. Then she gave them a dismissive wave. "Bye-bye," she said.

Darlene and Lynette turned away and headed down the road, Rex dragging his leash behind them. If he'd had a tail to tuck between his legs he would have done it.

I got the collar off my neck, tossed it and the leash aside. I walked to Barbara and put out my arms. She put up her hand again.

"Not just yet," she said. "You really do need to explain."

She walked past me to the cottage. I grabbed her luggage and took it inside while she checked out the place. She wasn't impressed. I couldn't blame her.

She sat down in a chair on the porch. I sat down beside her.

"OK," she said. "Start talking."

I dispensed with Darlene and Lynette right away, starting with how I'd been trying to walk off the effects of the Ama Aji. Then I told her about everything that had happened since we'd last spoken. It had been three days, since before I'd returned to Florida for Monk's funeral. So much to tell.

And then it was Barbara's turn. For starters, the deal was off with Aaron Hockelmann. At least for the time being.

"The money was dazzling, but beyond that it all seemed rather hollow," Barbara said. "I think he wanted to buy *Tropics* just for window dressing, another pretty mare in his big stable. He would have taken the heart out of it. And then probably turned around and sold it to someone else."

"So how did he react to you jilting him?"

"Oh, he was quite the gentleman about it. I mean, he did make use of his private jet so that I might fly directly here."

"Helluva guy," I said. "Look, I'm sorry the accommodations aren't any better. I mean, they've been fine for me, but I know they aren't much, so tomorrow I'll see about getting us one of the villas."

"Oh, Zack, that's sweet, but don't bother. You have far more important matters to deal with tomorrow. Besides, I've already booked a place down in Negril, at Tensing Pen. You remember the last time we stayed there."

"The smoked marlin and ackee quesadilla," I said. "Hard to

forget a place that serves something like that. Ranks among the top-ten best things I've ever eaten."

"And might I ask what's number one?"

I didn't bother to answer. I got out of my chair. I knelt on the porch in front of her. I took her hand.

"I've missed hell out of you," I said.

Her gaze drifted downward to my shorts.

"So it appears," she said. "And I know the cure for that."

Yes, there are many reasons why I love Barbara Pickering.

76

Barbara was up long before me the next morning, her clock still running on European time. When I stepped onto the porch of the cottage, I found her sitting at the table with a pot of tea and a tray of fruit that she had brought back from the resort's breakfast buffet.

I came up from behind, leaned over, and kissed her on the forehead, then helped myself to a slice of mango. Then I tried some of the pineapple. I felt the self-righteous glow that comes from eating fresh fruit first thing in the morning. When this is all over, I told myself, I will be a paragon of healthy living. I will cut out the drinking. Stay away from heavy foods. Knock off the pounds and get back to my old playing weight. I had another slice of mango. I wondered: Didn't the breakfast buffet have bacon?

Barbara said, "I've called for a car to take me to Negril."

"Already?"

She nodded.

Before finally falling asleep—note to pharmacologists: Rigorous, gleeful, it's-been-a-long-time sex reduces the effects of Ama Aji—we had talked some more about the delicate matters that lay ahead that day. It had put a bit of a damper on the afterglow.

"You sure you don't want to hang out here until . . ."

"Until what? Until word comes that there's been another bomb and this time it was marked for you? Or another shooting? No, Zack, I flew here hoping that this mess would be straightened out and that we might spend some time together. I don't want to hang out here, just waiting and dreading."

"So you'll hang out somewhere else, waiting and dreading."

"I prefer Tensing Pen. It's quiet. The yoga pavilion is perched right above the sea. I'll be staying in Cove Cottage," she said. "Should you survive."

"Nothing like cutting to the quick," I said.

She shrugged.

I said, "Everything's going to be OK, baby."

She finished her tea. She folded her napkin. She squared it on the table.

She said, "I cannot tell you not to do this."

"No," I said. "You cannot."

"Even if it is tearing at me, tearing at me worse than anything has ever torn at me before?"

"Even if."

"And if I were to insist that you not do it?"

"That would change things."

"Between us?"

"Yes," I said. "Between us."

"Because neither of us has ever made demands?"

"Because that," I said.

"Is that what it is then, what makes it work, the never-demanding, the always-trusting, the ever-hopeful?"

"I think so, yes. That and the fact that you're great in the sack."

Barbara smiled.

She said, " 'A madness most discreet, a choking gall and a preserving sweet . . .' "

"Shakespeare?" I said.

"Someone," she said. "Someone who knew."

She stood. We kissed. We went inside.

77

Later, after the car came and took Barbara away, I tidied the cottage and tried to figure out what I should wear. Big decision. It was Game Day.

I went through my suitcase, put on shorts, put on pants, nothing worked. Everything was too tight and made me feel constricted.

Back when I was playing ball, tight was good when it came to a uniform. Made you look sleek and cool. Unless, of course, you were a lineman, in which case it just made you look even more overgrown and thuggish.

I needed something loose, something that would give me freedom of movement. Just in case. Just in case of what, I wasn't sure. But if I was going down, then I was going down in comfort.

I stepped next door to Monk's cottage, rummaged through his closet. A pair of khakis hung from a knob on the door. I put them on. Baggy but not too baggy. I could wear them and look semi-presentable. Or, if things got bad, I could run in them. I am brave when I need to be brave, but I am not stupid. Running should always be an option.

I put on running shoes and a polo, an orange one. Got the keys to the Mercedes. Put them in a pocket of the khakis. Felt something else in the pocket—a slip of paper. Pulled it out. A rumpled receipt. I unfolded it and looked at it.

The receipt was handwritten and it was from Darwin's Stationery in Mo Bay. There had been a single purchase—one Ideal Executive Daybook. Cost—440 Jamaican dollars. I noted the date at the top of the receipt—September 4th. The day before I arrived in Jamaica.

The green backpack was sitting on the kitchen counter. I unzipped it and pulled out Monk's Ideal Executive Daybook. I flipped back to the earliest entry, June 14, about the time Monk started working for Darcy Whitehall. It was written in neat block letters: "D.W. 11 a.m."

The rest of the entries were written in the same neat hand and were just as innocuous, noting other meetings with Whitehall, through June, July, and August. Nothing really stood out until the two last entries—September 4th, the one that ultimately led me to Martha Brae and the home of Ida Freeman, Kenya Oompong's mother; and the entry on September 4th that listed the Dover Street address of Equinox Properties.

But according to the receipt I was holding, Monk hadn't bought the daybook until September 4th. Had he faked the earlier entries? Apparently. But why?

I was still mulling it over when I arrived at Darcy Whitehall's house. Alan was sitting in the kitchen with Otee, drinking coffee and watching the news on TV.

I said, "Anything about Kenya Oompong?"

"She turned herself in early this morning," said Alan. "She's in jail with her mother."

"She make a statement?"

Alan shook his head.

"Police haven't let her," he said. "Must be driving her crazy."

Otee said, "Where is Boggy?"

"He stayed in Camp Hill," I said, then told them about seeing Scotty Connigan leaving Cuddy Banks' house and finding the bodies on the floor.

"You a damn fool, go up Camp Hill without no gun, mon," said Otee. "You lucky you be standing here alive. When you going back dere to get Boggy?"

"Well, I was hoping you might do me a favor and go get him for me. I want to be here if there's any phone calls."

"Yah, dat be alright, mon. I go now," said Otee, standing from the table. "We gonna need all us together when dis shit start to fly."

I looked at Alan.

"Where's your father?"

"Still a little early for him yet," said Alan. "He'll make a showing soon."

I said, "They told him they'd call first thing in the morning."

"Only call come in so far be from dat JCP man," said Otee. "Dunwood his name."

"Dunwood called here?"

"Yah, mon. Maybe ten minutes ago." Otee grabbed a notepad from the table and handed it to me. "Said you to call him at dis numbah. He sound vexed."

"Vexed?"

"Yah, he agitated, mon."

I stepped to the phone and dialed Dunwood's number. He answered on the first ring. And yes, he did sound vexed.

"I want you to meet me at the Bird's Nest," he said. "Now."

"Sorry, I really don't have time to sit down and eat," I said, realizing as I said them that such words had never before spilled from my mouth.

"This isn't about sitting down and eating," he said. "It's about a murder. Two of them, as a matter of fact."

I said, "Look, if you're talking about what happened up in Camp Hill, I didn't have anything to do with that."

There was a long silence on Dunwood's end.

I said, "Is that what you're talking about?"

"No," said Dunwood. "What happened in Camp Hill?"

This time the long silence was on my end. I didn't want to tell Dunwood what had happened because I didn't want the police to come swooping down on Scotty Connigan. At least not yet, or at least not until I needed them. Which I was hoping I wouldn't because that would throw a big wrench in everything—especially in everything having to do with money—and likely bring down the roof on Darcy Whitehall.

But if Dunwood didn't know about the murders in Camp Hill, then what murders was he talking about?

"Chasteen?"

"Yeah."

"Get down here," he said, and hung up.

78

The bodies had already been removed from the car and hauled away by the time I arrived at the Bird's Nest. The parking lot swarmed with police, along with a contingent of guys in suits and shades who looked like Americans and fit the Fed profile.

Most of the activity centered around the car—a white BMW.

Eustace Dunwood spotted me as I pulled in and waved me to a parking spot away from the crowd. I got out and leaned against the Mercedes as he approached.

"Thanks for coming," he said.

"You didn't make it sound as if I had a choice," I said. "Mind telling me what's going on?"

"Manager noticed the car when he came to open up, about two hours ago," said Dunwood. "Best guess is it happened just after midnight. That's when a waitress saw them leaving."

"Saw who leaving?"

Dunwood took a moment to answer, studying me. He pulled out a notepad and read from it: "James C. Skingle and Laurance S. Connigan."

"Holy shit," I said.

Dunwood didn't say anything. He kept studying me.

I said, "Why didn't you tell me that over the phone?"

"Hasn't been released to the public yet. Didn't want it getting out," he said. "But mostly I wanted to see how you took the news."

"Read my face," I said. "I'm surprised. Shocked is more like it. How did it happen?"

Dunwood didn't answer. He flipped through his notepad.

"According to a Mrs. Janeese Simmes—Mr. Skingle's secretary—you threatened Mr. Skingle with bodily injury three or four days ago. Is that right?"

"Oh, jeez. Is that what this is about?"

"She also said you came to his office and she overheard what sounded like an argument between the two of you. Is this true?"

"No, I didn't threaten Skingle. All I did was mention to his secretary . . . what's her name?"

"Mrs. Simmes."

"I told Mrs. Simmes that if Skingle wouldn't make time to see me then I was going to whack him in the head with a two-by-four, but . . ." I stopped. It did kinda sound like a threat. "That's not how he died, is it?"

"No," said Dunwood. "It was a pistol shot to the back of the head. A .22 caliber."

"Same with Connigan?"

"Side of the head. We think the shooter must have gone for Mr. Skingle first and Mr. Connigan was turning around when he was shot. We suspect the shooter must have gained entry to the car and surprised them."

"You don't honestly think I was the shooter, do you?"

"No, but I am interested in why you and Mr. Skingle might have had an argument. I'm interested in anything that might shed some more light on this."

I didn't say anything. The fact that Skingle and Connigan were dead was coming at me from so far out of the blue that I didn't want to blurt out something that I'd later regret. Such as telling Dunwood that the two of them had been trying to extort five million dollars from Darcy Whitehall.

Part of me was relieved. I no longer had to worry about how I was going to deliver the money, pull some kind of double cross on Skingle and Connigan so Cumbaa could nab them and lock them up, and then get the money back. And getting the money back had been essential, since it would have been Freddie Arzghanian's money and that was not something to lose. There were only a zillion details about the whole thing that we hadn't worked out, and that had made it dangerous. I was relieved that the danger side of it was now gone.

The other part of me was confounded.

"Any idea who killed them?"

"Couple of thoughts on that front," said Dunwood. "Connigan was DEA so there's the possibility it could be drug-related. The other thought is that it was the NPU."

"The NPU? Why them?"

"Retaliation for arresting Kenya Oompong and her mother. If you remember, it was Jay Skingle who led the charge to get us to crack down on the NPU."

"You favor one over the other?"

"The garrison drug lords aren't shy about shooting each other because no one really cares about how many of them die. Killing Skingle and Connigan though, two Americans, that would bring down more heat on them than it was worth. They wouldn't want any part of it," said Dunwood. "So me, I'd put it on the NPU. Kenya Oompong might not be tied directly to it, but with all her other problems—stolen guns, the bomb-making material—she'll be out of commission for a while."

"No third-party possibilities?"

Dunwood shook his head, said, "No, what about you? Any thoughts on it?"

"No," I said, although I had thoughts aplenty.

Dunwood's colleagues called for him from across the parking lot. Before he stepped away, he reached into a pocket, pulled out a plastic evidence bag, and handed it to me. Monk's Super Bowl ring, the one Dunwood's men had found at the airport.

"Investigators are finished with it," Dunwood said. "Thought his family would like it back."

"Appreciate it," I said.

I got into the Mercedes. I put the key in the ignition, and then I just sat there. I pictured this: Ramin the Gentle rising up in the backseat of the BMW, just like he'd risen up behind me, and putting a pistol to the heads of Skingle and Connigan.

Was that the way it had happened? Had Freddie Arzghanian trumped everyone? Had he figured out a way to cut to the chase—simple, straightforward, problem solved, no outlay of cash?

I thought about how that might have worked. Or not.

Then I opened the evidence bag and took out Monk's Super Bowl ring, held it in the palm of my hand. It seemed none the worse for wear—hardly scuffed, a heavy thing, diamonds sparkling. I picked it up, resisted the temptation to slip it on my finger, just to see how it might feel to wear a Super Bowl ring. I admired it, so bright and shiny; the inside of the band, smooth and unblemished.

I kept looking at it.

The cell phone was finishing its third ring before it dawned on me to answer it. It was still on the floor of the Mercedes, where I'd left it the day before. The voice on the other end was subdued. Hard to believe it belonged to Lanny Cumbaa.

"Get the money," he said.

"What are you talking about?"

"The five million, Zack. Get it."

"But Skingle and Connigan, someone killed them."

"Yes, I know."

"But . . ."

"Don't argue, Zack. Just get the money. Or else I'm a dead man, too."

79

For the record, five million U.S. dollars in one-hundred-dollar bills weighs slightly more than one hundred ten pounds and can be divided easily between two large canvas duffel bags that will fit neatly in the trunk of a big black Mercedes.

We were standing in a narrow alley beside Freddie Arzghanian's office. Ramin and Hamil had just finished the packing and the loading.

Freddie Arzghanian said, "I must tell you, yes, I did consider killing the two of them, Skingle and Connigan, but I feared it would create more problems with your government than it was worth. Now, though, I have some regret, especially since I am risking all this."

He gestured to the canvas duffels. I closed the trunk.

"You have to pay to play," I said.

"Yes, I suppose. A most interesting game," he said. "And you are quite certain of what you tell me?"

I nodded.

"It is the only way the pieces fit," I said.

"The only way they fit for you, perhaps. For me, I still could just walk away."

"And leave two innocent people taking the blame?"

"Not my concern," said Arzghanian. "Besides, how do you know they are innocent?"

"Because I know Scotty Connigan planted that stuff under Ida Freeman's house. Just as I know he hired Cuddy Banks to wreak havoc and frame the NPU. Connigan and Skingle might be dead, but Kenya Oompong and her mother are taking the fall for them."

Arzghanian said, "Plus, there is the matter of your friend, Monk DeVane."

"Yes," I said. "There's that."

"You wish to resolve it."

"Once and for all."

Arzghanian's thin lips curled into a smile that wasn't really a smile.

He said, "And if you are lucky enough to walk away, then . . ."

"Then we'll discuss that when it happens."

"Not if."

"Hell no, not if," I said. "You'll be seeing me again."

"Because there is the matter of the money."

"Yes," I said. "There's that."

The cell phone rang. I answered. It was Cumbaa. He told me the route to follow.

"That will get you to the intersection of the C-3 and Dunkirk Road. Should take about twenty minutes. I'll call again then," Cumbaa said. "And, Zack, remember. Just you. Don't bring anyone else. That will only make things worse."

I opened the driver's door on the Mercedes.

"No one follows me," I told Arzghanian.

He shrugged.

"As you say," he said.

80

I pulled out of the alley and drove north on Dover Street. The route Cumbaa had given me led into the hills east of Mo Bay and toward the mountains. The further I went the more the road twisted and turned. I watched the rearview mirror. The road curlicued behind me, and when I hit the top of a hill and looked back I could see all the way down the road for the better part of a half mile.

A road like that, it's hard to follow someone without being seen. Ramin and Hamil weren't doing a bad job of it. They were hanging back in the white Range Rover as far as they could without chancing me making a turn and them not spotting it.

I knew they'd be back there. I knew Freddie Arzghanian wasn't about to give me all that money and let me go it alone. It had to be what it had to be. All we could do was see what happened next.

It was a lot like playing football. Especially defense, my side of the game. You huddled, made your best guess, and set your formation. Then out came the other side with its secret plan, trying to score, reading what you had going, maybe juking things around, calling an audible if they perceived a weakness. Then backs went in motion and you were countering that, stunting and shifting, maybe showing a blitz.

God, I loved to blitz. Zack the Sack, that's what they called me. Got six in one game against the Jets, just one shy of the record. Good timing, a fair amount of guts, then feets don't fail me now and go straight at 'em. When it worked you were a goddam hero; when it didn't, they'd pick your back door and hang you out to dry.

So I was stepping up to the line of scrimmage, showing my formation, waiting to see what they would throw at me. Stunt and shift, wait for the snap, and don't you dare screw up.

I pulled off near the intersection of the C-3 and Dunkirk Road and waited. Ramin and Hamil didn't appear behind me; they were keeping a safe distance. The phone rang. I wrote down more directions. I headed south on Dunkirk Road and turned where I'd been told to turn—a dirt road barely wider than the Mercedes, branches and thornbushes playing hell with the paint.

I was getting close now. One more turn, between a pair of crumbling stone columns, and I was heading downhill, toward a wooden bridge that spanned a gully maybe twenty feet deep with a clay-colored stream trickling through it. Two hundred yards beyond the bridge, at the crest of a low hill, sat the house. A stand of cotton trees and mahogany started near the house and ran down one side of the dirt road, all the way to the stream, and from it back to Dunkirk Road. The other side of the dirt road was overgrown field.

I drove slowly across the bridge, its timbers creaking and moaning. Then I was back on the dirt road again and heading up the low hill toward the house.

The house was in shambles but not unsubstantial. Two stories, walls of quarried limestone, a mossy slate roof that had caved in on one corner. Old, a couple of hundred years or more, it had been built when colonial plantations once ruled the Jamaican landscape. Behind it, the ruins of a few outbuildings, a tumbledown stone tower that once was a sugar mill. Another road, gashed with washouts, ran out the back of the property, through fields high with wiregrass and weeds. Once these same fields had been planted with cane. Great fortunes had sprung from them. It had been a long time ago.

Cumbaa's green Honda was parked outside the house. I stopped the Mercedes beside it and got out. No sound but the wind blowing through the trees and across the field.

I walked to the front door. It was halfway open. I stepped onto the threshold, waited. Nothing. I stepped all the way inside.

The place was musty and damp and dark. It was cluttered with old furniture, none of it worth anything, just big heavy pieces that took up space. Some old rugs on the floors.

In the room to my left, in the middle of what once was a Victorian-era parlor, I could make out a figure sitting on a wooden crate.

Lanny Cumbaa was bound and gagged now, duct tape around his hands, his mouth. He sat very still, not struggling against the bindings.

He wore a black BCV, a buoyancy compensator vest, the ones scuba divers use. The weight pockets were stuffed with something that was definitely not lead weights. I'd seen images on television of similar devices. Used by suicide bombers. Yes, someone had wired Lanny Cumbaa to blow to Kingdom Come.

His eyes were wide. He was looking past me. The door swung shut. I turned around.

There, with a pistol pointed at me, stood Monk DeVane.

81

If I hadn't been expecting to find him there, I might not have recognized him. The head was shaved, the beard was gone. Bruises marked his cheeks and jawline, along with the puffy reddish traces of stitches recently removed. He didn't necessarily look better, but he did look different. Just walking down the street, unsuspecting, I might not have picked him out.

"Like my new look?" Monk said. "Found this Indian guy, Dr. Ghogawala, did it on the sly at his clinic after hours, a discreet little place near Negril. I'd highly recommend him. Except for the fact that, well, he's no longer in business. After he was done with me, I had to revoke his license."

"You won't get away with this," I said.

"Sure I will," said Monk. "As soon as we're finished here, I'm heading to Kingston, boarding a freighter bound for Argentina. It's a private charter, actually. Paying the captain $50,000 to haul me down there, no questions asked. Then I think I'll head for Bariloche, up in the lake district. Buy a little ranch, run a few cattle, maybe find an Argentine honey. Amazing what you can do with money. Speaking of which . . . it's in your car, right?"

I nodded.

Monk kept the pistol aimed at me while he stepped to a window in the parlor. A big desk sat by the window, filled with all sorts of tools and contraptions, along with a dozen or so cell phones and a pair of binoculars. Monk looked out the window, then he picked up the binoculars and peered through them. He scanned the road, then the stand of trees and the field that flanked it. No telling where Ramin and Hamil might be. And no telling what Monk might do should he spot them heading our way.

Cumbaa hadn't moved a whisker since I'd walked through the door. He was taking long hard deep breaths, like he couldn't get enough air.

I said, "Can you at least take the tape off his mouth?"

Monk ignored me, kept looking through the binoculars.

If Ramin and Hamil were out there, it was time for them to do something. Then it occurred to me: They didn't care what happened to me. I couldn't count on them to save my butt. They were only interested in the money. They would lay low and let Monk do whatever it was he intended to do to us, then try to grab him when he made his move to leave. It would be much simpler for them that way, no sticky hostage situation to deal with.

Satisfied with what he saw outside, Monk set down the binoculars and stepped my way. He said, "Knew I could count on you to play it straight, Zack. Although you should have left here when you had the chance. I didn't plan on it ending like this for you. Really, I didn't. I only needed you at the beginning."

"To do what? Verify that you'd been in the van when it blew up at the airport parking lot?"

"Bright boy," Monk said. "See, the problem, the whole sticking point in the plan, was physical remains. I figured if I created a big enough blast, then that would explain why there wasn't anything to find. Still, there would be questions, and I needed someone who would be a credible witness, who could tie me to the scene and let the world know that Monk DeVane was no more."

"Four people died there that day, four innocent people who just happened to be in the wrong place at the wrong time."

Monk shrugged.

"Collateral damage. There was no other way. That bomb had to blow everything to hell."

"Except the fake Super Bowl ring."

I glanced at the real one, still on the ring finger of Monk's right hand, the hand that was pointing the gun at me.

He said, "Come on, Zack, you didn't really expect me to just toss my ring away, did you? I flew to St. Martin, found a jeweler there, and paid him a shitload of money to make a copy, a pretty damn good one, you ask me. My only worry was that someone would find it and keep it instead of giving it to the police. I mean, it wasn't a deal breaker if that happened, but it helped nail the notion that I had headed off to the hereafter. And it all worked out, didn't it? I just love it when a well-laid plan comes together."

"Only, you forgot the initials in the fake one."

Monk looked at me.

I said, "Rina told me you had her initials and yours engraved on the inside of the band. I saw her at your funeral."

Monk smiled.

"How was my funeral, Zack? Did I get a good turnout?"

"Not bad. I mean, for someone who ran off and left his wife and kids, set up an old friend, and killed anyone who got in his way. Put it this way: you got a lot better than you deserve."

Monk tensed, glaring at me.

"Don't get all high and mighty with me, Chasteen. I saw my chance and I took it. Now I get to reap the rewards."

He stepped back to the window, checking the road, then scoping through the binoculars again. He seemed a little jumpy. I didn't need him jumpy.

When he was finished looking outside, I said: "So how'd you do it?"

"You mean, the bomb in the van?"

"All of it," I said.

I was already fairly certain of how he did it, but I just wanted to keep him talking while I figured out what to do next. I had to deal with that gun of his. And the bomb that was strapped to Cumbaa. Brilliant ideas were not presenting themselves.

"All the bombs—the one that blew up the maintenance shed, the one in the skybox, the one at the airport—they all worked the same way," Monk said. "Very simple. I just used an SCR."

"Silicone-controlled rectifier."

"My, I'm impressed." He reached in his pocket, pulled out two cell phones, looked at them, then put one back in his pocket. "This is the little baby that will light up your friend, Mr. Cumbaa. Got it set on speed dial. Just press 'one,' it dials the number, completes the circuit and . . ."

He pretended to thumb the number; Cumbaa's eyes went wide. He grunted from behind the duct tape, squirmed in the chair.

Monk laughed at him, said: "What, you think I'm really going to be standing nearby when I punch your button? Unh-uh. I'll be long gone, but it will be quite the show."

He stuck the cell phone in his pocket.

I said, "So that's what you did in the skybox? Just reached in your pocket and dialed the number while you were talking to Kilgore, the bomb-squad guy?"

"Yeah, that was a lot of fun. Emptying the whole stadium; the bomb squad rolling in there, like they had it dicked; the look on that bomb tech's face when she saw the SCR engage. Then Darcy Whitehall, trying to act his cool collected self, all the while he was probably shitting his pants. And you, Zack, hurling yourself across the counter, knocking everything all to hell. Everyone just beside themselves when the bomb turned out to be nothing but a lot of smoke. Yeah, that was fun."

"One thing I didn't figure out—how did you get it in there?"

"Ali Whitehall."

"She was in on it?"

Monk shook his head.

"No. I mean, I briefly considered bringing her in on it, but that was me letting my dick do the thinking. She was just a little side treat, nothing else," said Monk. "You see all those shopping bags she had in the skybox? Before the game I just slipped it in one of those, looked like another box of shoes, and I offered to carry it in for her. Then when everyone was going around, glad-handing and being social, not paying any attention to me, I stuck it up under the chair. On the way down to the stands to get you, I called Scotty Connigan, told him it was in place, and then he made a call to Whitehall."

"Seems like a lot of trouble to go to, just for a dud bomb."

"All for you, Zack, all for you. I needed a way to hook you into coming down here to Jamaica. Make it seem like poor old Monk was in a jam and really needing an old buddy to help him out. Plus, it made it a little bit more plausible when the bomb went off in the van. Just another little nudge to convince Whitehall he needed to cough up the money."

"And the bomb at the airport cinched it."

"Sure did. And it gave me my exit strategy," Monk said. "I left you at the terminal, walked to the van, and just kept walking. Had a car parked outside the gate. Got in it, started driving, and I was on Queen's Highway heading to the late Dr. Ghogawala's clinic when I dialed the number and it blew. I would have liked to have been a fly on the wall when Connigan and Skingle first heard about that. I bet they were freaking out, wondering who could have done such a thing to me. Bet it really spooked them. They were probably beginning to believe it really was the NPU."

I said, "Connigan snuck into your room, took all your files."

"Wasn't anything in them, but they didn't know that. They thought they had to get rid of them in case anything in there pointed in their direction. But it was just a smoke screen, something to keep them guessing."

"Like the daybook you left lying on your dresser."

Monk cocked his head, said: "So you figured that out, huh?"

I pointed at the pair of shorts I was wearing and said: "Had to borrow some clothes out of your closet."

I reached for my pants pocket. Monk raised the pistol.

"Easy now," he said.

"It's just a piece of paper."

I pulled out the receipt from Darwin's Stationery Store. "I didn't find that until this morning. That's when I realized that everything you'd written in the daybook was just a setup."

"Yeah, well, it's like this, Zack. I had to throw a little bait out there, just in case you decided to stick around. So I wrote down the address of that old lady up in Martha Brae because she didn't really know anything. It was just a false trail, something to waste your time."

"She knew someone had been sneaking around her place," I said.

"What good did it do her? When the time was right, I made the call to the JCP, told them they needed to check out what was hidden under that old woman's house. Now she and her daughter will be taking the blame for everything that has gone down."

I said, "And you stuck in that legal ad about Whitehall's property off Old Dutch Road, along with the address of Equinox Investments, just so I would start sticking my nose into Freddie Arzghanian's business?"

Monk grinned.

"Pretty slick of me, wasn't it? I thought if you sniffed around Freddie's business long enough he would get rid of you himself and I wouldn't have to do it," said Monk. "It was the old misdirection play. Get everyone moving the wrong way while you slip off to the other side. So you caught on. You get the gold star, Zack, but what the hell good did it do you? If you had it all figured out, how come you drove up here and got yourself in this mess?"

I let it ride. "When did you decide to double-cross Skingle and Connigan?"

"Oh, I knew from the beginning that it was going to have to come down to that. My share wasn't going to be big enough to disappear on; they were cutting me short. Plus, I knew they had a little stash hidden up here from their shakedowns at those other resorts."

Monk stepped behind Cumbaa, to the rear of the parlor. He pushed aside a chest of drawers then lifted the edge of a threadbare rug to reveal a hatch door in the wood floor. He kneeled down and pried it open.

I could see a steel vault sitting inside the hidey-hole. The original click-wheel lock was gone. In its place was a heavy-duty padlock.

"The way Skingle and Connigan were talking, I'm guessing there's nearly two million inside. Haven't had a chance to count it yet. Still need to bust off the lock," he said. "But before I do that, why don't we step outside, Zack. I'm dying to take a look at what you brought me."

82

Monk waved me out the door with the pistol and followed me to the Mercedes. As we walked, I tried to gauge how far behind me he was by the sound of his feet crunching rocks, tried to visualize how I could spin and hit him. I'd have to hit the gun first, knock it away. What hand had it been in? His right. Was it still there, or had he switched hands? That would determine which way I had to spin.

But he was keeping a healthy space between us. If I spun around I'd hit air. Then I'd have to lunge. And he would shoot me.

I said, "Money's in the trunk."

"Pop it," he said.

He followed me to the driver's door. I opened it, reached in, and pulled the trunk release. Then he followed me to the trunk.

"Unzip the bags," he said.

As I did, Monk stepped in closer, and I felt his pistol against my ribs. He picked up a packet of bills, tossed it in his hand.

"Working a tight schedule here, so I'm gonna trust the count," he said. "I mean, what's a few thousand among friends?"

I felt the pistol move from my ribs; heard Monk step back.

Monk said, "OK, turn around, face me."

So this was it. Make your move, or make your grave.

I whipped around, slicing my left arm ahead of me. But Monk caught it with his free hand and held it while he arched back and brought a foot down on the worst possible place he could plant it—my right knee.

I heard the cartilage tearing, felt the pain in every nerve ending. I went down in agony, grabbing my leg. Nothing could make the hurt go away.

Monk looked down at me.

"It was the right knee, wasn't it, Zack? The one you blew out against Tennessee? Damn shame," he said. "Guess you won't be dressing out again."

And then, from inside the house, came an insistent, high-pitched buzzing sound—on-off, on-off—like you hear on a home burglar alarm when you punch in the wrong code.

Monk looked down the hill, toward the road.

"Godammit," he said.

He grabbed one of the cell phones from his pocket, punched at it.

"Come on, come on, come on," he said. "Do it, do it . . ."

I lifted myself off the ground just enough to see the white Range Rover as it rolled onto the wooden bridge. And then came the explosion. The bridge split apart, timbers flying in all directions. The Range Rover flipped twice, then landed upside down at the bottom of the gully, wedged above the stream.

Monk watched, transfixed by his own handiwork.

"Cool," he said.

83

I grabbed the bumper of the Mercedes and pulled myself up. Tried to put weight on my right leg, but my knee wouldn't take it. I braced myself against the car.

Monk opened a back door. He grabbed a duffel out of the trunk and tossed it onto the backseat. Then he grabbed the other duffel and tossed it in there, too.

"Now don't go running off anywhere," he said. He hurried into the house.

I considered my options. The stand of cotton trees and mahogany began about fifty yards away, down the hill. I could make like a log and roll there. But then what? Crawl on my belly like a snake until Monk caught up with me? I didn't want to bow out that way. I'd take what he was serving, spit it back at him if I could.

Cumbaa came out of the house, legs free but with his arms taped together behind him and tape still over his mouth. He walked slowly, testing each footfall, as if he didn't want to jiggle anything in the BCV. Monk nudged him forward with the pistol. He was carrying a roll of duct tape in the other hand.

When they reached the rear of the car, Monk said: "OK, the two of you, stand back-to-back."

Monk turned Cumbaa so that his back was facing me. I didn't move. Monk stuck the pistol to Cumbaa's head, said: "Kill you both now or kill you both later. Really doesn't make a whole lot of difference to me."

Cumbaa gagged, struggling for air.

I said, "Just let him breathe, OK?"

Monk reached out, ripped off the tape over Cumbaa's mouth, and Cumbaa let out a shriek, pieces of skin torn from his lips, which began to bleed. Cumbaa gasped and spewed.

I said, "You alright?"

Cumbaa turned his head and muttered: "Dumb fucking question."

Monk pointed the pistol at me.

"Now stand back-to-back and let me do this," he said.

I pulled myself behind Cumbaa and stood, as best I could, with a hand gripping the edge of the open trunk. And Monk began with the tape. I was at least a head taller than Cumbaa, so the first few wraps went around his neck and my shoulders. Then Monk worked his way down, binding our arms, our waists, our thighs.

He finished and said, "OK, into the trunk we go."

He gave us a shove and toppled us over. My forehead cracked against the side of the trunk, gashing me somewhere above my right eye. We thudded together onto the floor of the trunk, my face jammed against the back panel, Cumbaa facing out. I heard him groan as he went down.

Then Monk was picking up our feet, angling and wedging us in. He had left plenty of play in our lower legs, and now he twisted and turned us, folding us up inside. My knee broke through to a new level of pain, and I buried my mouth against the rough wool carpet of the back panel, muffling the anguish, not about to let Monk hear just how much it hurt.

"Don't you boys worry. That's a sturdy package I built into the diving vest. It won't go off until I want it to go off," Monk said. "Just so you know the plan, as soon as I finish up inside the house, we're going to take a nice leisurely drive to the freight docks at Kingston Harbor. I'll get on the ship, you'll stay right here, in the trunk, two bugs in a rug. Then when I get a half mile or so offshore I'll give you a ringy-dingy. How's that sound?"

Cumbaa said, "Go fuck yourself."

"Aw, don't be bitter," said Monk. "It'll be over real soon." And he slammed shut the trunk.

84

Until the moment the trunk lid went down I'd never been bothered by claustrophobia. But now the panic set in. I fought it off, squeezed my eyes shut, told myself it was just like sleeping, and then I'd open my eyes and I could not see a thing and my nose was jammed against the back panel and I was tasting blood from the gash in my forehead. Cumbaa all the while bouncing around, wiggling his legs, making it even more uncomfortable.

I said, "Just hold still, dammit."

"I'm trying to find it," he said.

"Find what?"

"The inside trunk lever. All the new models they have them. What's this thing, a year old?"

"Maybe that."

"So you're the one who's been driving it. Where's it at?"

"Beats hell out of me. I never looked for it."

Cumbaa kicked and squirmed some more, said: "I think it could be in that corner down there, by your feet. See if you can't feel something might be it."

I probed with my good leg, then said: "Nah, nothing."

"Probably it's in this other corner, up by my head, and what am I going to do, grab it with my fucking teeth?"

He lay still. I did, too.

It was stifling. The tape made it worse. A five-hour drive to Kingston. Probably die from the heat before we got there.

I said, "How did he get you?"

"The easy way," Cumbaa said. "Knocked on the door of my room. I opened it. That was fucking that."

"Guess he was just sitting back, watching all of us."

"Easy to be invisible when everyone thinks you're dead."

We lay there. We listened to each other breathe. It got hotter.

Cumbaa said, "At least it'll be fast. No warning. It'll just happen. Boom fucking boom."

"That's a comfort."

Minutes passed. We heard nothing except each other. Monk was still in the house.

Cumbaa said, "I didn't have a choice. He dragged me up here. But you knew what you were walking into. Why'd you do it?"

"Didn't want you to hog all the glory."

He said, "That's good. Because for a minute there I thought you cared about me."

"Well, I have grown attached to you."

Cumbaa groaned.

He said, "That was fucking awful."

"Best I could do."

And then, a slight motion of the car. We went quiet, waiting.

The trunk lid popped open, rose just enough to let in a sliver of light.

We waited.

The trunk lid rose, letting in more light. I couldn't see out; Cumbaa could.

I heard him rasp, "Who the fuck are you?"

And then a quiet voice: "I am Boggy."

85

After that, we didn't talk. Boggy's knife made quick work of the tape, and Cumbaa scrambled out of the trunk. It was tougher for me. Every movement was pain, but I managed to roll over, onto my back, then onto my side. I hung one leg over the trunk gate, then the other, and I was out, Boggy easing me to the ground.

Otee crouched by the rear fender, the Browning in his waistband, a rifle trained on the door of the house.

Through the big window I could see Monk inside, gathering tools from the table, maybe having more trouble opening the vault than he'd imagined. Then the sound of him hammering away.

Boggy tapped Cumbaa on the shoulder and pointed to the trees: Go there.

And Cumbaa scurried off, keeping low, letting the Mercedes stay between him and the house.

Boggy came to my bad side, got one arm around me, and together we followed Cumbaa. Otee brought up the rear, backing away from the house.

I stumbled once, almost went down, but Boggy kept me steady. When we were out of earshot of the house, I said: "How'd you find us?"

"The boy, Terrance," he said. "He drove up here once with his brothers and Cuddy Banks. They thought maybe to rob the place, but the two men were here and they turned around."

We made it to the woods and a small clearing. There, stretched out under a gumbo limbo tree, was Ramin. He was bloody and battered, just barely conscious. Hamil was tending to him. The boy, Terrance, sat nearby.

Boggy said, "We were just turning on to the dirt road when we heard the explosion. We stopped the car and got out and came through the trees until we met the stream. The two of them had already pulled themselves out of the car. We helped them out of the gully. I think the one, he will be alright."

I looked at Terrance.

"Thanks for your help," I said. "Wasn't for you we wouldn't have gotten out of there."

He nodded.

"I'm going to make it worth your while," I said.

He nodded again, this time with a little more enthusiasm.

Otee moved into the clearing.

He said, "Dat man back there in da house, dat Monk?"

"Yeah," I said. "That's him."

Otee let out air.

"Cho, mon. First ting me saw him me tink dat's Monk's duppy, 'cause him look like Monk but him don't. Got dem scars on his face and what-all. Dat da way a duppy look, all torn up and put back together. Gave me a mighty chill, mon," said Otee. "Because today, you know, it marks nine days."

Nine days. I didn't understand at first. And then I thought back to the evening I arrived at Libido, when Otee had come to my cottage and sprinkled the salt and tobacco seed around the porch.

After someone dies their duppy has nine days to roam. Nine days until the duppy can rest.

Cumbaa moved to where I was standing with Otee and Boggy. He said, "So what now?"

The answer came for us—a mighty explosion that shook the trees and rocked the ground.

We looked to the house—windows blown out, a gaping hole

where the door used to be. We watched as the roof collapsed onto the second floor and the walls fell in on themselves. Rubble and dust and doom.

Then silence.

Nine days since Monk had "died." Now he could rest.

86

Three weeks and one arthroscopic surgery later, the knee had mended to the point where I could get in a car and go somewhere as long as it wasn't me doing the driving.

It was the first Saturday in October and nothing short of glorious. Barbara wanted us to put down the top on Yellow Bird, her sweet little 450 SL, a 1979 that had just notched 130,000 miles. But I couldn't stretch out my leg in it, so she drove my Wagoneer.

It was a good day to bail out of LaDonna. The place was swarming with members of the International Palm Society, all there to witness the wonder of my fruiting carossier. What had started as Karly Altman's little gathering had grown into a weekend-long event with guest speakers and seminars and guided tours through Chasteen Palm Nursery, conducted by Karly and Boggy.

Barbara and I had hosted a Friday evening cocktail party at the house, attended by half the staff from Fairchild Botanical Gardens, along with field horticulturists who had flown in from as far away as Kew Gardens in London, and some folks who could only be described as certified palm nuts. The wind was light and the bugs off the lagoon were bad, but there was plenty to drink and, in addition to oysters roasted under a burlap bag on the grill, I had gone all out and made a giant batch of my world-famous conch fritters. Everyone left late and left happy.

After road wins at Mississippi and Auburn, the Gators were at home again, this time against South Carolina. It was a 2 P.M. game, and we headed out early so we'd have plenty of time to tailgate before kickoff.

Earlier in the week Ed Kilgore, from the Alachua County Sheriff's Department, had given me a call. He'd wanted us to sit down and talk, just so he could wrap up things on his end. I wasn't much in the mood for dropping by the sheriff's department, so Kilgore came to me. We sat behind the Wagoneer, in the shade of the oak trees at Norman Hall. There was fried chicken, black-bean-corn-sweet-pepper salad, and Barbara's favorite—pimento cheese and arugula sandwiches on nine-grain bread.

Barbara looked dazzling. She was wearing a creation from Ali Whitehall, part of a line that would soon grace Ali's Place, Libido's newest boutique. And she was in an ebullient mood. Before leaving Jamaica we'd dined twice with Darcy Whitehall. Much as I expected, he'd been smitten with Barbara, and he'd signed a two-year contract to buy the back cover of *Tropics*. It was the kind of commitment that could only bode well. Barbara felt sure that other big advertisers would soon be coming aboard as well. To hell with Aaron Hockelmann anyway.

As for Ed Kilgore, he was mostly interested in how Monk had managed to sneak the fake bomb into the skybox at Florida Field. I went through everything with him, right up to the explosion at the old house off Dunkirk Road.

"Scotty Connigan was worried that someone would break into the house and find the money that he and Skingle had extorted from the other resorts. So he'd rigged the vault to explode if anyone managed to pry it open," I said. "It wasn't meant for Monk, but it got him all the same."

"Sounds like one hell of a blast."

"Yeah," I said. "It was all that."

"But what about the money? It get destroyed, too?"

I shook my head.

"Nah, there were two vaults. The one on top held the explosives. The one underneath it, the money. The second one got dinged pretty good, but it held."

"So what happened to the cash?"

I reached for a big Tupperware container in the back of the Wagoneer, and said, "How about some more fried chicken, Ed."

87

We got to our seats just as the band was playing the Alma Mater. Then came "The Star Spangled Banner." When it was over the guy sitting in front of us turned around to Barbara.

"Been looking for you," he said. He reached below his seat and came up holding a book—*A House for Mr. Biswas.* "I grabbed it on my way out when they cleared the stadium at the Tulsa game."

Barbara was beside herself. She squealed and gave the guy a hug. His ears went red. She has that effect on guys.

The teams lined up for the kickoff. South Carolina received and the ball came out to the twenty on a touchback.

Barbara tucked away the book and started reading a copy of *The Independent Florida Alligator,* only the best student newspaper in the world.

South Carolina tried a pass. It went incomplete.

"Oh my," said Barbara. "There's a story here about Alan Whitehall."

"About him winning the seat in Parliament?"

We'd already heard the news. It had come out of Jamaica earlier in the week. Alan had gathered nearly 60 percent of the vote in Northern Trelawny. In his victory speech, he'd reached out to Kenya Oompong and Nanny's People United, offering

Oompong a key position on a parish council for social reform. She'd turned it down, of course. Kenya Oompong was one of those pot-stirrers who works better from the outside.

"It mentions the election," said Barbara. "But mostly it's about his work with Homes for the People. Seems they've just received a major donation that will allow them to extend their work to other islands."

She read from the paper: "The donation, in the amount of one million dollars, came from Guamikeni Enterprises, LLC, a Bermuda-based philanthropic organization."

Barbara stopped reading. She looked at me.

"Guamikeni. Isn't that a Taino word?"

"It is," I said.

"And doesn't Boggy sometimes call you that?"

"He does," I said. "Means 'Lord of Land and Water.' It's a little joke between the two of us."

South Carolina went three-and-out and had to punt. The ball went out of bounds on the Gator thirty-seven.

Barbara folded the paper and put it under her seat.

She said, "So why Bermuda, Zack?"

"Freddie Arzghanian suggested it. He said the offshore banks that run out of Bermuda are the most reputable. They even provide top-notch accountants if the IRS starts asking questions, to prove that everything is on the up-and-up."

"As up-and-up as it can be if you are dealing with Freddie Arzghanian."

"Freddie's an honorable guy, at least to those who are honorable to him. Besides, it was a one-time deal," I said. "Call it a finder's fee."

"A nice one?"

"Very nice."

"So what other charitable organizations will Guamikeni Enterprises be making donations to?"

"Oh, we've made several already. Sent a nice check to Annie DeVane, enough to buy a house for her and her kids. Sent a little something to this woman Altycia Andrews and her son, Terrance, who live just outside of Mo Bay. Otee got a little something. We spread it around a few other places, too."

The Gators broke from huddle and came out to the ball.

Barbara said: "Well, that sounds very generous of you. But is there any left?"

"Oh, I've got a little cushion," I said.

The quarterback dropped back, pumped to the right, then hit the flanker, a true freshman out of Belle Glade, who went all the way for the score.

The crowd was on its feet. With Barbara's help, I stood up, too. Slowly because of the knee. But it would be alright. Everything would be alright.

We cheered.

Read on for an excerpt from
Bob Morris's

Bermuda Schwartz—

the new
hardcover from
St. Martin's/Minotaur

He knows he will die. No use fighting it now.

"Where is it, Ned?" his killer says.

The words sound far away, as if he were lying at the bottom of a well and someone was calling down to him.

It reminds him of when he was a boy. Three, maybe four. Delirious with fever. Meningitis.

His mother and sister stand by his bed.

"Is Neddie going to die?" his sister says.

"Shhh," his mother quiets her.

And then the sound of his sister crying.

He remembers how he pulled himself back to them, willed himself not to slip away, crawled out of that deep, dark well to where he belonged.

But now . . . there is nothing he can do.

"It's still down there, isn't it?" his killer says.

He doesn't try to answer. His body is shutting down. All that is left of him has retreated to a small safe place, a place beyond fear, beyond pain.

The boat engine idles. He can feel it throbbing through the deck, hear its low rumble. The sound is comforting.

It makes him think of Polly. Her and her yoga. How she talked him into practicing it with her.

It felt good to stretch, to sweat. And to watch Polly, so graceful, so beautiful.

What he couldn't handle was the part, at the very end of a session, when they had cooled down, and Polly would fold her hands, as if in prayer, close her eyes and start in with that "Om" business.

"You're supposed to chant with me," she would say. "It's the universal hum, our connection with the life force."

He would try, really he would.

"Ommmm. . . ."

But it was too hippy-dippy for him. He would start laughing. And Polly, unable to help herself, would start laughing, too.

He loves her. Their time together has been so brief.

The rumble of the engine. . . .

He tries to match its tone.

"Ommmm. . . ."

"What's that, Ned?" his killer asks. "You trying to tell me something?"

He feels his killer close to him.

"Ommmm. . . ."

"Sorry, Ned. You're not making any sense. But that's okay. I know what I need to know. And I think it's still down there. Else, why would you have come back, eh?"

He feels tightening in the ropes that bind his arms and legs.

"Up you go," his killer says.

He senses himself being lifted to the side of the boat.

And now—a touch of something against his ear, something cold, metallic.

"Sorry, Ned," his killer says. "This might sting a bit."

But the sting is brief, the blackness welcome.

He is dead before he hits the water.

1

Lunchtime at Ocean's Seafood—I'm eating a fried grouper sandwich and grappling with a major philosophical dilemma.

Barbara Pickering sits across the table from me. As usual, she is in tune with my innermost thoughts and desires.

"You are already contemplating a piece of the key lime pie, aren't you?" she says.

"Depends on what you mean by already."

"I mean, you are one bite into your rather large sandwich, there remains a rather small mountain of French fries to be consumed, plus that cupful of coleslaw, and yet there you are thinking about ordering the pie . . . already."

"It's good pie," I say. "They mix crushed peanuts with graham crackers for the crust. They use real lime juice in the filling, not the bottled stuff. Pie like that, there's a lot to contemplate."

Barbara smiles.

"I can read you like a book, Chasteen."

"Oh really?" I put down my sandwich, lean across the table and dial up my inner Clooney. "So what are you reading right now?"

Barbara feigns concentration, then surprise. She looks pretty cute doing it.

"Why you filthy, filthy man."

"Damn, you're good."

Barbara's cell phone rings. She looks at the caller ID.

"Oh my, it's Aunt Trula."

"The one in Bermuda?"

Barbara nods.

"The one who is richer than God?"

She nods again.

"Sorry, but I better take it."

No objection from me. I finish off the coleslaw while Barbara exchanges pleasantries with Aunt Trula.

"Why no, Titi, I haven't forgotten, it's your seventieth, isn't it? . . . Oh? That sounds lovely, just lovely . . . We'd be delighted . . ."

The two of them carry on. I eat my sandwich and take in the view outside.

Truth be told, the view from Ocean's is lousy. The Atlantic is nearly a mile away and the windows open on A-1-A as it slithers through Minorca Beach before dead-ending at Coronado National Seashore.

Just down the street from Ocean's sits a miniature golf course with a humongous pink plaster of paris gorilla as its centerpiece. Next to the golf course there's a strip mall anchored at one end by a chiropractor's office and at the other end by the Mane Event, which despite its name is a decent enough place to get a haircut.

In between you'll find Blue Cat Surf Shop, Barr's Bait and Tackle, the Wine Warehouse, and not one, but two real estate offices. This is, after all, Florida. By state law, the percentage of realtors must always be at a level three times that of any other so-called profession and there's not nearly enough room to store them all.

I finish the grouper sandwich and catch the eye of the curly-haired woman, Kim, who is working behind the counter. I mime my desperate need for pie and she delivers it.

Just as I am savoring the first bite, I hear Barbara say: "That sounds like a wonderful idea. I'm sure Zack can help you out. He's sitting right here."

Barbara hands me the phone. I look at it. Then I take another bite of the pie.

"Aunt Trula wants to speak with you."

"That would be rude," I say. "To the pie."

Barbara covers the phone with her hand.

"She's getting ready to celebrate her seventieth birthday," she whispers.

"We'll send flowers."

"It's not until April. She wants me to go early and help with the party."

"So go."

"She wants you to go, too. She has a business proposition for you. She has offered to buy our tickets."

"She doesn't even know me."

"I've told her all about you."

"Including the part about how I can stand by the bed naked and flex my butt in time with my dazzling a cappella rendition of 'Chantilly Lace?' "

Barbara gives me that look she can give. She sticks out the phone. I take it.

"Hello there," I say.

I think I sound fairly chipper, at least for someone who has just been unwillingly separated from his dessert.

"Hello, Mr. Chasteen. It's a pleasure to meet you."

"And you."

We go on like that for a bit. And I manage to nibble at the pie without making loud swinish noises.

Aunt Trula speaks in a British accent. She sounds a lot like Barbara. Understandable. She is the younger sister of Barbara's mother. And ever since Barbara's mother passed away a few years ago, Barbara and Aunt Trula have become particularly close.

"I understand that you are a horticulturist, Mr. Chasteen."

"Nope, I just raise palm trees."

There is a brief silence while I suppose that Aunt Trula is considering whether she really wants to continue a conversation with someone who is more dirt farmer than title-holding functionary.

I take the opportunity to grab another bite of pie. And to consider Dorothy Parker. You can lead a whore to culture, but you can't make her . . .

"Think you can help me with a little landscaping project that I have in mind?" Aunt Trula says.

"I'll try."

"If one wished to plant one's backyard with palm trees that made a statement, then which palm trees would one choose?"

"Depends on what statement one was trying to make."

"That one had lived for seventy years and wished to celebrate it," says Aunt Trula. "Majesty, splendor, that sort of thing."

No self-esteem issues for her.

"Then I'd say you should go with *Bismarckia nobilis*. Better known as a Bismarck."

"Like that German chap, the one with the mustache, the first chancellor or whatever he was."

"Like him exactly. Otto von Bismarck. Had lots of things named after him, including a battleship that got sunk and a city in North Dakota. I think he'd be proudest of the palm trees."

"Tell me about them."

"Broad silvery fronds that fan out like a crown. Grow to about eighty feet tall. Real showstoppers."

"Do you raise Bismarck palms, Mr. Chasteen?"

"Matter of fact, I do. There's a large stand of them at the nursery, several dozen. My grandfather brought back the seed pods from Madagascar and planted them years ago before I was even born. They're nearly full-grown. Just like me."

Another pause on Aunt Trula's end. She's a Brit. You'd think she'd appreciate my brilliant dry humor.

"Very well then," she says. "I would like eight of your very best Bismarcks delivered to me here in Bermuda—one for each of the decades in which I have lived. And one more for the decade yet ahead of me."

"Why cut yourself short? You might hit ninety. Or a hundred."

"I don't intend to," she says.

Before I can come up with a suitable response, Aunt Trula says: "So how much?"

"Well, it's not quite that simple," I say.

As palm trees go, Bismarcks are fairly cold hardy. So I'm not worried about them surviving winters in Bermuda, which, even though it is six hundred miles off the coast of North Carolina, enjoys the blessings of the Gulf Stream and gets no cooler than Minorca Beach.

Bismarcks are salt tolerant, so stiff sea breezes aren't a problem. And they're adaptable to a wide range of soil, so given a suitable pH range they can thrive in Bermuda's limestone marl.

The trouble comes with transplanting. Bismarcks don't take kindly to it. Once established somewhere, they prefer to stay put. Like too many people I know.

I spend several minutes explaining the downside to Aunt Trula.

"No buts, Mr. Chasteen. I want those Bismarcks. And I want them planted in my backyard in time for my party in April. How much?"

I come up with a price in my head. Then I double it. Because I don't really want to dig up eight specimen–quality Bismarck palms and ship them on a freighter to Bermuda. Especially if they are just going to die once they get there.

I tell Aunt Trula what it will cost her. It is hard to get the number out of my mouth without laughing.

"Splendid, Mr. Chasteen," says Aunt Trula. "What say I add another fifty percent for all your trouble?"

"Deal," I say.

But like always, I've underestimated the trouble part. And hauling palms to Bermuda is only the start of it . . .